THE CHRISTMAS TREE KILLER

THE CHRISTMAS TREE KILLER

CHRIS FROST

Harper
North

HarperNorth
Windmill Green
24 Mount Street
Manchester M2 3NX

A division of
HarperCollins*Publishers*
1 London Bridge Street
London SE1 9GF

www.harpercollins.co.uk

HarperCollins*Publishers*
Macken House,
39/40 Mayor Street Upper,
Dublin 1, D01 C9W8, Ireland

First published by HarperCollins*Publishers* Ltd 2025
1

A catalogue record for this book is available from the British Library.

PB ISBN: 978-0-00-870767-5

This novel is entirely a work of fiction. The names, characters and incidents
portrayed in it are the work of the author's imagination. Any resemblance to
actual persons, living or dead, events or localities is entirely coincidental.

Set in Adobe Caslon Pro by Amnet

Printed and bound in the UK using 100% Renewable Electricity by CPI Group (UK) Ltd

MIX
Paper | Supporting
responsible forestry
FSC
www.fsc.org
FSC™ C007454

This book contains FSC™ certified paper and other controlled
sources to ensure responsible forest management.

For more information visit: www.harpercollins.co.uk/green

This book is dedicated to the NHS and
everyone who works for it.

Prologue

MICHAEL BUBLÉ WAS RIGHT – *it was beginning to look a lot like Christmas.*

It was late, and the kneeling figure's anger flared – wrapping presents had never been their forte. Even basic rectangular boxes were a struggle, never mind the irregularly shaped object facing them now. Their frustration mounted as their thumb once again pierced the wafer-thin wrapping paper, patterned with robin redbreasts.

'Fuck,' they muttered, watching the tear widen. Not even the Canadian crooner's dulcet tones could smooth the rising irritation.

It didn't help that they were hunched on the cold, concrete floor of a disused warehouse on the brink of collapse. Snow drifted through gaps in the crumbling roof, and the wind howled through the many breaches in the brickwork. A flickering streetlight outside provided the only illumination, casting jittery shadows over the floor.

The figure shivered; the polythene SOCO suit they were wearing did little in the way of protection from the elements. Through its thin plastic, they could feel every little stone and lump and bump of cement digging into their knees. Once or twice, they shifted to inspect the suit, to make sure that one of the tiny, pointed pebbles hadn't made a hole. They'd watched enough crime dramas to know that so much as a flake of skin or a drop of sweat could condemn you to a life behind bars.

With a sigh, the figure stood and stretched out their back, feeling the knots pop and the muscles hiss a quiet thank you. Bublé finished, and there was a second of silence before Andy Williams took up the festive baton, singing about the most wonderful time of the year. The figure tsked, instinctively adding 'on the beach' in the appropriate places, the song having recently been bastardised by the eponymous holiday company.

After a few more glorious stretches, they returned to the task at hand, calmer now. The wrapping job wasn't perfect – far too much paper, far too much tape – but better excess than exposure.

Although, maybe that couldn't be helped. Studying the parcel, the figure noticed some blood dribbling out of a small tear. They clicked their tongue in annoyance. This was a lesson in consumerism if there ever was one – always plump for the expensive stuff.

They used scissors to snip some tape and pulled it across the hole. It was messy, but the thought of blood pouring out when the paper was torn open made them laugh. At first, a little chuckle that became a full-bellied guffaw that echoed around the vast open space.

Half an hour later, having spent some of that time admiring their handiwork and mentally putting the finishing touches to their plan, they slipped out of their SOCO suit, and set it alight on the concrete floor, watching as the flames ignited, chewed up the fuel and died again. Soon, the pile of ash was the only evidence that someone had used this place for nefarious means.

With the present tucked under their arm, they stepped out into the night, vanishing into the swirling snow.

1

MADDISON CAST A GLANCE back towards civilisation. In the distance, house lights and streetlamps glimmered against the late afternoon's darkness. The thought of a hearty meal and a soft bed almost convinced her to turn back. It would be easy enough to trek the couple of miles to Haltwhistle and book a guesthouse for the night. But if she did that, she'd more than likely succumb to that feeling the following day, too.

Instead, she turned her back on Haltwhistle and faced forward. In front of her was a section of the Pennine Way that looked like something from a child's picture book.

Towering fir trees rose from the earth, gathering to form a dense forest. A recent dump of heavy snowfall meant that the branches were frosted, the icy crystals shimmered in the light cast by the full moon hanging in the heavens. It should've been picturesque, but something about the scene frightened Maddison. The wind was blowing a gale, and the evergreen branches swayed violently, as if frantically warning her to turn and leave. Something a hastily made sign, half buried in the frozen ground was doing explicitly.

HIKERS TURN BACK

She'd overheard warnings the night before in the YMCA – talk of trees being plucked from the ground by the relentless wind, leaving their vast, ancient roots exposed. The chance that more could fall was high.

3

But what was life without a little adventure?

Besides, if Maddison *did* turn back, or seek an alternate route, she'd drift away from her meticulously curated schedule. Her plan was to make it to the end of the Pennine Way, and she had a firm end date for concluding her solo trek lodged in her brain. She didn't want to deviate. It was against her nature.

With a breath that misted in the frigid air, Maddison ignored the sign, the wind, and the gnawing unease in her stomach. She stepped into the forest.

The darkness was near absolute – the beam of Maddison's headtorch was paltry and was quickly swallowed by the blackness beyond. As her eyes adjusted, the scene that greeted her was a mish-mash of two worlds. Undisturbed snow lay before her like an almost alien landscape. And yet the rich, sweet scent of the trees' needles transported her to her gran's front room, always brimful of decorations at Christmas. An elaborate garland would be draped across the fireplace and presents would spill from below the enormous Norwegian Spruce her gran would insist on, despite the fact it took up too much space and blocked most of the television.

For a fleeting moment, the nostalgia was comforting. But the memories of happier times were soon clouded by fear. Several uprooted trees looked like props from a fantasy film. Monoliths from some distant planet. Their vast, tangled roots jutted from the ground like skeletal hands clawing toward the sky. The shadows they threw formed grotesque, unearthly shapes, contorting as her torch moved across them. Maddison shivered, convinced that something, or someone, was waiting for her in the darkness. Branches wavered and creaked, and more than once it felt like more of the almighty trunks would be torn from the soil and fall on her.

With her self-imposed deadline at the fore, Maddison scoured the forest, eventually finding the Pennine Way trail, and pressed on. She zipped her jacket to the top and tugged the toggles that connected to the hood, pulling it tight around her head like a second skin. Still, determined drops of rain squeezed through the opening, stinging her already raw cheeks as another gust of wind ripped through the treeline. She pushed through a tangle of low-lying branches and was swallowed by the forest – nothing more than a speck in the vast wilderness.

Pausing, she pulled out her map and consulted it. The swell of trees hadn't seemed like such a challenge before she came in, but now it felt like they crept on for miles and miles in all directions. Would she do better to turn back? After all, the schedule she had been following didn't *really* matter – it was just something lodged in her head. Her safety was much more important.

A shriek from above broke through her thoughts. She looked up to find a barn owl staring down at her with near-luminous eyes. It regarded her for a moment, before unfurling its wings and taking flight. Maddison took it as a hint that she should do the same. Maybe turning back to Haltwhistle was the best thing to do. Thoughts of a burger oozing with cheese and a fizzing pint in The Brew Bar sounded just perfect. She might even make the start of the quiz if she got a move on.

Decision made, she turned around and was about to set off when she noticed something from the corner of her eye. There, nestled under one of the vast pine trees and half buried in snow was a Christmas present. She looked around, as if trying to figure out who it could be for. But she was miles from the nearest house, and no one else was crazy enough to be passing through here. Had someone dropped it?

She approached it and saw that it was wrapped in red paper with cute little Robins on it. She also noticed the tag – thin, rectangular and slightly damp from the frost. The ink had bled slightly, but not enough to become indecipherable.

Maddison.

Her name had been written on the gift tag.

Was this some sort of bizarre coincidence? A gift for another Maddison, left behind by forgetful picknickers earlier in the day? Had it fallen from a fellow hiker's backpack? Or, had someone left it there for her?

Her heart pounded. Maybe Tristan, her fiancé, had done this. He *had* been oddly inquisitive about her route before she left, almost a week ago. At the time, Maddison assumed he was just worried about her safety. But now, it made sense. He'd planned this. A little surprise. A care package waiting for her in the middle of nowhere.

Which was odd, because Tristan hated Christmas. His mum had left his dad on Boxing Day when he was young; the first mention of the festive season was enough to darken his mood.

Maybe this year, things would be different. Maybe with wedding plans being sorted, he had mellowed, now he had something to look forward to. Maybe this was his way of showing that he was ready to put the past behind him.

She smiled as she peered at the present, and picked it up, expecting a new fleece or a pair of boots. Something she could use on her trek.

The smell was the first sign that something wasn't quite right; a rancid odour, jarring in a forest that otherwise smelled of fresh air and Christmas. The thick glob of blood that oozed from a small hole in the paper was the second.

Maddison recoiled, and threw the gift to the ground, streaking the pristine snow with crimson.

The darkness around her seemed to shift, closing in on her.

Without a second thought, she took off running, screaming bloody murder as she went.

2

'A FOOT?' SAID DR Dougan, arching an eyebrow.

Tom nodded.

Under normal circumstances, Detective Inspector Tom Stonem and Dr Daniel Dougan would never have met. Their worlds, policing and psychology, were meant to run in parallel, not collide. But in the aftermath of a previous case – one that had almost destroyed Tom both personally and professionally – his boss, DCI Natalie Freeman, had ordered him to attend therapy if he wanted to continue in his role.

And so, somewhat reluctantly, he'd agreed.

Dr Dougan's office was exactly as Tom had imagined it. Beige walls lined with framed certificates from prestigious universities, an organised desk with a laptop and an ornate carriage clock, and two wingback chairs, one angled just enough to create the illusion that Tom was part of a conversation, rather than an interrogation. Even the soft strains of peaceful music drifting from a speaker on a table by the door felt calculated. Tom had thought, on his first visit, that police stations should update their interview rooms to this kind of layout – it clearly got results. It had certainly convinced him to open up.

The only indication that normal life continued beyond these four walls came from the sole window, which overlooked a busy Durham street. Delivery vans rattled over the cobbles, and a seething mass of shoppers pushed and shoved their way to shop entrances, scowls etched on their faces.

'Care to elaborate?' Dr Dougan asked, his voice low, measured.

'A woman found a hand-wrapped present somewhere along the Pennine Way yesterday evening,' Tom said, shifting in his chair. 'It had her name on the gift tag. When she picked it up, she realised it stank and was leaking blood. She called the police, and when they arrived, they found that someone had wrapped up a human foot. Severed just above the ankle.'

'And no sign of the rest of the body?'

'Not yet.' Tom shook his head. 'As you could probably guess, they're a smaller operation up that way, so they've asked me to go up and lend a hand with the investigation. Natalie has okayed it, but she thought a session with you before I went might be helpful.'

Dr Dougan's eyes swept over Tom, a flicker of a smile playing at the edge of his lips. Tom knew what was coming – a question that would push him into territory he wasn't ready for. A place that was raw and sore to the touch, but that needed to be poked and prodded if Tom were to make progress.

'And how do you feel about that?'

'It's my job,' Tom said quickly, knowing that his answer would be deemed unsatisfactory. Sure enough, Dr Dougan didn't even open his mouth to reply. Instead, he fixed Tom with a look that suggested neither of the men were fools and simply waited for Tom to prove him right.

'I feel okay.' Tom exhaled, pulling at one of the chair's loose threads. 'Obviously the timing isn't ideal, what with it being so close to Christmas…'

Tom shivered. He hoped that festive murders were not going to become his professional speciality. He supposed the dark of winter was a good time for hiding dark deeds – but some were darker than others.

The Christmas List Killer.

That was what the media had dubbed the case that had nearly destroyed him a year ago. The investigation had hollowed out his soul; had forced him to question whether he even wanted to stay in the job. The ripple effects were still being felt, and would be for months, even years, to come. Tom had a sneaking suspicion that, no matter how long he lived, he would never really be able to outrun the repercussions of the case. And that, in a strange way, had been what had snapped him out of his funk, what had forced him out of his sabbatical and back into his role as Detective Inspector. There were other people going through what he had, caught in the wreckage of crimes like the one that had almost ended him. If he could give them answers, justice, or even just an understanding of why, then maybe it would all be worth it.

During his first session with Dr Dougan, he'd joked that he was a bit like Batman, delivering justice for those who needed it. Dr Dougan, as always, had seen through the macho bullshit and Tom's efforts at deflection, but he could also see that he was ready to get back to work.

'And how do you feel about leaving here for a while? Do you think that will be good for you?'

'I shouldn't be away for long. I'll miss the team, but DS Rea is coming with me.'

'Lauren?'

'Yeah.' Heat prickled the back of his neck. 'Natalie said Northumbria Police requested two detectives, but I'm not so sure. Part of me thinks she's ordered Lauren along to keep an eye on me.'

'Does that bother you?'

'No,' Tom said. Truth be told, he was thrilled that Lauren was coming with him. His partner was sharp, one of the best detectives he'd ever worked with. Almost as important, she was fun. If he was to be sequestered for a while, she was the best company he could ask for.

'You know,' said Dr Dougan, having scribbled something in the notebook that was glued to his hand, 'I think this could do you the world of good. Yes, you're going to investigate a heinous crime, but I think this presents an opportunity for you. The forests, the wide-open spaces, the endless paths and trails. I think you should use this time to work on you. Exercise and fresh air are excellent remedies for poor mental health...'

'I—' Tom started.

Dr Dougan held up a placating hand. 'I am not saying you have poor mental health; I am simply stating that exercise and fresh air are excellent *for* poor mental health.'

'Yeah, yeah,' Tom laughed, good-naturedly. 'You and your psychobabble.'

'Look, Tom,' Dr Dougan said, his expression softening. 'I know how intense investigations can be. All I'm saying is, you have to consider yourself, here. It's been a tough year, and Christmas is obviously going to throw up some very strong feelings. Be kind to yourself. Use the strategies we have discussed and practised. Get yourself a pair of decent hiking boots and get out into the hills when you have a spare hour. Honestly, your mind and soul will reap the benefits.'

Tom nodded. He knew everyone had different ways of unwinding. Hiking may work for Dr Dougan and his acolytes, but a large hot chocolate and a paperback had always been Tom's go-to for a bit of mindfulness. But then again, considering the slight softening around his middle, maybe it wouldn't hurt to try.

He checked his watch. Haltwhistle, where Tom was due to meet his new team, was around an hour away. If he didn't leave soon, he'd be late. Not the best first impression.

'You are not your brother,' Dr Dougan said, rather cryptically, though Tom knew exactly what he meant. As always, Tom offered his hand, and the two men shook.

Outside, loose flecks of snow were falling, much to the delight of shoppers. Perhaps the tumbling white specks were a little reminder as to why they were trawling through shops in bad moods in the first place. For Tom, the snow was an unhelpful reminder that it was December, and another killer was on the loose. He had work to do.

Before leaving the city centre, he stopped at an outdoors shop and paid a lot of money for hiking boots he wasn't sure he'd ever use. Still, best to be prepared, and it would make Dr Dougan happy.

Back home, he moved through the rooms, grabbing essentials and stowing them in his suitcase. He had no idea how long he'd be gone. That would depend entirely on what the present really meant – a one-off gory stunt, or the first move in a macabre game?

His new flat, just a stone's throw from Durham's city centre, had become his safe haven. After last Christmas, it had become imperative to move out of the house where he'd almost died. His new place in Durham had taken on a chrysalis-type quality, allowing him to build up his defences and shed some of the fear that had come with him from Kibblesworth.

But some fears didn't fade with a change of address. Some things followed you, no matter how far you ran.

3

USED TO THE HULKING, tiered brute that was Gateshead Police Station, Tom had to laugh at what passed for Haltwhistle's centre of command.

It was essentially a repurposed bungalow on a main road, sitting on the edge of a housing estate with red-brick walls and frosted windows like you'd see in an office from the 60s. If it wasn't for a small brass plaque by the front door bearing the police's insignia, it could've been mistaken for a scout hut or a village hall.

Tom had driven past it three times, swearing at his satnav with increasing gusto, before realising it had, in fact, led him exactly where he needed to be.

There didn't appear to be a car park, so Tom pulled up on a nearby kerb with double yellow lines. He scribbled a note on the back of a receipt, explaining why he had abandoned his car, and set it on the dashboard in full view of any traffic wardens. He got out and hurried through the station's doors.

Lauren was waiting for him in what passed for the reception area, beside a cheap polyethylene Christmas tree, likely purchased from a bargain bin, draped in tinsel. When he entered, she rose from the chair. Her dark hair was in a ponytail, and she was wearing a blazer, which Tom thought odd. Maybe she was trying to make a good first impression. Her light blue eyes fixed on his, and she smiled.

'How was your trip?' Lauren asked.

'Yeah, fine.' Tom said, before nodding his head slightly in the direction of the woman who was sitting behind the front desk. He mouthed "friendly?" at Lauren, who shook her head.

The woman, who had severe cheekbones and short blonde hair cut into a bob, was poring over a notebook, seemingly oblivious to them. She took her time, reading the rest of the page she was on, before sighing theatrically and retrieving a bookmark from her pocket. Only after tucking it neatly between the pages and closing the book did she acknowledge them.

Tom clocked the way her gaze moved from his face to the lanyard that hung around his neck. He might have imagined it, but he could've sworn that her eyes darkened a shade.

'So, you're the big guns from the big city, eh?' she said, her voice as dry as old parchment.

Tom laughed. 'Hardly. Gateshead isn't exactly New York! I'm DI Tom Stonem, and this is my partner, DS Lauren Rea.'

'Pleased to meet you,' Lauren said. 'And you are?'

'DS Deborah Simpson.'

Jarvis Cocker and the video for *Disco 2000* immediately filled Tom's mind, but he doubted singing the 90s classic would endear him to his new colleague. And, in any case, she was still talking.

'As you can see, we're a small team, but we take pride in our work.'

'We're not here to ruffle feathers,' Tom assured her. 'We've been asked to be here, and intend to work alongside you to find… whoever is hacking off feet.'

'One foot, for the moment, thankfully,' Deborah said, as she stood up. 'You'll want to meet the boss, I assume?'

Deborah led them out of the small foyer. Trailing in their new colleague's wake, Tom shot Lauren a bewildered look. She looked like she was trying to not to laugh.

They walked down a narrow corridor, past a couple of offices. One held two tables that looked like they'd been saved from a salvage yard. The computers perched on top were thankfully in much better nick. A whiteboard stood at the front of the room, displaying some crime-scene photos, and a blown-up image of a pretty brunette.

Another door led to the sole interview room.

At the back of the building, in an office seemingly untouched since the day the place was built, sat DCI Martin Jones. A thin layer of dust covered every surface. There were no personal touches: no pictures on the walls, no framed family portrait on the desk, nothing of note to help put a picture together of what made the man sitting behind the desk tick.

Martin himself looked like his genes had come straight from the Stone Age, skipping every evolutionary step along the way. His bald pate was served by a thick, elongated forehead. Though there was a smile on his face, the jutting brow and sloping eyebrows gave the impression of someone who you wouldn't want to fuck with. Tom extended his hand, and waited for the DCI to motion to the seat before lowering himself into it. Lauren followed suit.

'Are you putting the kettle on?' Martin said to Deborah.

'I wasn't planning on it.'

'I'll apologise on behalf of my colleague,' Martin said to Tom, at the same time shooting Lauren a faux-exasperated look. 'We don't get a lot of visitors, and it seems Debbie's hosting skills have dropped to levels Basil Fawlty would find lacking. Debbie, if you'd be so kind, I'd love a cup of tea. Tom will have...'

'I'll just have a water, cheers.'

'And Lauren?'

'A water would be perfect, thanks.'

Deborah gave a mock salute before sloping out of the room.

'Pleased to have you both on board,' Martin said. 'Hell of a situation we've got here.'

'What can you tell us about the case so far?'

'Well, you know about the foot, don't you? Did word reach you that it's from a male?'

'No, but good to know,' Tom said.

'SOCO reckon it's not the kill site. Not enough blood. Whoever did this killed the poor bastard somewhere else, lopped the foot off, and brought it into the forest – wrapped in colourful paper.'

'Any ID on who the foot belongs to?'

'Not yet.'

'Have you interviewed Maddison yet?'

'Briefly. She was, understandably, in a right state when she came in. She's staying in the village. We thought we'd hold off questioning her properly until you two got here. Figured you'd want to be in on it, and there's no point making the young lass go through it more times than necessary.'

'Good idea,' Tom said.

'Do you want me to get her over here now?'

Tom shook his head. 'I'd like to see the crime scene first, if that's all right?'

'No problem. I'll get Deborah to take you there right away.'

* * *

It didn't take them long to reach the car park near the spot they needed on the Pennine Way. Perhaps sensing that neither Tom nor Lauren was interested in a pissing contest, Deborah had shed her haughty persona like a snake sloughing its skin.

From the car park, the incline was steep. The kind that burned your calves if you weren't used to it. Tom had forgotten to change into his new hiking boots, and before they reached the top, his trainers and socks were drenched.

At the top of the hill, a lone officer stood just inside a stretch of fluttering police tape. Happy with their credentials, he let them into the outer cordon. Inside a tent, they pulled on plastic suits, boot covers and gloves, and then signed the logbook.

Beyond the tent, SOCOs moved through the trees, heads down, methodical, combing the woods for the slightest trace of evidence left behind by the perpetrator. Something that might give the dead a voice.

'This way,' Deborah said, leading Tom and Lauren across the stepping plates to where the foot had been found.

Tom, who had rarely been this far north, was overwhelmed by the sheer majesty of the forest. The enormous trees, the vast blue sky and the ancient land beneath his feet combined to create a sense of otherworldliness. Deborah shook him from his reverie by pointing out the pine tree under which the human foot had been found.

Presumably, the tree itself, and the area surrounding it, had been the priority search area for the SOCO team. The tree stood alone, as if shunned by the rest of the forest for its part in the macabre spectacle that had brought every SOCO and his dog here today.

'Tony, one of the crime scene techs, said that there was nothing much to find here. As Martin said, it's believed the site was solely a deposition site, due to the low level of blood found. The baubles...'

'Baubles?' Tom echoed.

'Yes, baubles. Red and silver ones hanging from some of the branches. None of the other trees were decorated, so it stands to reason the person who dumped the foot also dressed the tree. Anyway, Tony put them through as priority for tests, but there weren't any fingerprints or DNA on them.'

Of course there weren't, Tom thought bitterly. Every channel on the television seemed to have a programme about police work, showcasing the ins and outs of crime-scene management and DNA analysis. Criminals these days essentially had a personal streaming service of dos and don'ts.

'We did get something,' Deborah said, as if sensing Tom's darkening mood. She pointed to the ground. The mud was marked here and there with footprints of varying depth. With some, the tread and design of the sole were easy to make out; with others, there was only the vague suggestion of an outline.

'We've got the shoes Maddison was wearing so we can eliminate her prints from the scene. Tony has photographed the others, and catalogued them. Hopefully it'll help nail whoever did this.'

'And still no word on the rest of the body?' Lauren asked.

'Not so far,' said Deborah. 'The SOCOs have combed a good portion of the forest. No sign of a body. But if this *is* the deposition site, it's unlikely the foot was cut off in another part of the forest, right?'

Tom nodded his agreement.

'More likely,' Deborah continued, 'the poor soul is at the bottom of the Tyne, or shoved in a freezer somewhere.'

This time, it was Lauren who nodded. Tom simply puffed out his cheeks.

The thought of a person, someone with a life, a history, dreams and goals: reduced to this. A severed foot in the woods. A missing body possibly discarded in a river. Any premature end to life was a tragedy, but the fact someone had ended a life and was playing a game with the hacked-off body parts was utterly maddening.

Tom felt a small ember of anger spark to life in his stomach. He had committed himself totally to every case that had been put in front of him, but there was something about some self-entitled bastard thinking they could toy with him that made his blood boil.

Game on, he thought, as he marched back towards the car.

4

A TRIP TO THE morgue on the way back from the forest didn't yield much, but Tom and Lauren did get to see the foot itself.

At first, Tom thought it odd that an entire mortuary cabinet had been devoted to the severed foot. When he mentioned it to the assistant, the man merely shrugged and said, 'Where else are we going to keep it?'

It was a good point, well made. Tom simply nodded and turned his attention to the body part in question. While he did, the assistant gave him a rundown of the headlines.

It belonged to a male, probably between twenty and forty, who would've worn a size nine shoe. So far, so unhelpful. Size nine was the most common footwear size for males in the UK. The toenails were neatly clipped and there was a tuft of thick, dark hair on the top of the foot. There was some cracked skin on the heel, but otherwise it was a foot that had been well looked after. Until it had been hacked off, that is.

The foot had been removed from the body after death, probably with a hand tool – likely a saw – judging by the tiny teeth marks and torn flesh left behind. With nothing else to learn, Tom thanked the assistant for his time, before leaving with Lauren in tow. Deborah had waited outside, having already seen the foot at the initial scene.

'Maddison is at the station waiting for us,' she said, as they left the mortuary.

'Best step on it, then,' Tom said. Deborah gave him a look that suggested she would not be disobeying the speed limits on the way back.

At the station, Tom and Lauren watched live footage of Maddison sitting in the interview room on a computer screen. The room was spartan, with just a foldable table and a couple of chairs. There was a water cooler pushed against one of the walls, with a tube of Styrofoam cups lying beside it, wrapped in a length of clear plastic. A small recording device sat on the table, and the CCTV camera whose footage they were watching seemed to be attached high up in the corner of the wall, presumably with a fisheye lens to take in everything that happened below.

Maddison sat patiently, possibly aware that she was being watched. Her legs were crossed, and she was tapping absentmindedly on the tabletop, possibly in time with a song that was playing in her head.

'You ready to give it a go?' Lauren asked.

Tom followed her into the interview room, where they slipped into chairs opposite Maddison.

She had her long, dark hair scraped back into a ponytail. Her face was make-up free, and there was a friendly upturn at the side of her mouth. Tom presumed that she had showered since being out in the forest, but there was still dirt packed under her fingernails, and the clothes she wore gave off the unmistakable scent of damp earth and pine.

Tom offered what he considered his most affable smile, while Lauren started the recording device and stated the names of those present, along with the date, time and purpose of the interview. She added that Maddison had declined the offer of legal representation.

After that, Tom took up the mantle.

'Can I just say, before we get started, how sorry I am that you've had to go through this. And that we are making you relive it now. I hope you can see why we have to.'

Maddison nodded, and a little of the nervous energy seemed to die away.

'Are you from around here, Maddison?' Tom asked.

'No, I'm from Newcastle.'

'And what do you do?'

'I'm a hairdresser. I work at a salon in the city centre.'

'And what brought you out this way?'

She considered the question for a moment before answering. 'I'm engaged. To a wonderful man, I should add.' But a lot of my married friends have settled down and have had kids. Their lives revolve around swimming lessons and trips to the farm. I want that stuff too, eventually, but I also like my own space. I don't know if I'm ready to give that up just yet. I've always wanted to walk the length of the Pennine Way, and thought that, if I waited until I was married, then I might never get the chance. My husband-to-be isn't much of an outdoorsman.'

'What does he do?'

'He works in IT. I think he helps make websites or something like that. He works in a proper office, though.'

She said it in a way that suggested any IT droid working from home wasn't worth their salt. There was a note of pride in her voice.

'Okay, Maddison, please can you talk us through last night?'

Maddison proceeded to give a measured, almost detached account of her trek through the forest, from considering turning back to the moment she found the grisly, blood-soaked present. The only time she wavered slightly was when she mentioned the sign warning hikers to turn back. Tom respected her for not omitting it to save face.

'Why do you think the present was addressed to you?' he asked.

'It had my name on it! Well, I mean, I was in the middle of nowhere, and of course, it could've been for a different Maddison, but what are the chances of that?'

Almost zero, Tom thought. He wasn't a big believer in coincidences, especially not in remote places with uncommon names scrawled on mystery packages. Someone had left that foot for her. He just needed to find out why.

'Who knew that you were doing your walk?' Lauren asked.

'Well, obviously Tristan did. That's my fiancé. My parents, my sister and her husband. I've told nearly every one of my clients and colleagues, so half of the North East probably knows. You know what us hairdressers are like!'

He had an inkling. His short back and sides came from middle-aged barbers who barely exchanged words, but he knew salons were different. He couldn't even name his barber, let alone imagine confiding his holiday plans to him.

'We'll need a list of your clients,' Lauren said.

Maddison scoffed. 'You can't seriously think any of my ladies could hack a foot off and address it to me.'

But then, reality seemed to hit as she clutched her mouth. Someone *had* hacked off a foot and wrapped it up for her. Someone who knew she would be passing through that particular part of the forest; someone she had probably passed that information to first-hand.

'This is going to sound over-the-top,' Tom said, 'but do you have any enemies?'

'Enemies? God, no. I've never had a serious argument in my life.'

'What about Tristan?'

'I don't know,' she said, averting her gaze. 'I don't think so. He works in IT, for God's sake. He's hardly going to be upsetting some nutter who collects body parts, is he?'

Tom wouldn't be surprised if he had. He'd seen a lot of things on his time on the force, and people these days were very easily offended.

'Thanks, Maddison,' he said. 'I think we have everything we need for now. If you think of anything else that might've slipped your mind, or you think might be important, please do get in touch. I assume you've already given your contact details to Deborah or Martin?'

She nodded.

'Great. Then we'll know where to find you, should we need to ask you anything else.'

'Best bet is my mobile. It'll probably be a week or so before I'm home.'

'What do you mean?' Tom asked.

'Well, I've got a fair few more miles to go before I call it quits.'

'You mean, you're going to continue on the Pennine Way?' Lauren asked, incredulous.

'Aye.'

'Maddison,' Lauren said, leaning forward. 'I'd seriously advise against that. There's a maniac delivering body parts to you, who clearly knows where you're going to be. I think it would be foolish to continue.'

Maddison sat up straight, squaring her shoulders. 'And I think it's foolish for you to explain the dangers to me like I'm a three-year-old. If whoever sent the foot wanted to kill me, they would've done. They could've waited in the trees and knifed me, instead. But they didn't. So save your breath.'

With that, she stood. Clearly the interview was over. Lauren spoke into the recorder to formally conclude the session, and then clicked the device off. She walked to the door, let Maddison exit first and then followed her out.

Tom sat for a moment, collecting his thoughts.

A minute later, Lauren reappeared.

'Pub?' she said.

'God, yes.'

5

THE HADRIAN WAS A striking building, built in the Tudor style with white walls and exposed black timber beams, perched on the edge of a small village green. A few picnic tables were scattered across the grass, but due to the low temperature and driving rain, they were currently unoccupied.

Inside was a cosier affair. A mahogany bar ran the length of one wall, its dark surface gleaming under the amber glow of brass fixtures. Behind it, a variety of spirits dominated the wall. The top played host to a series of pumps, some of which were given over to local brewers – colourful clips with playful names like Barley Legal Blonde Ale and Stout of Control. The room was fairly small, though mostly empty. A couple were playing cards at a table by the door, their voices stolen by the classical music that played from unseen speakers. An elderly man sat alone in a snug near the back, nursing a pint while a Red Setter snored by his feet, occasionally twitching in some dream chase.

The only nod to Christmas was a modest tree in the far corner, its sparse decorations twinkling half-heartedly. Tom appreciated the restraint. No loud, overbearing crooning of festive tunes, no over-the-top tinsel explosions or blinding lights. Just a peaceful place to relax.

The cellar door opened, and a man with thinning ginger hair emerged, rubbing his hands on a towel that had been slung over his shoulder.

'Sorry to keep you waiting, mate,' he said. 'What can I get for you?'

'A pint of Coke, a Diet Coke, and two cheeseburgers with chips.' Tom hesitated, then added, 'And two sticky toffee puddings.'

The barman nodded. 'Good choice.'

Tom thanked him, waited for the drinks to be poured, then retreated to a table near the crackling fire where Lauren had taken up residence.

'Cheers,' he said, as he passed her drink across.

She lifted her glass aloft and clinked it against his.

'Is this where we're staying?' Lauren asked.

'No, we're at a guesthouse about a ten-minute walk away.'

They each took a long sip of their drink, and a wave of exhaustion rolled over Tom. It had been a long day – his appointment with Dr Dougan that morning felt like a lifetime ago. Food would help, and he was looking forward to a good night's sleep.

Until then, he appreciated Lauren's company.

'What do you reckon, then?' Tom asked. 'About Maddison?'

'There's something fishy about the whole situation,' Lauren said, shaking her head. 'Imagine finding a fucking human foot, hacked off with bone showing in the middle of a creepy-ass forest, and not wanting to call it quits.'

'Some people are stubborn.'

'Some people are reckless,' she shot back. 'Fuck that. I mean, I get wanting to walk the Pennine Way. And I get wanting to do it on your own terms. But, go in the summer, when there's all the sun you need. She barely has eight hours of sunlight now. It's a death trap. She could catch hypothermia, or get lost or...'

'Someone could jump out from behind a tree and kill her.'

'Exactly!' Lauren said. 'I reckon there's something not quite right at home, if you ask me. She's supposed to be spending Christmas with her boyfriend, and instead, she's trudging through the wilderness?'

'Fiancé.'

'You're proving my point for me,' she said. 'Fiancé. Not even married yet, and she's craving space. You mark my word: there's something rotten here. I think we need to speak to this Tristan. See what his part is in all of this.'

'Agreed,' Tom said. 'Maybe that's where we start tomorrow.'

'Sounds like a plan.'

At that, their food arrived. The cheeseburgers stacked high on wooden trays, triple-cooked chips served in little metal baskets that looked more like pen holders.

'Fancy,' Lauren trilled, as the barman walked away.

'Very Instagrammable,' Tom replied, earning a snort of laughter from his partner.

They ate in silence for a while, each realising just how hungry they'd been. The fire crackled, the music played, and if it weren't for the severed foot in the back of their minds, it would've been a perfectly amiable evening.

* * *

The rain had eased slightly, so Lauren and Tom walked through the drizzle towards their guesthouse on the edge of the village, using Google Maps to guide them. The blue dotted line led them to Mulbury Cottage, a charming place that wouldn't have looked out of place in St Mary Mead. The house was modest – red brick with a gabled roof, its large windows dressed in net curtains. The front garden was served by a rickety gate and a flickering streetlight. The flower bed was empty, and the lawn was bisected by a narrow stone path.

'How much do you want to bet it doesn't have central heating?' Lauren said.

'How are you with fires?'

'Not great.'

Tom pressed the doorbell. A moment later, a woman who looked uncannily like Miriam Margolyes opened the door and greeted them warmly. She ushered them into the hallway, which was more modern than either of them had expected. It was decorated in neutral creams and beiges, with framed panoramas of sunsets and vast hills on the walls. A miniature frosted white Christmas tree was nestled by the entrance. A comforting wave of heat hit Lauren as she shrugged off her coat.

After a short tour that included a common room with a TV, a stack of old DVDs and a couple of board games, their host showed Tom to his room on the first floor, before leading Lauren up another flight of stairs.

'I thought I'd give you the bigger room,' she said, nudging Lauren playfully. 'Us girls have to stick together.'

Lauren smiled. 'Much appreciated.'

Once alone, she unpacked her things, splitting her clothes between the chest of drawers and the wardrobe. She undressed and pulled on a pair of thermal pyjamas. After arranging her toiletries on her bedside table, she fell onto the bed with a grateful sigh and grabbed her phone. When she found the number she needed, she hit call.

'Mummy!' Sophie's voice came through, bright and excitable despite it being past her bedtime.

'Hey, kiddo. How are you?'

'I'm in my pyjamas.'

'All ready for bed?'

'Yes, Granny's taking me now.'

'That's good. I'm glad I caught you just in time,' Lauren said. 'Why don't you give the phone to Ben, and I'll call tomorrow after you've had a big sleep?'

'Okay, Mummy. I love you.'

'I love you too,' Lauren said. 'Sleep tight, angel.'

With that, Sophie handed the phone over. In the background, Lauren could hear her daughter singing "Heads, Shoulders, Knees and Toes" while Granny told her to calm down.

'Hi, love,' Ben said.

Lauren smiled at the sound of his voice, even if it was a touched strained. Ben was a relatively new fixture in her life. They'd met the previous January, just after the conclusion of the Christmas List Killer case. Ben was tall and good looking, and very easy to talk to. He owned a gym and had sidled up to Lauren during one of her workouts and asked if she wanted a drink. She'd held up her bottle and told him she already had one. After a sheepish look, he said he meant would she like to have a drink, in a bar, on a date. They'd laughed over the misunderstanding, and Lauren had said yes, despite feeling bad that Tom was in hospital and she was out in the real world, accepting offers of dates from handsome men.

The date had gone well, as had the second and third. Soon, they were seeing each other regularly, though she didn't tell anyone at work. Lauren had always been secretive about relationships and wasn't about to change her ways, even though Ben had soon become an important part of her life, and was fast becoming a father figure to Sophie, whose own father had abandoned them not long after impregnating Lauren.

When Ben had proposed just a few weeks ago, Lauren had said yes without hesitation. She had been caught up in the whirlwind of rose petals and glittering diamonds. But, in the days that followed, doubts had crept in.

Was it too much too soon? Was a ten-month relationship a solid enough foundation for a lifelong commitment?

So far, she had kept her doubts to herself. Ben treated her like a princess, and doted on her daughter as if she were his own. He was driven and worked hard, seemingly didn't mind that she was called upon at all hours and got on well with her friends.

True, she hadn't introduced him to Tom or anyone else from work, and only her parents knew about the engagement. Those were surely signs that she wasn't 100% convinced, but she'd told herself that her insecurity was probably a hangover from her previous relationship. That she was just guarding her feelings in case things went south.

'Hi, Ben,' Lauren said. 'How are things?'

'All good here. Sophie is just on her way to bed. We stayed up a bit late to watch some *Bluey*, but she'll be down soon.'

'What episode did you watch?'

'We finished with the cricket episode.'

'Solid choice.'

'I thought so,' he laughed. 'How are things in Haltwhistle?'

'Not quite so rosy. The severed foot doesn't have an owner yet, and the way it was presented was very performative. It feels like we're dealing with someone who fancies their chances of us not catching him.'

'They're taunting you?'

'Seems that way,' Lauren agreed. 'We're off to interview Maddison's fiancé in the morning, I think.'

'Do you think it was him?'

'Well, Maddison isn't going home to him. Even after finding a foot addressed to her, she'd rather walk through a frozen, creepy forest in the middle of nowhere than go back to him. And at Christmastime, too. Something fishy there.'

'You realise you're describing our situation too.'

'Give over,' Lauren said, rolling her eyes. 'I'm here for work, and not by choice. Don't say things like that.'

'Sorry,' Ben said. 'I was just joking around. I know you'd rather be here than shacked up in the middle of nowhere with another man.'

'We're not shacked up. If you must know, I have the suite, and Tom's confined to the servants' quarters on the floor below.

Anyway,' she said, 'I've had a long day and it looks like I've got another one tomorrow. I'll call when I can.'

'Just a sec…' Ben said. She heard him move through the house, and then the sound of a door closing. 'Do you fancy sending me a picture of you in those cute little pyjamas you have on? Or without?'

'How do you know what pyjamas I have on?'

'I assume, since it's freezing, that you've got your thermals on? The ones that drive me wild.'

'And you want a picture of me wearing thick thermal PJs, do you? What do I get in return?' Lauren asked.

'You'll have to send a picture first to find out.'

Lauren didn't have time to reply. Before she could, there were two sharp knocks on her door.

'Give me a minute,' she said to Ben, throwing her phone down on the bed.

She moved to the door, now fully aware of how her thermal pyjamas made her look like a little old lady.

'Who is it?' she said.

'Tom. Open up.'

She opened the door a crack. When she caught sight of his face, she knew he was about to deliver bad news.

'There's been another suspicious package found in Kielder Forest. Martin wants us there, pronto.'

'Another body part?'

'He didn't say,' Tom shrugged. 'But I'd hazard a guess at yes. Shall we take separate cars in case we need to split up?'

'Sounds like a plan. Text me the address and I'll see you there.'

With that, he took off towards the stairs.

Lauren shut the door and picked up her phone.

'Sorry, Ben,' she said. 'Those pyjamas pics are going to have to wait.'

So much for an early night.

6

IF TOM HAD HAD time to take in his surroundings, he would've been blown away. Here, far from the light pollution and endless noise of the city, it was beautiful. The sky was alive with light: stars danced, planets spiralled, distant galaxies flickered like the dying embers of a fire. The universe above him was vast and full of life, but the land that Tom drove through was peaceful, save for the faraway wail of an emergency service vehicle cutting through the silence.

As it was, there was no time to appreciate the wonders around him. Instead, he sped through country lanes, his grip tight on the steering wheel, eyes glued to the windscreen. Not that he could see much at all. Rain poured and fog clung stubbornly to his headlights, swallowing the road in front of him, reducing visibility to mere inches. The radio Deborah had given him earlier kept bursting into life with updates from the crime scene, so he turned it off. He didn't want a preconceived idea of what he was about to encounter. He'd already lost that advantage with the first crime scene, and wanted to be one of the first on the ground at the second. He needed to see it fresh. Raw.

As he crested a low hill, the fog gave way, pulling back like a stage curtain to reveal a road closed by police tape. A smattering of cars and vans were parked in a layby, their lights washing the tarmac blue.

Pulling in beside a Ford Mondeo, Tom turned the engine off, got out, and was immediately soaked by the deluge. A uniformed officer stood just behind the tape, attempting to shelter under the branches of a tree. Judging by his sodden uniform and the hair plastered to his forehead, the tree wasn't doing a great job.

Tom ducked under the barrier and suited up in the makeshift tent to avoid contaminating the scene. Though, with the continuous downpour, Tom imagined a lot of potential evidence had been lost to the elements already. When he was ready, he signed the logbook, peeked through the flaps and steeled himself for a long, cold night.

With an exhalation that fogged the air, he stepped out into the night once more. The action was a little further up the hill, in a field ablaze with the harsh glare of forensic floodlights. Their glow carved unnatural shadows into the ancient landscape, causing Tom to shiver.

He briefly thought of a kitchen light swinging, its bulb reflected in a carving knife. His breath hitched for a moment, until he forced the memory away before it could take hold.

Instead, he began trudging up the lane, adrenaline battling against the fatigue to keep him alert. As he came to the gate that led to the field, with another officer stationed at it, his eyes caught on something along the wire fencing that bordered the stretch of farmland. A line of small, lifeless bodies strung up at intervals.

Moles.

Dozens of them, dangling like a perverse garland, swaying silently in the breeze. Tom's stomach tensed. He wasn't much of a country-dweller, but he knew one thing: moles don't hang themselves.

Cautiously, he stepped down into the sopping ditch and pulled himself up on the other side. The beam of his torch skimmed over their lifeless bodies, their fur slick and matted, tiny pink paws curled tight in rigor mortis. The display was deliberate. Precise. Could this be another message? Another breadcrumb in the killer's sick trail? What did moles and severed feet have to do with each other?

He snapped a few photos on his phone and then climbed back onto the narrow road. When he reached the gate, the officer who was guarding it nodded at the collection of moles with a smirk on his face.

'Finding our way of life interesting, sir?'

'What do you mean?' Tom asked.

'That's got nothing to do with what's happening up there.' He pointed at the field.

'How do you know?'

The officer chuckled. 'That's called a murder rail. Moles are a pain in the arse for farmers. Their digging damages crops and contaminates silage. They're buggers, so the farmers either get rid of them themselves or bring in mole catchers. They used to say mole catchers strung them up to warn off the other moles, but that's a load of bollocks. It's just to show the farmer they've done a decent job. It's tradition now.'

Tom glanced back the row of tiny, furry corpses, his tension easing ever so slightly.

'Thanks for the education.'

'You townies need it,' the officer laughed, clapping Tom on the shoulder.

Shaking his head, Tom plodded past him into the field. The ground was like soup in places, quicksand in others. The oozing mud grabbed at his new hiking boots, threatening to pull him down, trying to keep him from reaching the mass of bodies ahead.

If he was a superstitious man, he might've taken it as an omen. As it was, his mind was still on the moles. For a moment, he thought he'd been onto something. But really, it was just a rural quirk. A commonplace event for those who dwelled here. He was jumping at shadows. Dancing to the tune the killer was playing. He felt powerless, but knew from experience that killers usually slipped up. Their confidence, or arrogance, led to mistakes. And, judging from the note left behind at the first scene, as well as the theatrical display of the present, they were dealing with someone with an inflated ego. They wanted glory, for the world to know what they were doing. He just had to trust the process and follow the clues where they led him.

As he neared the forensic team, dodging puddles of mud as he spotted them, he heard his name on the wind. Turning and squinting back towards the gate, he saw Lauren picking her way towards him, slipping once or twice on the uneven terrain.

'Did you see the moles?' he asked, when she'd finally reached him.

'Yeah. Fucked up or what, eh?'

'Standard practice out here, apparently. I don't think I'm made for the country.'

'Nor me,' she said, a wry smile on her face. 'Though, don't you think it's funny that we're repulsed at some dead moles when we're potentially walking towards another severed human foot like it's just another day at the office.'

Tom laughed at that.

'Yeah, good point. I'm sure Dr Dougan would have something to say about that. Maybe I'll ask him what it says about me next time I see him.'

As they looked ahead, at the rows of pine trees, they spotted something odd: one of them had fresh baubles and tinsel strung upon its branches. All spruced up for Christmas.

They crossed the last stretch of field, stopping just short of the forensic team. They both knew from experience that interrupting the SOCOs with questions mid-flow was never a wise undertaking. Instead, they hovered by the treeline, watching the action unfold.

Eventually, they were called over by a forensic pathologist who introduced herself as Claire. A photographer and videographer were by her side, ready to capture the unwrapping in real time. The high-powered lights, the crowd of people and the various lenses combined to give the event a macabre spectacle – like a particularly grim reality show finale.

Claire spoke to the camera from behind a face mask, narrating each move she made. In front of her was a package, wrapped neatly in festive paper. Presumably, it was retrieved from beneath the unusual tree they'd spotted. Little robins covered the surface, their vivid red breasts striking against the rain-slicked paper. A thin silver ribbon was tied around it, shimmering in the flood-lights. Claire cut through it with a slow, practised movement, as one might disarm a bomb.

A small cardboard tag fluttered loose.

'To Niall,' Claire read, holding the label up for the photographer.

Tom felt his pulse quicken.

Who was Niall?

He didn't have time to ponder that question just now, as Claire was already moving on.

She peeled back the wrapping paper to reveal another layer. Tom hadn't been at the first crime scene, but he knew from the photos and the report that the foot had been wrapped in a single layer. This was a deviation. A deliberate one? One made from necessity? A taunt?

Only time would tell.

After bagging the first layer, Claire moved onto the second, meticulously removing strips of Sellotape again. The videographer adjusted his position ever so slightly, to make sure he had the right angle for the grand reveal.

After taking a breath, Claire peeled back the layer.
A hand.
Pale.
Lifeless.
And missing its ring finger.

7

TOM THANKED THE FARMER, reiterating that he believed the incident (on his land, at least) to be a one-off occurrence, before striding outside. The rain still bore down in heavy sheets, but he was already so soaked he barely noticed it. His boots squelched against sodden ground as he made his way back down the lane towards his car. Just as he reached for the door handle, a nearby car flashed its full beams on and off a couple of times.

Lauren.

He slipped into the vacant passenger seat, apologising for the flood he was bringing with him. The warmth inside the car was a euphoric relief.

'What did he say?' Lauren asked, her gaze flicking to him as he lowered his hood and brushed stray hairs from his forehead.

'He claims that a couple of another farmer's sheep had escaped their field and found his. When he went to try and sort it, he saw the present under the pine tree. Word spreads like wildfire around these parts, so he knew all about Maddison's present. That's why he phoned it in.'

'And he'd been in all evening?'

'Yeah, they have CCTV at various points around the farmhouse.'

'Any on the field?'

'No such luck,' Tom said, shaking his head. 'Anyway, I had a quick look so as to rule him out. He was in for most of the night, went out at just after eight o'clock to sort the sheep, and then returned once the SOCOs had told him to go home. He's in the clear.'

'Does he know anyone called Niall?'

'No, he doesn't think so. I told him to give us a call if he suddenly remembered a second cousin or a man from the pub, but I think the farmer is a dead end for us.'

Lauren let out a frustrated sigh, and said, 'So, what's next?'

'Well, Claire is pulling an all-nighter to try and get us some answers. She's invited us along to the hospital to watch her do the examination on the hand. I'm very happy to go alone and relay the information back in tomorrow's briefing if you don't feel up to it.'

'Don't be soft,' Lauren said, smiling at him. 'Shall I drop my car off at the guesthouse and we'll go in yours?'

'Sounds like a plan.'

* * *

The hospital was in Carlisle, half an hour away. Having never heard of it before today, this was the second time both had visited within twenty-four hours. The life of a detective – death dragged you where it wanted you.

Despite the late hour, the car park was bursting. Tom found a space and paid handsomely for the privilege before setting off alongside Lauren to the mortuary.

Inside, Claire had pulled together a small team on short notice. The assistant who had walked them through the foot earlier was off shift, but the examination was proceeding regardless. Tom and Lauren were handed the necessary protective clothing, which they pulled on before being admitted to the mortuary proper.

Usually in these circumstances, there was a gurney with a body lying on it waiting to greet them, the harsh light from above exposing every imperfection and injury. This time, though, the scene that awaited Tom and Lauren was like something from a sci-fi movie – a single hand, palm up, on the brushed steel surface. Tom half expected it to twitch, to flip onto its fingertips and scurry off like Thing from *The Addams Family*, but of course it didn't.

'Thanks for pushing this through at such short notice,' Tom said to Claire.

'If it was a body, there was no chance. A hand, on the other… well, you know, shouldn't take too long,' she replied, before turning to her team. 'Are we ready?'

Everyone around her gave their ascent, and she clicked on the recording device. Just like at the deposition site, she was followed by a videographer and a photographer. For a while, she directed the duo to various parts of the hands, calling for close-ups from various angles, all the while narrating her findings. She took scrapings from under the nails, the severed wrist, and from the ragged wound where the missing finger should've been. Finally, she turned to Lauren and Tom.

'Are you ready for some preliminary findings?' she asked.

'Born ready,' Lauren said.

'Obviously, this is best guess,' Claire caveated, 'but I would say that both the hand and the foot belonged to a healthy, white male, aged between twenty and forty years old.'

'From the same person?' Tom asked.

'Now that is not something I'm prepared to take a punt at just yet,' Claire said. 'What I *will* say is that the severing of the foot took place while the victim was alive, while the hand was severed post-mortem. Rigor mortis had set in, meaning the victim was already dead. The cold weather may have skewed decomposition time a little, but we can probably hazard a guess that time of death was roughly twelve to thirty-six hours before the present was found.'

Tom frowned, and said, 'So between half a day and three days?'

That time frame, evidentially speaking, was enormous. If the victim had died twelve hours before, it spoke of an efficient killer – one that selected, snatched, murdered and mutilated in quick succession. If it were three days, though, that showed a killer who preferred to play with their victims. Psychological, and perhaps physical torture were a real possibility. If the police psychologist wanted to put together a profile, the time frame would need to be narrowed down. Tom asked the question, already knowing the answer. As he expected, Claire shook her head.

'I can only work with what I've got. If it wasn't snowy and freezing outside, maybe I *could* narrow it down for you. As it is, the elements are skewing the findings too much. I'm giving you what I can.'

'And I appreciate it,' said Tom. 'Really, I do.'

Claire's blue eyes glinted as she nodded. 'Well, since you appreciate me, let me give you some more.' She gestured to the space where the missing finger should be. 'Can you see that scabbing around the wound? That suggests to me that the ring finger was severed while the victim was still alive, too.'

'Why would the killer do that?' one of the technicians asked.

Tom could think of a few reasons.

It could be that the ring finger carried a distinctive mark that would make identifying the owner easy. A scar, a tattoo, perhaps a birthmark. Maybe an accident on a rugby pitch or a car crash had broken the digit, leaving it with a distinctive curve or arch.

The chosen finger itself was telling – the ring finger was symbolic. It could be that the victim had wronged the killer in some way. The choice of finger suggested an affair. Perhaps the victim had cheated on the killer, and they'd been found out. Then, the killer had lopped the finger off as a message, killed them, and then severed the hand for good measure.

Which made Niall, who the wrapped hand had been addressed to, someone of interest. Had Niall been the man the victim had been having an affair with? Or was this another way the killer was trying to throw the police off the scent? Had the ring finger been picked to lead the police on a wild goose chase?

'Any way to tell what the finger was removed with?' Tom asked.

'It's a clean cut, compared to the wrist,' Claire said. 'I'd say the wrist was severed with a handsaw, on account of the teeth marks that were also present on the foot. This fits the MO, linking the kills…'

'As if the presents hadn't already,' muttered Lauren.

'The finger is different. It's a clean cut, which can't have been easy with the victim alive and probably squirming. Although, the killer might have drugged the victim to keep them still. The wound is too clean for any self-defence.' She looked closely at the hand again. 'I'd say something like a pair of secateurs might be likely.'

'A handsaw and secateurs,' Tom said. 'We're looking for a green fingered, DIY enthusiast.'

'Good start to the profile,' Claire chuckled. 'You could put that on the wanted poster.'

'What's next?' Lauren asked.

'Well,' Claire said, 'we'll feed the fingerprints from the hand into the system, see if we get a match. That's the quickest way we can hope of identifying who the hand belongs to. If we get a match, we can test DNA from the hand and the foot to see if they are a match. But, I have to warn you, it's going to be a while. Everything is backed up.'

'How long are we talking?'

'Fingerprints shouldn't take too long. Couple of hours, maybe. I'll make sure to send them as a priority. The DNA test will be a significantly longer wait. We're potentially looking into the new year, though.'

'Well, let's hope we get a hit on the prints, then. That it for now?'

'That's it,' Claire agreed. She passed him a card with her number jotted on it. 'That'll be easier than trying to get me through the office.'

Tom nodded and pocketed it. He thanked the team, and then he and Lauren left the mortuary, both grateful for the clean air outside.

'Claire could be bit more subtle, don't you think?' Lauren said, glancing at him as they got into Tom's car.

'What do you mean?' he asked.

'She gave you her digits, man.'

'For professional use.'

'You think she's handing out her personal mobile number to other detectives?'

Tom shrugged, though he fought the twitch of a smile.

'And what about the whole "since you appreciate me" thing?' Lauren asked, flicking her hair behind her shoulders in mock flirtatiousness. 'She was flirting up a storm in there.'

'Oh, stop it,' Tom laughed.

'Honestly, dude, she's into you.'

'Well, hopefully you and I won't be staying long enough for her to fall totally in love with me. I wouldn't want to add a broken heart to the crimes being committed in the Haltwhistle area, would I?' He shot her a grin, and then checked his phone. 'I've had a message from Martin. He wants to have a quick briefing at the station before calling it a night. I'm very happy to drop you off at the B&B if you want?'

'No, it's fine. I'd prefer to hear what goes down.'

'You're just worried that I'll drop you off and then call Claire for a late-night coffee, aren't you? You're keeping tabs on me, detective. I know your game.'

41

Lauren laughed, and then gave him a playful punch on the arm. Tom set the satnav for Haltwhistle and pulled out of the car park. The roads were quiet, and Lauren fell asleep less than five minutes into the drive, her head lolling against the window. Tom turned the radio off, hoping that the silence would let her stay asleep for longer.

With nothing to distract him, and against his better judgement, his mind drifted to Claire.

8

DESPITE THE HOUR, THE briefing room in Haltwhistle station was packed. Deborah, Martin, Lauren and a host of DCs Tom had not yet been introduced to were crammed in, taking up whatever space was available. Some sat on chairs, others leaned against the wall, a few of the younger lads had hoisted themselves up onto the windowsills. It made Tom feel like he was giving a talk at a high school assembly.

'For those that don't know me, my name is DI Tom Stonem, all the way from sunny Gateshead.' He paused as a titter of laughter rippled through the room. Tom noted that Deborah remained stony-faced. Perhaps a murder briefing was neither the time nor place. Eager to move on, he motioned to Lauren, who waved timidly. 'This is my partner, DS Lauren Rea. I know it's late, but Martin and I just thought a briefing now would be handy, so that we can hit the ground running with this first thing.'

He gestured to the whiteboard plastered with crime scene photos, maps of the area, and a picture of Maddison.

'Let's take it from the top, shall we? On the fourteenth of December, Maddison Cassidy passed through a section of the Pennine Way just north of Haltwhistle when she stumbled upon a present addressed to her. It contained a severed foot. On the fifteenth of December, a second present was found in a farmer's field just off the Pennine Way near Bellingham. We've just

43

unwrapped it.' Tom pointed to a printed picture of the hand. 'You might have noticed that it's missing a ring finger.'

'Same vic?' someone asked.

'At the moment, we're not sure. Claire, the pathologist,' he said, studiously avoiding Lauren's gaze, 'is doing us a solid and speeding through the tests to find that out, though it may take a while. In a strange way, we should hope that it is a single victim, nasty as it sounds, because that would mean only one person has been killed.'

A murmur of agreement thrummed through the crowd.

Tom could hardly bear to think of the other option – that multiple people had been murdered in order to harvest their limbs as presents. It was a chilling thought; one he tried not to linger on. In any case, he had a roomful of people waiting for him to speak.

'There's obviously the tags on the presents. Maddison found the one addressed to her, but it was a farmer called Jacob who found the second present that was addressed to Niall. The farmer is clean.'

'Are there any Nialls on missing persons?'

'None. It's been checked as a matter of priority, and there are no Nialls.'

'So what are the next steps?' another DC asked.

'Our first priority is identifying the victim, as that will provide us with vital clues – who they were, possible motives for murder, connections. That's the key, and thankfully Claire is on it. The fingerprints should be in by the morning. If they don't yield anything, then we're back to square one. We're also testing the wrapping paper for prints or DNA, but I'm not holding out much hope. Whoever is doing this is unlikely to make such a careless mistake.'

Tom paused to sip his water, before continuing.

'Our second priority is finding Niall, who the present was addressed to. With only a first name to go on, it's not going to be easy, but we can start in the local vicinity and work our way outwards. In the morning, we can start compiling a list of all the Nialls in the area and begin tracking them down. Until then,' he said, 'I suggest we all go home and get a good night's sleep, because tomorrow is going to be pedal to the metal. I'd like everyone who's on shift in the building at nine a.m. so that we can get started.'

That allowed for roughly six hours sleep, by the time people got home and into their beds. Tom thought he caught a few mutinous looks as people left, but he didn't care. He was here to catch a killer, not make friends, and if he could do that quickly, he might save lives.

'Deborah,' he called to the DS who was loitering by the door. He thought that handling Deborah with kid gloves might be the way forward: make her feel like a vital team member and she'd yield the best results.

'Yes?'

'Would you mind drafting a missing persons appeal to go out to local press? I know it's late…'

'Leave it with me,' she said.

'I'd like something in print for the local newspapers, as well as the bigger Carlisle and Newcastle outfits.'

'What about social media?'

'Yeah, plaster the information anywhere and everywhere. If someone has been at the toilet for too long, I want to know about it.'

She gave him one of her sceptical looks.

'Not literally, obviously,' Tom added quickly, 'but any information is good information.'

She nodded and left.

'She thinks you're a pervert now,' Lauren said, following Tom out the door.

'Haltwhistle is bringing out the comedian in you, DS Rea,' Tom laughed, as they made for his car. 'I must see if there's a theatre nearby. When all this is done and dusted, you might have found a new calling.'

* * *

In his guesthouse room, Tom lay staring at the ceiling. He was beyond exhausted, could feel the ache in his muscles from the day's exertions. But his mind was racing, refusing him any respite.

He knew that every killer was different. Knew that each had their own pattern they adhered to – the length of time between kills, the level of planning for each, potentially a memento of their crime – that many thought they were doing something monumental by taking a life: the hero in their own story.

Somewhere out there, beneath the same sky Tom could see through the net curtains of his bedroom window, a killer slept.

Or maybe they didn't.

Perhaps right now, as Tom tried to drift off, the killer was at work again. Maybe another victim was drawing their final breath. Maybe they were hunkered down with a roll of wrapping paper, preparing a bloody offering to be crudely patched up with Sellotape and ribbons. A fresh gift tag and name.

It was enough to drive a person mad.

Tom rolled over, the unfamiliar bed creaking beneath him. He tried to clear his mind by jamming his earphones in and playing peaceful piano music. Dr Dougan had told him that focusing on the melody while visualising the notes tinkling off the ivories was a good way to induce sleep. For a while, Tom lay there, duvet bundled over him, concentrating on make-believe crochets and minims.

In the end, it worked, though not until the first streaks of scarlet were lighting up the sky.

9

THE MOUNTAINS SWALLOWED THE last of the daylight, their black ridges and valleys piercing the bruised December sky. Dark clouds smothered the stars, but the moon was doing its best to cast faint light into the world. The wind was strong, rattling through the branches, whispering secrets for anyone wise enough to listen. An owl's shriek ripped through the gale, high and sharp – a banshee's wail carried on the wind.

The figure in the forest did not seem to notice.

They walked as though enjoying a leisurely stroll on a summer's day, though their boots crunched over ice-laced mud rather than golden sands and foaming turquoise waves. They were dressed for the elements, at least: a bobbled hat, a thick coat, a pair of black leather gloves – the kind Santa Claus himself might wear.

A worn backpack was slung over their shoulders. This, sadly, was not the kind of sack Father Christmas would load onto his sleigh. Rather, it looked like something an eighteen-year-old trying to 'find himself' would carry as he stepped onto some far-flung trail in Southeast Asia. It was old and tatty, but more than up to the task.

At the start of their mission, there had been a fair bit of weight to it. Now, after two deliveries, it was somewhat lighter. Not enough to affect their pace, but enough to remind them of the season.

A time for giving.

For sharing.

The first two deliveries had gone more smoothly than expected. Smoother, even, than they could have dared to dream. Though, they could imagine the unwrapping hadn't been a fully joyful event.

A foot here, a hand there.

Fitting, really. A finger in every pie. A foot in every grave.

A ghost of a smile flitted on the figure's face. They might just get out of this in one piece.

It was soon extinguished by the icy wind and daunting thought of what was to come next.

They stopped in a small clearing and pulled a tattered map from their back pocket. Google Maps would be far easier, but they were no fool. No technology on a mission like this. That was the rule. Otherwise, they might as well amble into the nearest police station and hand over a signed confession.

No, no. There were plenty of miles yet.

They gazed at the map, their eyes tracing the undulating hills and the dark masses of trees that lay ahead of them. They located where they were, and plotted where they needed to be before the sun came up.

Time was tight. They needed to move.

They folded the map with care, slipping it back into their pocket, then adjusted the straps on the backpack – Santa's Sack, as they liked to think of it. Santa's Sack for Santa's helper.

A little lighter, yes, but not empty.

Not yet.

There were more deliveries to be made before Christmas.

The season of goodwill, and all that. A time for generosity. For sharing.

A chuckle threatened to rise in their throat, but they tamped it down. It would do no good to become hysterical. Instead, they moved forward, one step, and then another. Soon, they were in an easy rhythm. A steady march, like a soldier on a mission, which they were. They pushed branches out of their way with one gloved hand, while navigating the treacherous, gnarled roots beneath their feet, with only the moon as their guide.

Up ahead, the path wound deeper into the hills, where the sky darkened further and the wind conjured up voices and silhouettes in the shadows.

But it wasn't ghouls in the woods that the figure feared.

That was the least of their troubles.

They had work to do.

And the night was still young.

10

Tom studied the HIKERS TURN BACK sign, and pictured Maddison standing in this very spot just a few days ago, her fingers brushing the timber before pressing on, unaware of the horrors that lay ahead.

Tom, however, was not here on official business.

Another flurry of nightmares had wrenched him from sleep long before his alarm was due to go off. Instead of lying in bed, sweating and restless, lingering on dreamscapes of floating feet and bloody handsaws, Tom had changed into his clothes headed outside before he could talk himself out of it.

He had stood in the grey light, assessing his options, the town still wrapped in a pre-dawn hush. Some houses had lit-up windows, but most stood in darkness. He had considered going to the station, getting a jump on the day ahead early – but he knew burning the candle at both ends was a recipe for burnout. Working himself into the ground wouldn't bring about justice any faster. And if he wanted to catch the killer, he needed his wits about him.

And then, he'd heard Dr Dougan's voice in his head: the wonder of the great outdoors. So, with a sigh, he'd grabbed his new hiking boots from his car, laced them up, and started walking. Before he'd even fully registered his destination, he had ended up here – where Maddison had last stood, her path about to turn from routine to tragedy.

Tom had not spent any great deal of time outside. A handful of camping trips in his youth had been enough to put him off for good. Sure, he'd been on walks through parks on sunny summer days, but found the crowded paths and kids whizzing by on bikes like they were Evil Kinevil annoying. Besides, his work didn't really allow for long windows of time out and about. There was always a crime to solve, and he was only too happy to oblige.

But now, with a few hours to himself, he was heeding Dougan's advice.

His boots crunched against the dirt path, the morning dew clinging to the soles. The air was sharp with the scent of pine, crisp enough to sting his lungs. Though he was loathe to admit it, a few minutes into his walk, he began to enjoy it. Focusing on the rhythm of his steps, on each gust of wind that swept through the trees, on the deep, steadying pull of his breath — it was taking his mind off his fitful sleep, each step scrubbing the fragments of nightmares that flashed behind his eyes.

By the time he reached a steep incline, he was breathing hard. His calves and hamstrings – muscles that hadn't been properly worked since he had given up five-a-side football nearly three years ago – burned, and he liked it. He welcomed the ache. He leaned into it, pumping his legs like pistons as he navigated the hill.

At the summit, he stopped, hands on his hips.

Silence stretched before him. There were no cars for miles. No voices. No DCI barking orders, demanding more. The sky was shifting from deep blue to a soft pink, streaked with purple. It was stunning. Below, the valley unfolded, and he watched a lone bird push off from a branch, its wings silhouetted against the rising sun.

Tom caught his breath. His heartbeat steadied, and a tightness that he hadn't known to be sitting in his chest unravelled.

For a fleeting moment, he considered phoning Dr Dougan to thank him, or maybe just to share this unexpected moment of tranquillity with the man who had suggested it in the first place. But he had no service, and the therapist would likely be asleep anyway.

He checked the time, and realised that if he didn't get a move on, he'd be late for his own 9 a.m. deadline. With one last glance at the sweeping valley and the vast, endless sky, he turned and started back towards civilisation.

* * *

Tom made it to the station with a few minutes to spare. On the way, he'd planned to pick up a load of pastries – croissants, pains au chocolat, and whatever else he could get his hands on – as a morale booster, but the village shop wasn't open yet.

The desk sergeant greeted him warmly as he passed. Perhaps murder was the thing to bond people in the frozen north – nothing like a dismembered hand to bring people together.

Imagine what a pain aux raisins could do.

He found Lauren in the office, phone pressed to her ear, frustration etched across her features.

'... Call me when you get this,' she said, before disconnecting and placing the phone on the desk with a sigh.

'Someone avoiding you?' Tom sat down opposite her.

'Maddison,' she replied. 'I thought I'd phone to see if she knew anyone called Niall, but she's out of range, I think.'

'She'd be beyond Bellingham by now, right?'

'Depends how quickly she's going. It makes you wonder how close she was to the hand addressed to Niall. Maybe it was intended as a message for her. Maybe she knows who Niall is.'

'Maybe,' Tom said, 'maybe not.'

'Thank you, Confucius, for those words of wisdom.'

'I'm here all week.'

Lauren drummed her fingers on the desk. 'I've been thinking this over all morning. I know it's unlikely, but could Maddison be behind it?'

'Why would she do that?'

'I don't know,' Lauren admitted. 'Maybe she's done something bad and is trying to draw the attention away from herself. Maybe she's killed her boyfriend—'

'Fiancé.'

'Fiancé, yeah. Maybe she's killed Tristan, and this is a double bluff. Maybe that's why she's so comfortable finishing her trip as planned – because she knows no one is actually after her. Because *she* is the killer.'

'It's far-fetched,' Tom said, 'but stranger things have happened.'

'Jesus, you really are full of sage advice this morning. What's up with you?'

'Nothing,' Tom shrugged. 'I've been for a walk, that's all.'

'*Just a walk?*' Lauren said. 'Or did you smoke a joint on the way? Is that why you're so Zen?'

'I'm like a duck,' he replied. 'Calm above surface, legs flailing below.'

'Good to know.'

'Look, it's a theory. And it's as good as anything we have right now, so thanks for sharing. Do you think—'

Tom didn't get to finish his question. At that moment, Deborah bustled into the room and wedged between him and Lauren. She was as subtle as a sledgehammer to the bollocks, but he had to hand it to her: it got results.

'Debbie, how are—'

'Please don't call me Debbie.'

'But Martin—'

'Martin is a DCI who called me Debbie on my very first day. I didn't feel I was in a position to correct him, but you're a different matter. I much prefer Deborah, thank you very much.'

'Deborah it is,' Tom said. 'What have you got for me?'

She handed him a sheet of A4 paper and stepped back, right onto Lauren's foot. As Lauren swore loudly and Deborah mumbled apologies, Tom examined the paper.

It was a printed spreadsheet listing men called Niall, along with corresponding addresses, and other pertinent information. There were fifteen within a six-mile radius. Tom dreaded to think how many there'd be if they were forced to expand their search to Carlisle or Newcastle. For now, he tried to focus on the positives – they had a decent jumping-off point.

One of the men on the list had been to prison for GBH over a decade ago. He also noted that the addresses were listed in order of proximity to Haltwhistle. Someone had been sufficiently thorough, and he said so.

'It was one of the DCs,' Deborah said. 'Seems like he stayed up half the night pulling this together.'

'Good on him. Pass along my thanks,' Tom said. 'So, are we planning to visit?'

'I am,' Deborah said. 'Martin wants to conduct a press conference, and he wants you in on it. He's wearing his smartest suit and you—'

'Are not,' Lauren finished Deborah's sentence, still behind her.

'Ouch! Double-teamed by Trinny and Susannah.' Tom pulled a mock-offended face. 'So, you two get to go on a jolly while I have to smarten up for the journos?'

'I thought I might go alone,' said Deborah.

'I'd prefer if you went as a pair,' said Tom, acknowledging Lauren shaking her head vigorously while scowling. 'In fact, I think there could be a blooming partnership in the making here. An English Cagney and Lacey. A more northern Scott and Bailey.'

Deborah looked delighted at the comparison to Suranne Jones. Lauren, on the other hand, was not nearly as pleased.

'No time like the present,' Tom said, and Deborah hurried off. 'And, if this takes all day, then so be it. This is our strongest lead yet.'

'You're a dick,' Lauren muttered as she passed, though she was smiling.

'I'll see you for a pint tonight,' Tom called after her.

'Only if I'm not behind bars for murder,' Lauren muttered, before disappearing around the doorframe.

Tom was assessing his only-slightly creased shirt and drab tie when Martin walked in, looking immaculate. He was dressed in a fitted suit, a shirt that looked as though it was lifted straight from a hanger and a partnered tie. Tom could practically see himself in the DCI's shoes. Martin wore a vague look of disgust.

'Are you changing before the presser?'

'I was just on my way to the guesthouse,' Tom assured him.

''Atta boy,' Martin replied.

Back at the guesthouse, Tom's day went from bad to worse. The landlady informed him that his room was double-booked so she needed him out. Luckily, she had a spare flat a few minutes' walk away, one that was usually very popular on Airbnb but for some reason remained vacant this year, and she offered him that instead. He said that would be fine, asked to borrow her iron, then proceeded to his room where he showered.

After shaving, he threw on his smartest shirt and fanciest tie, giving himself a once-over in the full-length mirror. Dark bags framed his eyes, and his cheeks looked hollow. You couldn't polish a turd, apparently.

He checked his watch, but there was no time for a facemask. His appearance would have to do.

11

LAUREN AND DEBORAH HAD struck out three times and decided to cut their losses, opting for an early lunch in the hopes that nourishment from the café might turn their luck around.

Deborah, somewhat reluctantly, forewent the sandwiches she had prepared that morning, pushing the boat out by ordering a chicken caesar salad. Lauren, on the other hand, chose a ham and cheese panini with crisps. They retreated to a seat by the window, watching a sleepy Haydon Bridge drift by: an ancient stone church with a tall steeple, a railway crossing with an absurdly short platform. Aside from that, not much to observe.

'So, nothing to show for our efforts this morning,' Deborah said.

'I wouldn't say that,' Lauren countered. 'In policing, I often find you have to take the wins where you can. We may not have found *our* Niall, but we were able to narrow down the list by three. A good morning's work, in my opinion.'

A good morning's work, sure, but hardly a good morning. Deborah had insisted on staying five miles per hour under the limit, refused to turn the radio on, and responded to Lauren's attempts at conversation like she was undergoing a cross-examination. Lauren had finally relented, leaving Deborah to it. She'd taken to gazing at the passing countryside of vast fields and grazing sheep, counting down the minutes until lunch. Throw in Deborah's intense interview technique, and Lauren was ready to call it a day.

'How many more do you think we can fit in?' she asked.

Deborah consulted the list. 'There are a few in Hexham, so we could easily manage three or four after this one. Then, back at it tomorrow if we don't get anything today.'

Great, Lauren thought.

Tonight, if the day ever ended, she'd make sure the pints were on Tom. She might even plump for the most expensive steak on the menu, to truly underline the suffering she had endured because of him. She glanced over at Deborah and felt a tad guilty about her negative attitude. She was a good detective, she just had … quirks. Maybe Lauren just needed to get to know her a little better. Perhaps, now that she wasn't behind the wheel, she'd be more open to conversation.

'So, are you married?' she tried.

'No.'

'Got a partner?'

'No.'

'Do you like ABBA?'

'Not really.'

Lauren sat back in her chair, mentally adding a bottle of the house red to tonight's order.

Then, seemingly from nowhere, Deborah said, 'What's the deal with you and Tom?'

Lauren blinked. 'What do you mean?'

'Is there something more than a professional partnership there?'

'No. Why would you think that?'

'You seem close, that's all,' Deborah shrugged. 'Do you have a boyfriend?'

'No,' Lauren said, just as their food arrived.

As she picked open the panini to allow the steam escape, she wondered why she had denied having a boyfriend. Technically, she had told the truth, as she actually had a fiancé. But that only made the lie seem worse.

It was true that she and Tom had their … moments, but that was before the Christmas List Killer and Ben. Tom was a good man, and funny when he made an effort. True, she found herself increasingly enjoying their time spent together. But he was her partner. That was all.

They finished their food in silence, not quite companionable, but close enough now that Lauren knew Deborah was capable of occasional flashes of humanity. Lauren paid the bill and followed Deborah to the car.

'Who is the next Niall, then?' Lauren asked, as Deborah started the engine.

'Niall Wampler, of North Bank Road.' She pressed some buttons on the satnav. 'He's five minutes away.'

* * *

Deborah parallel parked in a tight space, without so much as a glance at Lauren for acknowledgement.

That was the true mark of a confident person. Lauren had once reverse parked into a space an articulated lorry could've navigated with ease, and her struggles almost demanded a ticker tape parade.

They were on a street of terraced houses on the outskirts of the village. The houses overlooked a green – complete with a NO BALL GAMES sign – though there were two goals stood at either end of the grass square. Three tall trees grew slap bang in the middle, making football a tricky proposition. Lauren could tell from the patches of dirt in front of each goal that where there was a will, there was a way.

They checked the address on the list before opening the gate to number 18. The front garden was bare, save for a small window box, the flowers long dead. Deborah climbed the steps to the door and rapped loudly.

'Deborah, maybe I should take this one,' Lauren suggested, having witnessed Deborah's bullish manner of questioning.

Before Deborah had time to pass judgement either way, the door opened.

'Niall Wampler?' Deborah asked.

'That's me,' he nodded.

Niall appeared in his mid-twenties, with dark, tousled hair and a layer of carefully cultivated designer stubble. He wore a shirt and tie with a pair of pyjama bottoms, worn slippers on his feet. He grinned when he caught Lauren giving him the once-over.

'Hangover from Covid,' he said. 'I have a Zoom meeting in half an hour.'

'You look ridiculous,' Deborah said. 'We're from Northumberland Police. May we come in?'

He opened his mouth to answer, but Deborah had already stepped across the threshold.

'Come on in.' He extended an invite anyway, before holding the door wide for Lauren and then closing it behind her. Lauren followed Deborah down a short hallway and into a busy living room. Wires were sprawled everywhere: chargers sprouting from wall sockets, HDMI leads snaking across the wooden floor, PlayStation controllers blinking in a cradle beside a huge TV. There was tasteful artwork on the walls and (strangely, to Lauren's mind) a diffuser, which saved the room from appearing like student digs. A moulting Christmas tree sat in the far corner, smelling of pine. Lauren couldn't help but quickly scan beneath it for any parcels wrapped in robin-patterned paper.

'Sorry,' Niall said, rubbing the back of his neck. 'The place is a bit of a tip at the moment.'

'You can say that again,' Deborah muttered.

'It's fine,' Lauren cut in quickly. 'Is it okay to call you Niall?'

'Sure.' He flopped on the sofa. 'What's this about? Am I in trouble?'

'Do you know a Maddison Cassidy?'

He looked confused. 'Yeah...'

'How?'

'We went out in high school. That must be, what, seven years ago now? Eight, maybe.'

'Do you still keep in touch with her?'

'God, no,' he said, a beat too fast. 'I haven't spoken to her since she broke up with me.'

'Why?'

'Do you keep in touch with your exes?' he countered. Lauren shook her head. Deborah sat as rigid as a statue. 'It was a silly high school thing. We only went out for about five months in sixth form. That was it.'

Deborah pulled a photo of Maddison from her bag and passed it to Niall.

'Is this her?'

He took a moment to consider the photo of love lost.

'That's her,' he said eventually, passing the photo back to Deborah. 'Is she okay?'

'She's fine,' Lauren said. 'But she was walking the Pennine Way when she found a severed human foot in wrapping paper. It was addressed to her.'

'Jesus,' Niall exclaimed. 'And what? You think it was me?'

'Not exactly. On the fifteenth of December, we were called to a field near Bellingham where we unwrapped a severed human hand. This one was addressed to Niall. We've been trying to track down a Niall with a connection to Maddison, as we believe the crimes are linked.'

'Wait,' he said. 'Someone sent a human hand to me?'

'Yes. Minus the ring finger,' Deborah nodded.

Niall looked like he might throw up. He sat back on the sofa, screwing the balls of his hands into his eyes.

'I know it's a lot to take in.' Lauren shot Deborah a look. 'Do you have any idea why someone might do that?'

'No,' he stammered, lowering his hands. 'Not at all.'

'What do you do for work?'

'I'm a recruitment consultant.'

'Have you annoyed anyone in the past month or so? Made any enemies?'

'Not to my knowledge,' he said, before choking on a laugh. 'And if I had, a fucking severed hand hardly feels like a reasonable complaint procedure.'

'Agreed,' Lauren chuckled. 'HR wouldn't be too happy.'

'Niall, where were you on the evening of the fourteenth of December?' Deborah asked.

'I was in London on a course. I've been down there a lot lately.'

'Do you have the dates?'

'I think I was down there between the tenth and the fifteenth.'

'Do you have proof?' Lauren asked.

He sat up straight.

'Why? You can't seriously think I had anything to do with this.' He stood up and started pacing. 'Why the hell would I send a hand to myself? A severed hand! And why would I send a foot to a girl I barely remember from years ago? Someone I haven't thought about in nearly a decade?'

'Niall, we—' Lauren started.

'Look,' he said, cutting across her. He rubbed a hand down his face. 'Can I have a minute?'

'Of course.'

Niall strode out of the room, the front door opening and closing a few seconds later. Deborah looked nervously at Lauren, but Lauren shook her head. Niall wasn't about to do a runner from his own house. Instead, she watched him through the window as he slipped a cigarette from his jacket pocket, lit up, and exhaled a plume of smoke skywards.

Deborah and Lauren sat in silence, waiting.

A couple of minutes later, he reappeared, bringing with him the stench of tobacco.

'Sorry,' he said, retaking his place on the sofa. 'It's just a lot of information to take in, you know?'

'We do,' Lauren said. 'And if you need any professional help in dealing with it, or you want to talk to anyone after, we can arrange support.'

'Thank you.'

'Now, we just have a few more questions and we'll be out of your hair.'

Niall nodded.

'Why did you and Maddison break up?'

'I think she was cheating on me. I can't be sure, but she started going out with someone else immediately after breaking up with me. Makes sense there was some overlap, right?'

'It's a possibility,' Deborah said. 'Do you remember his name?'

'Tristan. He was a dick to me for most of my school life. And not just to me – he was just one of those massive twats who got a kick out of intimidating people. Called you gay if you liked certain music, or because you didn't play football. Your classic arsehole, basically. Actually, now that I think about it, I'm pretty sure he dumped a dead guinea pig in someone's locker. I'm pretty sure he claimed it as a prank, and that he hadn't killed the animal or anything, but it's the mark of a weirdo, for sure.'

'Do you know if they're still together?' Lauren asked, though she knew the answer.

'No idea. As soon as I left school, I never gave either of them a second thought. Maddison was nice, though. I never knew what she saw in him. Alpha male, maybe. As they say,' he motioned to himself, 'nice guys finish last.'

'That's a Green Day song,' Deborah said.

Lauren and Niall both turned to look at her. Despite the situation, a grin spread across Niall's face. He laughed, and said: 'One of their better ones, too.'

Lauren stood, handing him a card. 'As I mentioned, if you need any support, please do get in touch.'

'Do you think whoever's doing this will target me?'

'We don't think so. However, we'll station a patrol car nearby for a few nights just in case. Purely precautionary,' Lauren added, noting the colour drain from his face.

With that, she thanked him for his time and headed to the front door, Deborah in tow. Back in the car, Lauren cast one last glance at the house. Niall watched them leave from the open doorway, looking as though he'd just seen a ghost. Lauren waved as Deborah pulled away from the kerb.

'Back to the station?' Deborah asked.

Christ, yes, Lauren thought, *and step on it.*

12

SUCH WAS THE INTEREST in the case that news agencies from far and wide braved the journey to Haltwhistle. Big players from the cities had requested for the presser to go ahead that afternoon, to allow time for travel. Second-hand news or replays were not good enough in their line of work – the frontline was where the action was. And, right now, the action was in a tiny village in the north of England.

The delay offered Tom much-needed time to ruminate.

He remembered a journalist – Archie Walker – from the Christmas List Killer case. At one of the press conferences, he'd made some comments that got under Tom's skin. Days later, Archie had caught Tom in a particularly bad mood. He'd asked a question that had provoked a reaction: Tom had pinned him to a wall, his arm on the journalist's throat. It had earned him a suspension, while Archie had walked away with a Fortnum & Mason hamper in way of an apology. Tom hadn't been asked to sign the card.

He couldn't afford to lose control like that again. He'd been sent to Haltwhistle as a safe pair of hands, an experienced detective who knew his way around a crime scene, one who commanded respect from those working around him. It would do him no good to blow up if – or rather when – a question he didn't like came his way.

The station wasn't big enough for the number of guests they were expecting. Luckily, Martin had managed to secure the keys to a scout hut, where a couple of eager volunteers were arranging rows of chairs, filling urns with tea, and buttering scones.

Tom wasn't asked to get involved.

He was sitting in a dusty back room, half-filled with rusty sports equipment and camping supplies, with the lights off. His hand was on his chest, palm flat, concentrating on the rhythm of his heart.

Breathe, he told himself.

In for four.

Hold for four.

Exhale for four.

Dr Dougan said exercises like this would help. Supposedly, it calmed the mind and focused the senses. Supposedly, it eradicated feelings of anxiety.

Supposedly.

But it wasn't working. His mind was spiralling. It twisted and turned, pulling him twelve months into the past, back to his kitchen. He saw the cold glint of the knife: the unsteady hand wielding it.

He felt his breath hitch; his chest rising and falling like a spasm. It wasn't working – he could barely draw enough oxygen onboard to stay alive. The room was closing in. The walls suffocating.

Breathe.

Tom fought against the rising tide, engulfed by panic, counting to four over and over again while forcing breaths in and out, trying to keep his head above the water. He was hot and cold at the same time, sweat pooling on his forehead and in the small of his back. His stomach churned, and he thought he might be sick.

Fuck, how he longed to be on the brow of the hill he'd visited this morning, rather than in a musty hall feeling like he was awaiting trial.

Music. He needed music.

Fumbling in the front pocket of his bag, he found his headphones and shoved them in his ears. 'Remember Me As A Time Of Day' by Explosions in the Sky filled his head, blotting out the world. He sank back into his chair, eyes closed as he let the soundscapes wash over him. He clung to each note like it was a lifeboat, dragging him to safety.

His collar soon felt looser.

His chest unclenched.

The kitchen and the knife seemed a little further away.

Then – a knock on the door. Tom paused the music as Martin poked his head in.

'It's starting to fill up,' he said. 'Ready in five?'

Tom nodded, and then hit play again.

* * *

The main hall was almost full, with only a few sporadic seats empty. Cameras on tripods lined the back of the room, their red recording lights signifying they were ready and waiting. Reporters perched on the edge of their seats, phones balanced on knees, notebooks and pens at the ready. There was a low hum of chatter among the journalists who knew each other, the big players who covered stories of this magnitude every day, and knew how to play the game. The less-experienced ones sat quietly, pens poised, ready to make their mark.

Martin and Tom entered through a side door at the front of the room, then made their way to a makeshift stage – the flimsy kind dragged out for nativity plays and summer fêtes. Tom took a seat while Martin approached the borrowed lectern, the wood scuffed from years of sermons and class assemblies.

Martin cleared his throat, welcomed everyone to Haltwhistle, and then read a prepared statement detailing the case so far – two body parts found twenty-four hours apart, no suspects. The press officer had done her best to pad it out, to make it sound more grandiose, but the bare bones of what they had managed to accomplish so far spoke for themselves. Any journalist worth their salt would be able to see it.

As Martin spoke, Tom scanned the room. He recognised some from past press conferences in Gateshead, and others whose names he knew only from TV. A few rows back, he spotted Archie. When they locked eyes, Tom nodded coolly and then looked away, tension immediately simmering in his chest. As a journo who wrote for one of the higher-tier papers, he was absolutely entitled to be here. But, Tom couldn't help thinking, if he had been investigating a lost trolley at the supermarket, Archie would've made it his mission to be there. There was no way he was going to miss severed body parts for the world. Tom just had to hope that he wasn't here to stir up trouble.

'Any questions?' Tom heard Martin say, and a volley of hands shot up.

Martin handled the first few easily – questions about the identity of the victim, and whether the hand and the foot belonged to the same person. Standard fare. It seemed a lot of people wanted to know the same thing, as after a few questions in this vein, hands lowered, beaten to the punch by the bigger outfits who knew how to work the press conference.

Then, Archie stood. Tom's inclination was to throw something at him, to stop him from asking whatever he was about to, knowing that it would not be good.

'DCI Jones, I'm just wondering about the wisdom of having DI Stonem on the team. I mean, everyone here is bound to know what happened to him last year.'

The hall seemed to shrink around Tom. He dug his fingers into his thighs, in an effort to hold his tongue.

Martin's response was smooth. Practised. 'DI Stonem is a valued member of the team. As the SIO, I trust him completely to resolve the case in a timely fashion, with the full support of the team.'

Archie wasn't done. 'Do you know what happened to him last year?'

Tom could feel the roar of his pulse in his ears.

'Believe it or not,' Martin said, his tone steady, 'this is not my first murder investigation. I do know how to read a file and am more than aware of Tom's excellent track record. Now, if there are any more sensible questions…'

Archie smiled – the kind that made Tom's blood boil. He considered leaving the room, but knew how that would look – like an admission of guilt, or weakness. Neither would be a good look. Instead, he focused on controlling his breathing.

'His record prior to moving to the North East *may* have been excellent,' Archie said, then made a show of checking his notes, 'but he hardly covered himself in glory last year. First, there was the frenzied attack on one of the area's best and brightest journalists.' This earned a big laugh from the room. Tom clenched his fists. 'And let's not forget how Tom and his team disappointed a number of families by failing to stop a killer.'

There was a shift in the room, unease settling. Some of the younger ones studied their shoes or checked their phones.

Martin cut in sharply. 'They did stop the killer.'

Archie shrugged. 'Some of those deaths were preventable.'

'In your opinion,' Martin countered. 'The police force can only work with the evidence it has. Any claim must be backed up by hard evidence, as you know. I will reiterate. DI Stonem would be a credit to any force, and we're lucky to have him. There'll be no more questions.'

'Could Seth, or one of his cronies, be behind this?'

Seth.

It was a name Tom had tried hard to blot out of his brain, to wish out of existence. But it was back now, clawing at his memory, unravelling something deep inside him.

His vision swam as white noise thrummed in his ears. From far away, he heard Martin end the press conference, the squeal of chairs on parquet flooring. He felt someone grab his elbow, guiding him gently off the stage and away from the hubbub. Someone was speaking to him, but he couldn't understand. They might've been speaking in a different language for all he knew. Something dampened his face, and when he lifted his hand, he realised they were tears. He was crying.

'Tom!'

His eyes snapped opened like he had been fast asleep. Martin was standing over him, a bottle of water in his hand, concern etched on his face.

'Get that down you.'

Tom took the bottle, twisted the cap with trembling fingers, and glugged it down. He wiped his face, and when he was more composed, said: 'Maybe he's right.'

Martin's expression hardened. 'That dickhead isn't half the man you are. What I said wasn't bullshit. I read your report, and I wouldn't have accepted you if I didn't think you were an asset. I know all about what happened last year, but I don't give a rat's arse unless it starts affecting what's happening *this* year. I trust it won't.'

'No, sir,' Tom said, his throat tight.

'I didn't think so. Now, I'm going to go and chase the vultures away, and then we've got work to do. Yes?' Martin straightened, turned to go, but then stopped. 'Tom, you didn't hit that prick Archie this year. I see that as progress. As far as I'm concerned, that's enough to earn your place here.'

13

TOM'S NEW ABODE WAS only a five-minute walk away – a nondescript flat above a bakery that smelled faintly of burnt bread. It had everything he needed, not that he would be spending much time there anyway; the case was all-consuming.

This place was sparse but functional. He walked through the living room, observing the small TV and comfy sofa. His throat closed at the sight of the small Christmas tree – thankfully, no gifts beneath.

The kitchen cabinets weren't empty, but he'd need to do a supermarket sweep sooner rather than later, especially now he didn't have a complementary guesthouse breakfast every morning. In the bedroom, he tested the mattress and peeked into the bathroom. The shower looked a decent job. He felt like he was in desperate need of one – the day's grime sticking to him – but if he didn't hurry, he'd be late for the pub with Lauren. He was eager to find out how she'd managed to endure a day with Deborah. But first, he had a phone call to make.

On the way, he called home.

His dad had been unwell for the past couple of weeks, and he'd attended a hospital appointment earlier that day. In the thrall of the press conference, he'd mostly managed to forget about it. But now, his worry churned in his stomach.

"A healthy work–life balance isn't just for the sake of your wellbeing. It's beneficial for everyone else in your life, too." Dr Dougan's sage advice played in his mind as he waited.

His mum answered, her voice cheery enough. At first, they danced around the topic. She asked him about his job and he told her he had been seconded to Haltwhistle. He asked about the choir she was part of, who were no doubt building up to some elaborate Christmas concert. A moment of silence led them down the path they'd both been avoiding.

'How did the appointment go?' Tom finally asked, dreading the answer.

'They've run some tests,' she said, her words measured. 'Took some samples. We just have to wait and see what comes back.'

'Did they say when?'

'Not really. They said it was busier than usual for this time of year, but they would try to be quick.'

He nodded to himself, eyes on the slick pavement beneath his boots.

'Do you still want me to come for Christmas dinner?' he asked. 'Would it be easier just the two of you?'

'It won't be the two of us. We have Danny, remember? We all want you here. He can't wait to meet you.'

Tom had been slightly taken aback when his parents had mentioned fostering again. But he was proud of them. They'd given him a life he could only have dreamed of before all the paperwork went though, and he was proud that they still wanted to make a difference.

'Would you prefer to book somewhere? Save you the stress of cooking?'

'I love cooking,' she said, and he could picture her shaking her head at the suggestion, a dishcloth slung over her shoulder, something rich and hearty in the oven waiting to be served up and enjoyed. 'Honestly, love, everything will work out. We don't even know for sure that it's…'

The word that neither wanted to linger on.

'Is he up for a chat?' Tom asked.

'He's asleep. Sorry, love. The day took it out of him.'

Tom massaged his temple. 'Well, pass on my love. And if you need anything, I'm only a couple of hours up the road.'

'From what I saw on the news tonight, you've got more than your hands full. Take care, son. Remember, you can bow out if it gets too much. No one will think any less of you.'

'I know, Mum. Speak to you soon.'

'I'll let you know if I hear anything.'

They said their goodbyes, and Tom pocketed his phone. The thought of his parents, one facing the prospect of a life-changing illness, the other attempting to keep things ticking along as per usual, even after adopting a foster kid, made him sad. Their cul-de-sac was famous for its festive lights, and he wondered if they had bothered to string theirs up this year. His mum was never one to back down from a challenge – she had probably doubled down in an act of defiance, especially to welcome their new lodger.

Ahead, the pub came into view, warm light spilling onto the cobbled street. Snow had begun to fall, swirling in the streetlamp's sodium hue. He imagined Haltwhistle would look postcard-pretty with a light dusting of snow, the type of village scenery made for Christmas cards.

Inside, the air was thick with the smell of roasted meat and beer. A beautifully-decorated Christmas tree stood beside a small stage, an acoustic guitar nestled in a stand. He scanned the crowd, eventually finding Lauren in a snug at the back.

It was the type of setting perfect for date night. There was a solitary table, with a flickering candle and a long stem rose at its centre. Soft music from a speaker hidden somewhere in the wall drifted over them, Adele's 'Make You Feel My Love'.

Lauren looked almost apologetic.

'It was the only table they had,' she said, in way of greeting.

'It's great. Private,' Tom added, as he shrugged off his coat. And then: 'What can I get you?'

Perhaps Lauren had seen the doomed press conference, or maybe she could just sense his sadness, for she went easy on him. Instead of a pricey glass of the Gott Napa Valley Cabernet Sauvignon she'd been eyeing up, she plumped for a pint of lager instead. Tom returned a few minutes later with their drinks, and they perused the menu. When the waiter came, Tom ordered a lasagne and Lauren opted for fish and chips.

'So, how was your day with Deborah?' he asked.

'An adventure,' she replied. She told him about her day – the questionable interview technique, Deborah's complete lack of filter, and her incredible prowess at parallel parking. 'And she likes Green Day.'

Tom raised an eyebrow. 'Green Day? As in, the rock band?'

'Yeah! She knew quite a deep cut, too, so I assume she's a fan.'

'That bumps her up in my estimations.'

'She's now at notch one.'

They said it in unison – quoting an inside joke – and both laughed.

After that, the weight on Tom's shoulders eased up. Lauren always seemed to have that effect on him. He looked over at her. As the candle's flame flickered, the reflection of its glow danced in her eyes. He looked away again a flush prickling the back of his neck.

They discussed the press conference, the sheer dickheadery of Archie Walker. Tom didn't mention the anxiety he had felt, or the suspected panic attack he'd suffered after. He *did* praise Martin for sticking up for him, mentally noting to buy him a bottle of something nice as a thank you.

Their food arrived, and they dug in. After, they washed it down with another pint.

'Are you sticking around for Christmas?' Lauren asked.

'No, I'm heading down to Manchester to see my parents.'

'I imagine that'll be nice and weird at the same time.' Lauren paused, weighing her words. 'No Seth.'

'No Seth,' he repeated, like a full stop. 'What about you?'

Lauren deliberated, making a show of gulping her lager, and then said, 'I think it'll just be Sophie, me and my parents.'

'Sounds nice. What is Sophie getting for Christmas?'

They talked for a while longer about Christmas tradition and family quirks, before inevitably circling back to the case. The development of the hand had thrown their plans off course, but paying a visit to Tristan was on the cards for the following day. Their stomachs full, with tiredness creeping up on them, they paid the bill and left.

Snow was settling. It grazed the roads and the windowsills, the moon casting its glow as more flakes twirled from the heavens like tiny falling stars. Tom and Lauren crunched down the street, content to take in their surroundings in silence. They paused outside the guesthouse. Lauren turned to him and, without warning, pulled him into a hug. Tom froze for a second, and then relaxed into her embrace. The appley scent of her shampoo washed over him, and he realised he hadn't had proper physical contact with anyone in some time. He felt something hitch in his stomach – not unpleasant, but a hint of a warning all the same.

When she drew away, she smiled. 'See you in the morning, Tom.'

'Bright and breezy,' he nodded, voice thinner than usual. 'Sleep tight.'

He watched her ascend the steps and wave, before disappearing through the door. He lingered for a moment. Snowflakes settled on his coat and melted against his exposed skin.

On the way back to his flat, he scolded himself.

Lauren was his partner. He had to be professional. It would do no good to consider anything else stirring under the surface. Though, he had to admit that she was his type: dark hair, confident, an endearing laugh.

No, Tom, he warned himself. There was absolutely no point in considering if things could go further. *You're damaged goods, and her superior*. It was a disciplinary hearing waiting to happen.

And yet, as he let himself into the flat…

He considered whether it might be a risk worth taking.

14

As Lauren trudged through the snow to the station, she mulled over her thoughts.

First, she realised that she kept denying the existence of Ben like Peter had Jesus – first to Deborah, and then to Tom. Soon, the cock would crow and she'd be outed. Of course Ben would join the Christmas Day festivities (if she managed to sew up the case in time), so why hadn't she just said his name last night?

Her second thought was that Debbie was cut from the same cloth as Derren Brown. With her demure appearance, yet unexpected knowledge of rock music and expert parallel parking skills, her contradictory nature occupied Lauren's thoughts. Maybe that's why she hadn't mentioned Ben. Maybe Deborah had hypnotised her when she'd failed to mention him in the café.

And then, there was the hug.

Lauren was an overthinker to the core. Tom had probably taken it at face value: a simple goodnight embrace. But Lauren had lain in bed, replaying it. Hugging each other wasn't something they usually did. Maybe it was the falling snow and the soft lighting. Maybe it was the fact he had seemed desperately sad. Or, maybe, she *was* missing Ben and had simply longed for the reassuring touch of another human.

Although, she could almost discount that last one. The missed calls from her fiancé continued to pile up, and she had almost no inclination to ring him back. She told herself that

76

she was embroiled in the case, that it was easier to forget about home for the duration, but that wasn't strictly true. She knew his routine off by heart, knew what time he'd be at work, and planned calls home to Sophie when he wouldn't be there, then claimed it bad luck that they appeared to be ships in the night.

She forced the hug out of her mind. She needed to be fresh for their meeting with Tristan.

Tom was already in the office when she arrived, Google Maps open on his monitor. A blue line snaked from their location in Haltwhistle to an address in Humshaugh, just north of Hexham.

'What's that?' Lauren asked, sitting down in the seat beside him.

'That,' Tom said, gesturing at the screen, 'is the address of Rosanna Price.'

'And who is Rosanna Price?'

'She called in this morning. Seems like she has some information for us, though she didn't say what. Only that she wants us to pay her a visit.'

'This morning?'

'Yeah, I figured we'd hit the road in a few minutes. Could stop for a bacon bap on the way. Though,' he added, standing up. 'I doubt you'll need one, what with being waited on hand and foot.'

'Poor choice of words,' Lauren said, as she ushered him towards the door.

One bacon butty and half an hour later, they were circling Humshaugh, searching for Rosanna's house. They trawled through the village a couple of times, realising on the third trip up Military Road that the turnoff they needed was partially obscured by overhanging trees, creating a Narnia-like aura.

Tom indicated and turned onto the lane, his tyres bouncing over the rutted track. After a minute, the track became smooth tarmac and the view opened up. The countryside was frost-covered and vast, the sky huge and pale – pregnant clouds promising more snow. It looked like a painting.

In the foreground stood Welbeck Cottage.

The word 'cottage' suggested something quaint, a cute little stone house nestled in the heart of a sleepy village. This was anything but. It was massive, like five terraced houses had been knocked through to create this monolith. It *was* constructed of stone, with two chimneys at either end puffing out smoke. Tom could almost feel the warmth of the fire on his skin and hoped that would be the room Rosanna escorted them into.

After Tom parked next to a spotless Range Rover, they climbed out. A woman stood at the threshold, a spaniel circling her feet, its tail wagging excitedly, though she paid it no attention.

Rosanna Price was in her late twenties, with sharp cheekbones and dark sunken eyes, as though she hadn't slept in days. Her long, chestnut-brown hair was pulled into a loose ponytail, strands clinging to her face in the cold air. She wore a thick cream jumper and dark leggings, a pair of Ugg slippers hugging her feet.

'Rosanna?' Tom said, as they made their way up the garden path.

'Yes,' she said, her voice thin. 'Good of you to come at such short notice.'

They took their shoes off in the boot room, setting them beside a muddy pair of walking boots, before following her through a sleek kitchen-diner. A huge bouquet of fresh flowers sat on a wood-topped kitchen island, a splash of colour in an otherwise muted room.

She led them down a short corridor and into a sitting room at one end of the house. The fire was flickering, heat emanating from its flames. Above the fireplace, a wooden stag's head surveyed the room, its horns an impressive show of craftsmanship. There was a bookshelf laden with paperbacks, a couple of deep sofas and a wall-mounted TV. Beyond the French windows, rolling hills stretched into the distance.

Lauren couldn't tear her gaze from the view.

'Please, take a seat,' Rosanna said. 'Can I get you a drink?'

'I'd love a tea, please,' Lauren said.

'A water would be great, thanks,' Tom added.

When Rosanna left, Lauren raised an eyebrow at Tom. 'How the other half live, eh?'

'I reckon I'm a good ten years older than her...'

'At least,' Lauren interjected.

Tom gave her a look. 'I just wonder how someone in their twenties can afford a place like this.'

Before they had long to speculate, Rosanna returned with a tray. She passed Tom his water and placed Lauren's mug of tea on a table near her. Rosanna sank into one of the sofas, her lips tight, cheeks blotchy.

'Rosanna,' Lauren said gently, 'can you tell us why you called this morning?'

Rosanna plucked at a loose thread on her jumper, as if a self-soothing gesture. Then, in a voice barely above a whisper, she said, 'My husband, Joshua, didn't come home from a work trip. He should've been here two days ago, but I've not heard from him and his phone is going straight to voicemail.'

'Is that unusual?'

'He travels for work quite regularly, and sometimes he misses connections so he's away an extra night and things like that, but he always lets me know.'

'Where was he travelling from?'

'Munich.'

'And what does he do for work?'

'He owns his own business that manufactures, develops and sells medical supplies. It's a family business, but his dad retired two years ago. After that, the company became Joshua's. Quite fitting, both of us in medicine. I think he found it useful being married to a surgeon. Sometimes, he brought home samples or prototypes for my opinion.'

Lauren reached into her bag and pulled out a photograph.

'Rosanna, I'm going to show you a picture. It's not overly graphic, though there is a missing finger. I know it's upsetting, but I just need you to look at it and see if you recognise it.'

She passed over the photo of the hand, taken from an angle that obscured the severed wrist.

Rosanna closed her eyes for a moment, working up the courage to look. Eventually, she stole a glance, and paused, as if she'd been unplugged. Then, the tears came.

'That's Josh's hand,' she managed to choke between sobs.

They gave her all the time she needed, letting her talk at her own pace. Sometimes, the job meant doing things that seemed unkind – but in this case, they needed more details. Lauren retrieved a box of tissues she spied on one of the shelves, handing them to their host. Rosanna took them with a grateful nod. Eventually, she composed herself enough to look at them, though tears still trailed her cheeks. She breathed deep and then nodded again to show she was ready.

'Rosanna,' Tom said, 'I know this is a very difficult time. I just need to know how you identified the hand as Josh's?'

She pointed an unsteady finger at a small scar on the palm, using the other hand to block out the portion with the missing finger.

'Three years ago, when he proposed, he popped open a bottle of champagne. While he was pouring, he knocked one of the glasses over and it smashed. A chunk of glass got stuck in his hand. He needed six stitches.'

Tom took the picture from her and studied the palm.

It seemed they had found their victim: Joshua Price.

15

HALF AN HOUR LATER, Tom stood beside Lauren in the garden, gazing out at the distant hills. Another car was now in the drive, that of Rosanna's mother. After the revelation, Lauren had suggested that Rosanna call someone who could provide emotional support. Joanne had arrived within ten minutes, still wearing a flour-dusted apron, carrying the faint scent of freshly baked cupcakes.

Tom had quickly explained the situation: that the hand likely belonged to Joshua, and that they still needed to question Rosanna. Joanne had flashed a brief understanding smile, then hurried into the house. Tom and Lauren remained outside, giving the grieving family the space they needed.

'Are you okay?' Lauren asked.

'Yeah, why wouldn't I be?'

'I don't know. A sadistic killer so near Christmas. It's a bit close to home, no?'

'It's the job,' Tom said with a shrug, though his heart thudded a beat faster. 'Right now, the only person whose feelings matter is Rosanna. She might have answers about Josh that can help us end this thing. On that note, you didn't happen to bring a photo of the foot, did you?'

'Only one with the ankle bone showing at the top. I think that might tip her over the edge.'

'Yeah, good call,' he nodded. 'Do you think we can obtain one that's less graphic? She could help us figure out whether both came from Josh or not.'

'On it.'

She pulled out her phone and searched for the number she needed. Finding it, she took a few steps away and held it to her ear.

Tom huffed out a breath, hands in his pockets against the cold, and pondered his line of work – the things he had to put people through for the sake of uncovering the truth. In a way, he reasoned, it wasn't really his doing. The dark side of humanity had to answer for something; it was their actions that forced his hand.

It's an important part of the world, keeping the peace, his dad always said.

At the memory, a lump formed in his throat. He fixed his eyes on the horizon and drew some of Dr Dougan's prescribed breaths. Before he had time to complete a cycle, Lauren was back, and thoughts of his dad's scan were thankfully forced from his mind.

'They've said they'll try to get a decent photo for us as soon as. They're pretty backed up with post-mortems today, so it might not be with us before we have to leave.'

'Do you think showing her the photo we have would be too hard on her, if we're out of options?'

'I think so,' Lauren said. 'She's the only real lead we have. We don't want her shutting down on us.'

'Yeah, good shout,' Tom said.

'They're the only shouts I make.'

Behind them, the front door opened and Joanne appeared. She'd taken off her apron.

'Officers,' she called. 'I think Rosanna is ready to talk.'

They trooped across the grass, their footprints marking the dew-covered lawn. Joanne stood aside to let them through, then closed the door softly behind them.

'Go easy on her, won't you?' she said.

'Of course,' Lauren reassured her. 'She can have as many breaks as she needs, but I can't imagine we'll be here much longer.'

'Thank you. I'll be in the kitchen if you need me.'

Tom and Lauren followed the corridor into the room they'd been in earlier. Rosanna was in the same place as before. The fire had been stoked, and fresh drinks awaited them. Joanne reminded Tom of his own mother – miraculously able to be in five places at once without breaking a sweat. Rosanna glanced up at them as they sat down, her face tear-streaked.

'I just can't believe this. When I heard about the hand on the news… How it was wrapped up… What sort of sicko…?'

'It's horrific,' Lauren agreed. 'And we're really sorry that we have to do this now, but we still have some questions.'

'If it helps catch the bastard who did this, I'll do anything I can.'

'Thank you.' Lauren opened her notepad to a fresh page. 'The hand was addressed to a Niall Wampler. Do you know who that is?'

'Yes, we went to school together.'

'Can you think of any reason why someone would send Joshua's hand to Niall?'

'No,' Rosanna said, an almost manic laugh escaping her lips. 'It's fucking weird.'

'Agreed,' Lauren nodded. 'I'm guessing if you know Niall, you'll know Maddison Cassidy too?'

'Yes, we're still close with Maddison and Tristan. We don't see them as often as we'd like to … Joshua is…' she faltered, '*was …* working a lot.'

This prompted a fresh wave of sobs. They gave her all the time she needed. A few minutes later, once she nodded at them, Tom took up the mantle.

'Rosanna, you told us before that Josh ran a medical company.'

'Yes.'

'What is it called?'

'Silver Skies Medical Supplies.'

'Can you think of anyone who would harbour bad feelings towards him?'

'I imagine any number of people. As you can understand, in his position as CEO, Joshua had to make some really unpopular decisions from time to time. He was, I suppose, what others would describe as ruthless. Truth is, since Brexit, selling to Europe has become a nightmare. In order to keep the company afloat, never mind in profit, he had to make some redundancies. Which, unsurprisingly, didn't go down well.'

Tom made a note to compile a list of people whom Josh had fired. He imagined losing a job before Christmas was enough to tip some over the edge.

'Did he mention any names in particular?'

Rosanna pondered for a few seconds, then shook her head. 'No, not really. Truth be told, I found discussing work terribly boring. I want to switch off outside work – not talk balance sheets and bandages. I tended to zone out, especially when he was on one.'

Tom took a sip of his water, deliberating which path to take next.

'When was the last time you saw Maddison?'

'At a charity event I organised at the start of November. But I was so busy that I barely had a chance to even say hello. The last time we properly got together was in the summer, probably. We went for drinks in Newcastle.'

'Did she seem worried about anything?'

'She had money problems,' Rosanna said. 'She was in the middle of planning her wedding, but she had to scale back on what she truly wanted. Tristan was being next to useless, and I felt bad for her. I spoke to Joshua that night, and we offered her some money.'

'For anything specific?'

'No. Planning a wedding is like spinning plates. You never know what you're going to have to pay for next. We just thought, if we could offload some of the stress, we would.'

'How much did you give her?'

'Ten grand.' The number was said casually, as though mere pocket money. Judging from the house she lived in, maybe it was.

'Was there a deadline for paying it back?'

'Oh, God, no. Nothing like that. Maddison is a good friend. I know she'll get it back to me at some point.'

'Was Joshua happy with the arrangement?'

'I can't imagine he gave it a second thought, if I'm honest.'

'But he did know about it.'

'Yes, I discussed it with him.'

Tom scribbled a few thoughts in his notepad.

'Rosanna, this part might be a little tricky.'

She braced herself.

'It's likely that the ring finger was severed as a message, and we do have to ask about it. Was your marriage a good one?'

'Yes.'

'Were there any arguments?'

'Every marriage has arguments.'

Tom felt like they were on shaky ground. Before, Rosanna had been open and helpful. Now, it felt like she was being deliberately obtuse. Was she withholding something?

'Rosanna, we know this is difficult, but any little detail might help us catch the killer.'

'I know,' she said, her hands covering her face. She pressed her fingers gently against her closed eyes and sighed. 'We had a good marriage. We were comfortable financially, we had a nice house, plans for kids, another dog. The dream! And now...' She lowered her hands again. 'All of that has been ripped away from me.'

'Did you ever get the impression that he was having an affair – or anything like that?'

Rosanna looked him dead in the eye. 'No, detective. If you must know, we had a very active sex life.' Tom felt his cheeks redden. 'Now,' she continued, 'is there anything else you want to know? Favourite position?'

'I think we've got everything we need for now.'

Tom and Lauren stood up, outstretching their hands, which she shook. Lauren offered the services of a family-liaison officer, which Rosanna accepted. She walked them to the door, Joanne loitering in the kitchen.

As they stepped outside, Rosanna called after them. 'Find the body, will you? I want to give him a proper funeral.'

'We'll try,' Tom called back.

Rosanna closed the heavy wooden door behind them. Suddenly, the woods that surrounded the house, alongside the silence, felt eerily oppressive.

'Let's get out of here,' Lauren said. 'Time for a briefing?'

Tom fiddled with his phone for a minute, and then held up the screen.

'Silver Skies is just over half an hour away. Maybe we should pay a little visit, as we're in the area.'

16

BALLIOL INDUSTRIAL ESTATE, ON the outskirts of Newcastle, was your standard business park. Tom drove past a recycling centre, a down-on-its-heels gym, a couple of nondescript factories, discount carpet outlets, and two dodgy car garages that looked like they would rip you off without any consideration.

As he pulled into the car park of Silver Skies, he pointed out a fried food van.

'You can't have another bacon bap today,' Lauren said. 'Think of all that salt, clogging your arteries.'

'I was actually considering changing it up. Sausage bap, maybe? Even a sausage roll, if I'm being really adventurous.'

'What a dramatic shake-up.'

They exited the car and made their way to the unit that belonged to Joshua's company. It was an enormous building, though it looked like it could do with a facelift. The walls were shabby, the plaque beside the door faded and watermarked. High up, a broken window had been boarded over, the wood covered in graffiti.

'How do you reckon they got to that?' Tom asked, pointing it out. 'Onto the roof and rappel down, or do it before it goes up?'

'Why would they use the wood if someone had already tagged it?'

'Yeah, good point. Excellent use of the word "tagged". I didn't know you were so street.'

Before Lauren could retort, Tom pressed a button on the intercom. A short, sharp trill emitted, before a cheery voice came through the speaker.

'Silver Skies Medical Supplies.'

Tom identified himself and asked to be let in. The door clicked, granting them entry into a waiting room that reminded Tom of his dentist's – sterile and grey. Plastic chairs lined three of the walls, and a coffee table dead centre was covered in magazines – some medical, others gossip, housekeeping, current affairs. There was a small hatch in the remaining wall, framing a woman with red hair and a cheery smile. If she was concerned about why the police were here, she didn't show it.

'How can I help you?' she asked, as they approached.

'We'd like to speak to whoever is in charge.'

'Usually, that would be Mr Price, but he's away on business at the moment.' She picked up a phone and scanned a laminated sheet next to her. 'I'll just check if Mr MacMaster is free.'

After a short conversation, she smiled. 'I can take you up to his office now.'

She let them through the door and into the building proper. The ground floor was filled with clanking, whirring machinery. Conveyor belts shuttled shining silver surgical implements some-where out of sight. A bored-looking employee manned the controls, his eyes passing over a digital display as though he was being forced to read the world's most boring book.

'This way,' the receptionist said, leading them up a set of metal steps. Their footsteps echoed around the cavernous space, attracting some looks from those working below. They walked along a corridor, past a number of offices and a large boardroom. Joshua's office door was garnered with a nameplate. Tom figured poking around in there after their meeting with Mr MacMaster couldn't hurt.

At the end of the corridor, they were ushered into the office of the man who was technically in charge of operations, though he did not know it yet. He was behind a desk, his eyes locked on his computer screen. He clicked a few times on his mouse and then stood up. He was in his early fifties, a pair of glasses perched on his nose. His grey hair was thinning, though plenty still clung stubbornly to the sides of his head. His shirt and tie looked expensive, as did the pinstripe suit jacket hanging on a hook by the door. Behind him, a vast window overlooked the factory floor below like the bridge of a ship. It felt like they were hovering; the effect made Tom's stomach lurch.

'Please, take a seat.' The man's sombre tones were softened by a Scottish lilt.

Tom and Lauren sank into the two seats on the other side of his desk, facing him. Once he reclaimed his seat, Mr MacMaster interlocked his fingers and rested his chin on the bridge he had created. Tom had seen Dr Dougan do this many times.

'How can I help you?'

Tom and Lauren had deliberated on how much to reveal. Currently, they only had Rosanna's word that the hand belonged to Joshua – they both knew from experience that emotional testimonies could often turn out to be unreliable. Tom took the lead.

'We have reason to believe that Joshua Price has been murdered.'

His complexion blanched.

'What? How?'

'Mr MacMaster—'

'Duncan, please.'

'Duncan, details are still being corroborated, so I can't say too much. Mr Price's wife has identified the deceased's hand from a photograph, but we will have to do a formal identification. We have a few enquiries that might help with our investigation.'

Duncan paled further. 'Hand? You're not saying that the one found at the farm was Joshua's?'

'Like I said, that's yet to be confirmed, but we have reason to believe it is.'

'Jesus!' Duncan slumped back in his seat, then reached for a desk drawer before pulling back like he'd been scalded.

Tom noticed. 'Everything okay?'

'Yes, it's … it's nothing.'

'Are you sure?' Duncan nodded, so Tom continued. 'In that case, do you mind if we ask you a few questions?'

'Of course. Do you have anyone in custody?'

'When did you last see Joshua?' Tom asked, ignoring his question.

'Let me see...' He swivelled in his chair and looked at a Silver Skies-branded calendar hanging on the wall. 'We had a board meeting on the tenth of December, and then he flew to Europe.'

'What was discussed?'

'It was just a standard weekly meeting,' Duncan shrugged. 'We talked about targets, a potential new deal with a company in Italy, what Trump's taxes mean for us.'

'What do they mean for you? Redundancies?'

'Not necessarily,' Duncan said, 'but it's not out of the question.'

'Who else was in the meeting?'

'There were about ten of us. Joshua, myself, some of the sales guys… Denise in reception can give you the full list on your way out.'

'What about minutes?'

'Yes, she should have those as well.'

Tom decided it was time to start really probing. 'Is money a concern?'

'Money is always a concern in any business,' Duncan said, though he looked uneasy discussing finances. 'We recently mislaid a batch of NovoRapid which costs an arm and a leg.'

'What's that?'

'Insulin.'

'Noted,' Tom said, and then got back to the line of questioning he wanted to pursue. 'There have been job losses in the past, is that correct?'

'There have.'

'Would we be able to have a list of those who have been let go?'

'Yes,' Duncan nodded. 'I'm sure that's something Denise can sort for you, too.'

'Thank you.'

Tom made a mental note to corner Denise before they left. As he was about to ask another question, Duncan reached for the drawer again, this time pulling out a bottle of whisky and a small glass. He unscrewed the cap and began to pour, the peaty aroma of the alcohol permeating the room.

'Duncan,' Tom said, 'would you mind holding off on that until we're finished?'

'Ah, yes,' he said, stopping mid-pour. 'Of course. Don't know what I was thinking.'

'Is that something you'd usually do during the working day?'

Duncan looked appalled at the accusation. 'Not at all. But most days don't involve the police showing up and informing me my boss has been murdered. You'll forgive me if it looks like I'm having an off day.'

'Why do you have alcohol in your drawer?'

'In case we have visitors, or the need to celebrate a good business deal.'

Tom wanted to take the bottle off him, but resisted. He didn't think it would please their host. Instead, he moved on. 'Duncan, what was Joshua like as a boss?'

'He was hardworking. Fair. Honest. He wasn't afraid of ruffling feathers if he thought it would be beneficial to the company.'

'Ruffling feathers how?'

'Just making decisions, really. In the old days, you'd hash it out with a colleague if you didn't agree with something. Now, everyone bottles it up, moans in the staffroom, posts about it on the internet…'

Tom wrote the word 'internet' in his notepad, and said, 'Did he ruffle feathers often?'

'Look,' Duncan said, his expression darkening, 'I know what you're getting at, but I can assure you no one here is capable of chopping their boss's hand off and wrapping it up. What would they stand to gain?'

'Promotion?' Tom suggested.

'Now listen here, sonny,' Duncan rose to his feet. 'I won't have you coming in here and throwing accusations around like that.'

'No one accused anyone of anything,' Lauren said. 'We're just trying to establish a motive.'

'Do you stand to personally benefit from Joshua's death?' Tom was sure Duncan was getting angry in an attempt to deflect any scrutiny. But Tom was like a dog with a bone. He wasn't about to give up that easily.

Duncan stared a hole through Tom, then released a deep sigh.

'I suppose so,' he shrugged. 'I'm second in command. Obviously, we had contingency plans in place, should something happen to any of the board of directors. But I don't want you thinking that this is something I would ever have wanted. Joshua was like a son to me.'

With that, the tears came. Real or performative, Tom couldn't be sure. He and Lauren thanked Duncan for his time, then got up to leave. Before they had reached the door, Duncan had necked the glass of whisky and was pouring the next.

Outside in the corridor, Tom paused by Joshua's office and tried the handle, but it was locked. He stuck his head through Duncan's door again, asking if he had a key.

'Not that I know of,' he said, glugging another glassful.

Back outside, Tom peered in through the window of the office. Frustratingly, the blinds were slatted and half-closed, which meant he couldn't see much. The desk was messy, with various piles of paper stacked on it. There was more paper on the floor, and an overflowing bin. Writing on a whiteboard wasn't discernible, adding to the mystery. It was probably nothing important, but it could help the investigation if there was something in there.

In the reception area, Denise printed the documents they had requested, organising the contents into folders and labelling them with a black biro. Maybe if Duncan drank himself into oblivion, Denise could take over. She seemed the most efficient person here.

'Do you know if there is a spare key for Joshua's office?' Tom asked, as he took the proffered folders.

'The cleaner has one,' she said, 'but no one else. Joshua liked his privacy.'

'Is the cleaner around?'

'No, she'll be here this evening, though. Around seven o'clock. Do you want me to call you when she gets here?'

Tom considered this. Haltwhistle to Silver Skies was a fifty-minute drive. There would be a briefing when they returned, with next steps doled out. He didn't think coming back here to riffle through a bin was the best use of their time, especially on such a busy day.

'Do you think you could ask the cleaner not to do Joshua's room tonight, but to leave it open for us? We'll be back first thing in the morning.'

'I'm sure that'll be fine,' she nodded.

Done, they thanked her and stepped outside. It was raining, and the owner of the fast-food van looked like he was about to pack up.

'Do you believe in fate?' Tom asked Lauren, already rummaging in his pocket for change as his stomach gave an almighty rumble.

17

ON THE DRIVE BACK, Tom called the station and requested that anyone involved in the case be summoned for a briefing. By the time he and Lauren returned, the station was full, anticipation crackling in the air like static. Instead of diving straight into the meeting, Tom veered towards Martin's office and rapped on the door.

'Any chance I could commandeer your computer for ten minutes?'

'Absolutely,' Martin said, eyes glued to the screen. 'Just let me…' He tapped on the keyboard for thirty seconds, and then logged out. 'All yours,' he said. 'I'll go get the troops rallied.'

Tom shut the door when Martin had gone, relishing the brief moment of quiet. He spent a few minutes trying to clear his head, figuring out the most concise, effective way to deliver the newest information available. He logged onto the computer, scoured the internet for what he needed, and sent some pictures to print. The machine juddered to life, and then proceeded to spit out paper very slowly. While he waited, he scribbled some notes, refining the order in which he would present the developments.

When all was ready, he collected the printed pages, and strode down the corridor to the incident room, which quietened as he entered. Officers sat with notepads and laptops ready, the air

94

thick with purpose. Tom stepped in front of the whiteboard at the front of the room and cleared his throat.

'All right, first of all, thanks for being here, everyone. There have been a few significant developments today, which have opened up some avenues to explore. I thought it would be beneficial for everyone to hear them at the same time.'

He flattened some Blu-tack to the back of a page and fixed it onto the board. A clean-shaven man with blond hair stared out at the room through hooded eyes, the top of his shirt collar and tie just visible where the picture cut off.

'This is Joshua Price. He is the CEO of Silver Skies Medical Supplies, and the suspected owner of the severed hand.'

'Suspected?' Deborah repeated, eyebrows raised.

'At the moment, yes. His wife pointed out a scar on the palm that Joshua sustained some time ago. We're going to ask her to come and identify it in person to determine if it's really his. We can show her the foot while we're at it, if the DNA results haven't come back by then. I'd say we're looking at the same victim for both the hand and the foot, but that's only a hunch at this moment in time.' He pointed at the picture. 'Joshua was due to fly to Munich on business on the eleventh of December. He was supposed to be there for two days, but has not returned home. I want to know whether he made the plane in the first place. If he did, can we track his movements in Germany? Hotels, meetings, what have you. If he didn't, then where did he go? Was he intercepted at the airport, or did he not even get that far?' He turned to one of the DCs and said, 'Can I leave that with you? I want CCTV from the airport. Check-in records, anything that tells us about his movements. Okay?'

The officer nodded, and scribbled furiously in his notepad. Tom turned to another DC.

'I'd like you to draw up a full profile on Joshua. What kind of person he was, his habits, any patterns in his routine that would've made snatching him easy. I want to know where he ate, what his favourite drink was, where he worked out. If our killer is a planner, these are the kind of things they would know. I want a report that makes me feel like I'm reading about my best friend. Can you handle that?'

The other DC nodded.

'While we're on Josh, let's get his name and picture plastered all over social media. No need to specify why – we can't confirm his death until Rosanna has been – but just make it very clear that we are worried and want to speak to him. Yes?'

A chorus of agreement rippled through the room.

Tom moved on. 'Now, let's talk about suspects.'

He fastened a second picture to the board, under the suspects heading.

'Rosanna Price is Joshua's wife. She reached out this morning to tell us Joshua was missing, so I'd say it's unlikely that she's involved. However, I'm sure we're all aware of the statistics. We know that a lot of disappearances and murders are committed by spouses, so it's worthwhile keeping her in the frame until we can rule her out. They have a big house, and had ambitious plans for their future – kids, dogs, the works. They were financially secure.'

'Mo money, mo problems,' Deborah said.

'Excuse me.'

'Mo money, mo problems,' she repeated. 'It's a song by Biggie.'

Tom caught Lauren's eye at the back of the room, and had to fight the urge to succumb to a gale of laughter. He moved on to the next picture quickly.

'This is Niall Wampler. The hand was wrapped and addressed to him, though it was found quite a distance from his home. This could be an error or deliberate misdirection. Perhaps it was actually meant for Maddison,' Tom gestured to her picture which was already on the whiteboard, 'who he dated in high school for a short time. He claims that he was in London on a work trip when the body parts were found and in the days before that. Obviously, that's something that we'll look into. Deborah, if you could do that, that'd be great.'

Deborah nodded while Tom fastened another picture to the whiteboard. A confident-looking man with dark, spiky hair and pale blue eyes stared back out at them, a hint of a grin playing on his lips.

'Tristan Watt. He is Maddison's soon-to-be husband. They borrowed money from Joshua and Rosanna for their wedding, so there may be some sort of money dispute there. Maybe Tristan felt emasculated and wanted revenge. Maybe he never agreed to borrowing the money in the first place, and felt Maddison went behind his back. We believe he may have "stolen" Maddison, for want of a better word, from Niall in high school. It was a decade ago, though, so likely means nothing. Lauren and I were meant to visit Tristan today, but our plans were waylaid. We'll prioritise a visit when we can.'

The last photo was of Duncan MacMaster.

'Temporary CEO of Silver Skies in the wake of Joshua's death. He's a lot older than our other players, but seems to enjoy booze and obviously stood to gain from Josh's death – promotion, presumably a pay rise…'

'Power,' Deborah said, ominously. This time, Tom made sure not to glance towards Lauren, safe in the knowledge that if they locked eyes, he was guaranteed to lose all composure.

From the back of the room, he heard a laugh-turned-cough.

'Power,' Tom repeated. 'Exactly.'

'While we were at Silver Skies, we also found out they have been experiencing financial difficulties. Staff have been let go – we have a list of those. We believe there may be more on the horizon, though that's not confirmed. And they recently lost a batch of insulin, which has caused them to lose money, too. Lauren is going to comb through the list of redundancies and see what she can find out about them. I imagine some disgruntled ex-employee has used social media to sound off or moan about the company. Let's see what it throws up.' He stopped, let them soak in the information, and then said, 'So, that's where we are. Suspects to narrow down, people to visit, research to be done. We're making progress. Let's keep pushing.'

He brought the meeting to a close, thanking everyone for their hard work. Deborah stalked out of the room with purpose, like she intended to personally track down every single one of the North East's CCTV's cameras and extract the data: her one-woman mission to determine if Niall had told the truth. The room emptied in twos and threes, groups divvying up work or discussing what had just been said, the station buzzing with the notion that the net could be closing.

Lauren lingered. 'What's your plan?'

'I think I'm going to try and dig a little deeper into Silver Skies and the enigmatic day-drinker, Duncan MacMaster. See if there are any secrets I can shake loose. Speaking of drinks, do you fancy the pub tonight?'

'I can't,' Lauren said, shaking her head. 'I really want to get through this list of people Joshua fired. I think there's gold to be found.'

'Very diligent,' Tom said, ignoring the brief lurch of his stomach at her words. 'I'll probably do the same. Spag bol and a night on the laptop.'

Lauren smirked. 'I think Amanda is making a stew.'

'Of course she bloody is,' Tom groaned under his breath. 'Maybe I'll get a takeaway instead.'

* * *

Tom had reflected on his poor diet since reaching Haltwhistle, which consisted mainly of fried meat in different breads, and had opted against a takeaway. Instead, he'd gone home via the Co-op and stocked up on some ingredients that would hopefully not result in a heart attack.

Back in his flat, alone, he stirred a bubbling bolognaise sauce while googling Silver Skies on his iPad. According to their website, they exported their wares all over the world – to America, the Middle East, Australia, and everywhere in between. Tom made a note of the organisations they sold to, with the intention of passing them along to a DC so they could call for a sort of character reference. Maybe someone, somewhere, had dirt on Joshua or knowledge of shady dealings that linked back to him.

A short dedication on the website caught his eye: a tribute to Joshua's father, the company's founder. Tom tried to pull on that thread for a while, wondering if the elder Mr Price had gone to his grave in debt to someone who thought killing Joshua was the way to get back what they were owed. However, newspaper reports painted a different picture: large charitable donations, humanitarian trips overseas, free medical equipment sent to remote corners of the world. A man who seemed to save lives, not ruin them. Obviously, Tom knew monsters could hide behind headlines. But Joshua's father genuinely came across like an angel. For now, Tom put that theory aside.

Instead, Tom focused his attention on Duncan. He wasn't active on any form of social media, and his biography on the website was short and sweet. Newcastle born and bred, he had studied engineering at Imperial College London before returning north to help set up the company. The 'fun fact about yourself' section was left blank – this somehow endeared him a little to Tom. A fun fact section might suit a trendy media startup trying to come across as hip and accessible, but surely a medical company would want to come across a bit more professional.

Maybe Tom was just getting old, but he found himself more and more confused by the digital-savvy direction the world was travelling in.

After reading a few more articles, none of which really mentioned Duncan except in passing, he locked his iPad. His eyes felt gritty, tiredness creeping up on him. He walked a few laps of the apartment, ending up by the window which overlooked Haltwhistle. The pub on the corner looked inviting, the golden windows glowing softly in the darkness.

He considered texting Lauren, asking if she was finished for the night, or if she fancied a break and maybe a pint to round out the day, but decided against it. She had already told him no earlier, and he didn't need those words to sting again. He didn't want to come across as desperate, or someone who couldn't manage an evening without a drink.

Instead, he settled on the sofa and channel-surfed for a while. He watched part of an old episode of *Mock the Week* and a few jokes from *Live at the Apollo*, though nothing sustained his attention for more than a few minutes. When the opening credits of *Naked Attraction* rolled in – bright, brash and filled with flesh he didn't want to see – he immediately switched off the TV and went to bed for a very sensible early night.

18

LAUREN KEPT CHECKING HER phone, hoping Tom would text to ask her if she wanted a drink.

She knew it was unlikely, having already told him of her intention to work through the list of fired employees, but her time in Haltwhistle had made her realise what a sociable creature she was. Living in a bigger community with friends and family close by, she had perhaps taken it for granted that she could nip out for a coffee with her sister or meet up with one of the mums from NCT when she fancied it. Now, trapped in a guesthouse bedroom with only a list of potential murders to distract her, she felt a little uneasy.

Like the walls were closing in.

Which was a silly notion, she knew. Amanda had given her the biggest room, after all.

She pushed thoughts of a fizzing pint of lager aside and focused on the task at hand. So far, she had sifted the list of fired employees through the internet, and hadn't found cause for alarm. Most of them were not overly security conscious, so she'd been able to access their Facebook pages. Most had, around the time of their dismissal, taken to social media to broadcast how pissed off they were, which was not unusual. It was their personal space, and if they wanted to shout their feelings into a void, that was up to them. Aside from some truly awful spelling and a couple of mentions of political parties

101

being culpable for the downturn in the economy, there were no obvious candidates, in Lauren's view.

She scored a line through James Silvester's name and turned her attention to the next on the list, when her phone started ringing. It was her mum. A quick glance at the time – 8:15 p.m. – meant Sophie would just be heading to bed, while Ben would be leading a spin class.

She scooped up the phone and answered, freezing like a deer in headlights at the sound of her fiancé's voice.

'She's alive!' he said.

'Ben,' she replied, attempting to inject her words with enthusiasm. 'Nice to hear from you. How are you?'

'Worried sick, and a little bit humiliated.'

'Why?'

'You've not been replying to my texts…'

'I have.'

'Not many of them.' With that, she couldn't argue. 'And you haven't returned any of my calls.'

'I've been working.'

'But miraculously, when I call from your mum's house, you do find the time to answer.'

'I thought it was Sophie.'

'And you thought I was at work.'

'No, Ben, that's unfair.' But it wasn't. He had her bang to rights.

He sighed. 'Look, I get it. You're busy trying to track down a murderer. But I'm worried about you. Worried about how much time you're putting into this, and worried about your safety.'

'It's my job.'

Lauren started pacing the room, phone gripped to her ear.

'I know, but these past couple of days have made me realise all over again how much I love you. The thought of something bad happening to you is terrifying, and this case isn't exactly a walk in the park.'

'Is this because you found out about the hand?'

'It's the missing finger. It's freaked me out.'

Lauren rubbed her forehead. 'Ben…'

'No, listen to me. It feels like an omen. You go away for a few days and find a hand with the missing ring finger. We've barely talked because you're so busy. If you put two and two together…'

'You get fifty billion,' Lauren said. 'Look, Ben, this is not about me and you. This is about a poor man losing his life in the most horrific way possible. This is about the families around him who lost a son, a husband… My job is to find out who is responsible and bring them to justice.'

'It's such a dark job.'

'So, what, you think I should give it up?' Before Ben could answer, she pressed on. 'Because that's not happening. I've worked my arse off to get to where I am. After what happened last Christmas, Natalie has been pushing me to keep progressing. These complex cases – killings, serial killers, rapes –they're making a difference to people.'

'I'm not asking you to give it up,' he said, quietly. 'I'm just asking if it's worth losing yourself over.'

She pinched the bridge of her nose. 'Ben, you read too much fiction. I have an off switch.'

'Oh, really. Are you relaxing right now?'

She thought about lying, but couldn't. 'Well, no, but I am about to finish for the day.'

When he spoke again, it was like talking to a different person. There was an immediate lightness to him, almost like the sharp words between the two had never been uttered. Instead, he asked questions about Haltwhistle, what her accommodation was like, how Tom was. In turn, she asked about his work, but both sides of the conversation felt like they were taking place to a different rhythm. She was waltzing but he was mid-rumba. Eventually, he handed the phone to Sophie, who had been yelling "Mummy" in the background for thirty seconds.

Talking to her daughter was a balm. Sophie babbled on about what she'd been up to that day, how she'd had a hot dog for dinner, and about the episode of *Little Lunch* she'd watched before brushing her teeth. Hearing the account of her daughter's day made Lauren's heart swell, and she longed for a hug. In lieu of that, she resolved to get the case sewn up as soon as possible so that she could get home.

After Sophie toddled away from the phone, Lauren expected Ben to take up the mantle, but was met only with silence. She stayed on the line for another fifteen seconds or so, but no one came, so she hung up.

She stared at the screen, thumb hovering over his contact. She did love Ben, and she was looking forward to marrying him (she thought), but she couldn't shake the fear that her job would always be a wedge between them. She had made it very clear from the outset that Sophie and her job were the two things she loved most in this world, and he had accepted that.

Or had seemed to.

Had he really just been waiting for the right moment to issue her an ultimatum? Ask her to choose between the job and him?

She thought about phoning him back right now, and hashing it out, properly, just as her phone started to ring. She answered without checking the display, and was surprised to hear a voice she recognised but couldn't immediately place.

'DS Rea?' the voice said.

'Speaking. Who is this?'

'It's Maddison.'

'Oh, God, Maddison.' Lauren sat down on the bed and grabbed a notebook from her bag. 'Are you okay?'

'Yeah, yeah,' she said, and then, 'no. I just got to my hostel and saw on TV that the hand belongs to Joshua. What the fuck?'

While they hadn't officially gone public with the ownership of the hand, the current unknown whereabouts of Joshua, plus the police's public appeal had obviously been enough for some journalists to join the dots – the word 'allegedly' no doubt doing a lot of the heavy lifting in their live reports.

'Maddison, Rosanna identified the hand from a picture. Obviously, we trust her, but we still need a formal identification before we announce it. You shouldn't have found out this way. I'm sorry.'

The signal was terrible, and Lauren really had to work hard to make out what Maddison was saying.

'I'm really scared someone is coming for me,' she spoke in hushed tones. 'I'm going to end my walk. I can't stand it anymore.'

'Where are you?' Lauren asked.

'At a hostel in Windy Gyle. I'm going to try and get home tomorrow.'

'Which hostel?'

There was static on the line, and Lauren had to ask Maddison to repeat the name.

'Can Tristan come and collect you?'

'That's why I'm scared,' Maddison said, on the verge of tears. 'I can't get hold of him. His phone is off, and it's never off. If the killer got to Joshua, do you think he'll find Tristan?'

'There's probably a perfectly logical reason,' Lauren said, trying to soothe her, while pushing away her own doubts. 'Tell you what, why don't I swing by in the morning and grab you. You can tell us what you know about Joshua, and we'll drop you back home. We can check on Tristan at the same time, together.'

'Sounds like a plan,' Maddison said. 'Thanks.'

'No worries. Look, get into your room, lock the door, and I'll call a friend who owes me a favour to beef up security for the night. All right?'

With that, she hung up and considered what she'd just learned.

The timing was certainly odd for Tristan to vanish off the face of the earth… Still. There was no point jumping to conclusions until they'd swung by in the morning. Instead of lingering on the point, she called Phil, a DC and one of the core team back in Gateshead.

'If it isn't Little Miss Countryside,' he answered. 'I think I'm actually all right for tips on how to plant carrots or advice on buying a tractor.'

'Ah, I thought I'd miss your little quips, but I was wrong. I was just ringing to say that, thanks to you, I'm handing in a transfer request.'

They both dissolved into laughter, and had a quick catch up. She saw Phil as her little brother, and was pleased to hear that he was chipper. Lauren filled him in on the case, and asked him to get to Windy Gyle for the night to keep an eye on Maddison.

'But I'm off this week,' he protested.

'She's hot,' Lauren said.

'Do you really think I'm shallow enough for that to make a difference to me?'

'I can hear you moving around your house like a Tasmanian devil.'

'Shut up,' he laughed. 'I'm only doing this because I owe you one. What she looks like is not important to me. I'm an equal opportunities employer.'

'She's a brunette,' Lauren said, knowing his preference, and then hung up, neglecting to tell him that Maddison was also engaged.

19

TOM AND LAUREN CRESTED a hill, and the Free Walkers Hostel came swimming into view. In the golden, early morning light amidst the vast wilderness that stretched in every direction, the building looked like a mirage.

They pulled into the small gravel car park and got out. The wind hit them immediately, the breeze stirring the long grass along the fence line. The hostel itself looked like a converted farmhouse, weathered by years of wind and rain. Its whitewashed stone walls were chipped in places, and the roof seemed to sag in the middle, a couple of tiles missing, like teeth in an old mouth. A wooden sign dangled crookedly from the porch, hand-painted with the name of the hostel. A black cat lay stretched across one of the steps, it's tail flicking lazily. It gave them a slow, disinterested blink before lowering its head again. Under a makeshift shelter made up of tarpaulin and sticks, a heap of mud-caked boots had been abandoned.

Lauren spotted Phil's car parked near the exit, where he was unceremoniously snoring up a storm in the driver's seat. She rapped smartly on the window, causing Phil to jerk awake, slamming his hand on the horn in the process. The blast echoed, scattering a few birds who had been loitering by a nearby bush.

'How long have you been asleep?' she asked.

'Five minutes, maybe ten,' he said. 'Not long.'

The yellow crust in the corners of his eyes told a different story.

'No bother?'

'None,' he said, as he stretched.

'You're excused, soldier,' she said.

'You mean I don't even get to kick around to see her.'

'She's engaged.'

'Could've told me that last night,' he huffed, before starting his engine and bidding them goodbye with a playful flick of the fingers.

'Charming as ever,' Tom laughed.

As Phil made short work of the winding roads, Tom and Lauren climbed the steps to the hostel and ventured inside to find a reception area with a counter, a spinning rack draped in tinsel which held maps of the local area and leaflets of nearby attractions, and a couple of vending machines. A faulty lightbulb flickered overhead.

A young guy with long dreads was slumped behind the counter, eyes closed. He wore a thick duffel coat, headphones covering his ears. Tom tried to gently tease him awake by knocking lightly on the wooden countertop, but had to resort to shaking the receptionist when his increasing volume failed. The receptionist opened bleary eyes, and looked around like he was seeing the world for the first time. Tom could smell that he had enjoyed a joint or two recently, though decided against mentioning it. That wasn't why they were here.

In the end, they didn't need him. Maddison emerged from the dining room, wearing a heavy fleece and slipping into her coat.

As they went outside, the receptionist pulled up the collar of his coat and sank back into the chair again.

Nice work if you can get it, thought Tom.

They followed Maddison to a gouged and graffitied picnic table in the hostel's garden. It overlooked sprawling hills bleached gold with the rising sun. Aside from the occasional passing car or the faraway caw of a bird, there was only silence. Just like the morning of Tom's impromptu hike, he felt the pressure in his chest ease, and he began to wonder if leaving Durham for somewhere more rural could be a smart move.

Plenty of time to consider that after the case. For now, there were more pressing matters.

'Did you manage to get some sleep?' Lauren asked Maddison.

'A bit. There aren't many people here. In fact, I think I might be the only one.'

'It *is* in the middle of nowhere, and it *is* nearly Christmas.'

'Yeah, both valid points.'

Lauren paused, brushing a decaying leaf from the tabletop. 'Maddison, are you okay if we ask you a few questions before we get going?'

'Yes, though I'm having second thoughts about stopping.'

'Why?'

'I'm so close, and I know that if I stop now, I'll never try it again. It feels like my one shot.'

'What about Tristan?'

'Well, I figure you're still going to check on him, right? And, like you said, there's probably a perfectly reasonable explanation. He's a massive gamer and usually has to rein in how much he plays when I'm there. He's probably just gone on a massive *Call of Duty* bender and lost all track of time and what's real.'

Lauren nodded. 'Well, it's your decision, but…'

'Yes, it is,' Maddison said, cutting off a lecture. 'And I'm determined. So, ask me what you want to know.'

'How well do you know Rosanna and Joshua?'

At the mention of Joshua's name, a little of Maddison's confidence seemed to falter. She looked down, tears suddenly springing to her eyes. Lauren handed her a packet of tissues and waited.

'Rosanna and I have been friends since school,' she said, eventually. 'We used to see loads of each other, but not so much anymore. Just because of where we live, not because anything has happened between us or anything like that. She's actually going to be one of my bridesmaids.'

'And Joshua?'

'He was part of our friendship group at school. It was always destined that he and Rosanna would get together. They were the posh, rich ones out of us all. It was simply a matter of time. Tristan hated the fact that they were the Posh and Becks of the North East, of course. Used to wind them up, crash their dates, steal Joshua's watches when we went round to theirs, and wouldn't own up until Joshua got really panicky. Their wedding was this big lavish affair with hundreds of guests.'

'Is that what you were hoping to have?'

'God no,' she laughed, wiping at her eyes. 'I want something small and simple, but even that costs a bomb. Dresses are thousands, catering is madness, even hiring a PA system to plug a bloody phone into is hundreds of pounds. Everything adds up. Tristan and I were scaling back, but even then, we couldn't afford what we wanted. That's when Rosanna stepped in, saying she would lend us whatever we needed. At first, I declined, but she was insistent. In a nice way,' she added, noting Lauren's raised eyebrow.

'Why would she offer you the money?'

'We've been friends for over a decade. I've helped her through a lot of tough times in her life. Her mum dying, her dad's cancer scare, her…'

The mention of the C word threw Tom, who conjured up images of his dad lying on a hospital bed, tubes pumping whatever it was they used during chemotherapy. He silently scolded himself, and forced himself to remember that while tests had been done, the results hadn't come back. It could be nothing… When he zoned back in, Maddison was still talking about Rosanna.

'… Well, I was just there when she needed me. Maybe that counts for something, but she's just generally a really lovely person. She did it because she wanted to.'

'With no strings attached?'

'No. Obviously I have to pay her back, but not until after the wedding. And I can do it in instalments.'

'She told us she is a doctor.'

'Yeah, at a hospital in Newcastle. Paediatrics.'

A cloud passed in front of the sun. The warm gold light was eclipsed, casting them in cold shadows instead. Maddison shivered and hunched her shoulders against the biting breeze.

'Do you think Rosanna would appreciate your support now? Isn't that a reason to stop the hike?'

'I called after speaking to you last night. I told her I wanted to give up on my hike and come and see her, but she told me she wants to be with her family. She's gone off to them for a few days. That's partly why I wanted to stop early – but now she's not there, there's nothing stopping me from going the distance.'

Lauren passed her notebook across and asked Maddison to write Rosanna's parents' address. She had to look at her phone to find the postcode but knew the other parts by heart. She then passed it back across the table to Lauren, who said, 'Did she ever refuse your support in the past?'

'Oh yeah,' Maddison nodded. 'Whenever she went through something, she'd insist on being alone, but I'd always drive over regardless, and she was always grateful.'

'Can you think of anyone who would want to harm Joshua?'

'Not really.' Maddison sniffed and took a few calming breaths. 'He's a nice guy, but I imagine he can be pretty cutthroat in business. He's confident, and I'm sure that can rub people up the wrong way.'

'So, you think it could be a business dispute?'

'Maybe, but that's just a guess. I've seen him give a few speeches at dinners I've been invited along to as Rosanna's plus-one, but I've never seen him in a boardroom or anything like that.'

'What about Niall Wampler?'

Maddison almost laughed. 'No way.'

'Why not?'

'He and I went out for like, five minutes. And that was ten years ago. There's no way he's going to suddenly start killing people I know after all that time. Why would he?'

'Revenge?'

'I don't see it. Niall was a sweetheart at school. Wouldn't say boo to a goose. No, you're barking up the wrong tree there.'

Lauren made a few notes and then flipped to a fresh page.

'Was Rosanna and Joshua's marriage a good one?' she asked.

Maddison chewed at her lip, and then said, 'Mostly.'

'What does that mean?'

'They were mostly good together, but when they had both had a drink, they could make cruel jabs at each other. She thought he worked too much. He thought she didn't under-stand the pressure he was under, and was ungrateful that it was his money that bought their nice house and allowed her to pursue her art. It was petty, but alcohol brings out the worst in people.'

'I mean, a surgeon's wage is hardly a pittance, is it?' Tom said.

'True, but Joshua was pulling in the big bucks.'

'Did Rosanna ever tell you if things went further?'

'You mean did he ever hit her?' Maddison seemed appalled at the prospect. 'Christ, no. They could be a bit lippy with each other, but that's as far as things ever went.'

'You know that for sure?'

'Well, not a hundred per cent,' Maddison admitted, 'but a girl can tell. Joshua would never do that kind of thing. And if he did, Rosanna wouldn't have stood for it. She would have left him.'

The black cat suddenly shot away from the door, running from the steps like it had been scalded. The receptionist was walking towards them, shivering. He offered them drinks, but they refused – there wasn't much more that they needed from Maddison. He seemed annoyed that he'd made the effort and got cold for nothing and stalked away without another word.

'Maddison,' Lauren said, once the receptionist had closed the hostel door behind him, 'Do you think Joshua ever cheated on her during business trips?'

'No,' she said, though she seemed less sure. 'I don't think so. Like I said, he was this confident, good-looking guy who could be a bit flirty when he'd had a few drinks. But, it was all bravado. I don't think he would ever have taken things further.'

'But you don't know?'

'No,' Maddison said, 'but what I do know is Rosanna has nothing to do with this. She's a lovely person. She adored Joshua with all her heart, and would hate to think of you asking such questions about her. She'd do anything for him.'

Lauren closed her notebook, and said, 'It's all just part of the process. We have to eliminate people, and what you've told us has been really helpful.'

They started to rise. Maddison unhooked her legs from the bench and strode towards the door, when Lauren said: 'Look, Maddison, are you sure about continuing? You seemed scared last night, and I just want you to make the right decision.'

'I'm going to set off in a minute and get to the next hostel before it gets dark. I'm so close.'

Lauren nodded. There was nothing either Tom or her could say to change Maddison's mind.

'You'll let me know about Tristan, right?'

'Right,' Tom said, 'as soon as we know anything.'

They lingered for a minute, waiting to see if Maddison might change her mind. Instead, she smiled and started back towards the hostel.

'Let's go see Tristan,' Lauren said.

'Might get a game of *Call of Duty* out of it,' Tom added, as they headed towards their car. As he reached for the door, his phone rang.

It was the station.

'You better get back here quick,' someone said when he answered. 'Debbie's gone rogue!'

20

JUST UNDER TWO HOURS later, Tom abandoned his car at the front of the station and ran inside, expecting chaos. He and Lauren had speculated wildly on what Deborah might have done, with theories ranging from commandeering the station for her secret line-dancing troupe, to hijacking the place, guns drawn, cowboy style.

When they pushed through the door, there was an eerie sense of calm. The phone was ringing, but there was no one attending the desk to answer it. Tom half expected a zombie to come lurching out at them from behind the furniture. When it did not, he swiped his keycard to open the back door, where the offices and interview room were. He and Lauren marched down the corridor to Martin's office, where the DCI and Deborah were locked in a serious conversation. Deborah sat across from him, looking pleased with herself, while Martin had the face of a man who knew he was locked in an argument with only one winner – and it wasn't him.

'What's up?' Tom asked.

'Tell them,' Martin muttered.

Deborah turned slightly in her chair. It looked like the theatrical move of someone in a Bond movie – a villain about to reveal their masterstroke. All that was missing was a cigar, a cat and a small tumbler of whisky.

'I've made an arrest,' she said.

'You've what?'

'Made an arrest,' she repeated, a smile on her face.

'Who?' Tom pushed.

'Niall Wampler.'

'Why?'

'Because he lied to us.'

Tom leaned forward. 'Deborah, start from the top. Tell me everything.'

'Niall was not in London when he claimed he was. He was here, in the north. I found that out from his employers. I then went through his banking details and found out that he was spending money in a bar in Newcastle. I tracked down the CCTV footage, and it's pretty damning.'

'Show me.'

Deborah looked at Martin, who spun his computer monitor so that Tom and Lauren could see it. There was a window open, paused at the start of a video. Martin pressed play, and the footage sprung to life.

It was grainy black and white, and showed the inside of a pub. The camera seemed to be positioned over a door, angled so it captured the bar's interior and some of the seating in the middle. The date and time were stamped in the bottom left hand corner, showing 10th December at 20:45.

The pub was quiet. A barman walked to and fro, cleaning glasses and restocking the fridges. He looked like he was at a loose end. In the centre of the room, at a table for four, were Joshua and Niall. It was the night before Joshua was due to fly to Munich, when Niall claimed he was in London on business. A third man, wearing a suit, sat with them, his features slightly obscured by shadow. Each nursed a pint.

'Nothing really happens,' Deborah said. 'They stay for another hour or so and then leave.'

'You said it was damning.'

'He isn't where he said he was. He lied to us.'

Tom nodded, and said, 'Do we know who the man in the suit is?'

'No. Not yet.'

'Is Niall here?'

Deborah motioned to the wall with her head. 'In the interview room.'

'Have you spoken to him yet?'

'No, marching into his office in Newcastle and arresting him hasn't exactly endeared him to me. I reckoned you would want to take the first crack, anyway.'

There was a note of challenge in her voice, as if she was expecting a rebuke for her actions. Having seen the footage, the fact that Joshua, Niall and the unknown male were together on a night Niall was supposed to be almost three hundred miles away and Joshua should've been getting ready for a flight to Europe certainly raised questions. While Tom might not have burst into a busy office and made the arrest there and then, the footage proved that Niall did indeed have some questions to answer.

'Thanks, Deborah,' he said. 'Lauren and I will take it. Has he asked for a lawyer?'

'Yes. Someone is on his way from Newcastle. Shouldn't be long.'

Tom asked for the footage to be sent to him, so he could watch it in its entirety before the lawyer arrived. With Niall in custody, it was his chance to grill him, and he wanted no stone left unturned. He left Martin's office alongside Lauren and found a space in the next room, where he booted up his computer and opened the video file.

For a while, they watched Niall, Joshua and the unknown male hang out. It seemed an odd atmosphere – not hostile, but not overly friendly either. There wasn't much laughter, no leaning in, no physical ease. It wasn't like watching mates hang out. Instead, the conversation looked formal and stilted. Of course, it was difficult to know if this was accurate without any sound. He made a note to follow up with the barman, to see if he remembered the trio or overheard any of their conversation.

Tom sped up the playback, keeping an eye out for anything of worth. An hour after the footage began, the men got up and walked towards the door, leaving the pub in single file.

Tom went back to Martin's office, where Deborah was.

'Did the pub have any other CCTV? Anything outside?'

She shook her head. 'No, that's all we've got.'

'So there's no way of tracing where they went next?'

'No. There's no more payments on Niall's card until the following day, when he is in London.'

'What time?'

'Late afternoon,' Deborah said, pulling a notebook from her pocket. 'sixteen-thirty-three at WHSmith in King's Cross.'

'So he has plenty of time to leave the presents for Maddison and himself, and then get to London, too.'

'That's my thinking.'

'Good work, Deborah. Lots to ask him about here.'

He left the room again, just as the locked door at the end of the corridor clicked open. A DC was leading another man through. He looked like a pencil, tall and thin with his dark hair gelled straight up, like he'd stuck a fork in a plug socket to achieve the look. His suit was expensive, his shoes more so. He had a leather briefcase in one hand and a scowl on his face.

'I'd like fifteen minutes with my client,' he was saying to the DC, as they eased past Tom. The DC showed him into the interview room where Niall was waiting and closed the door behind him.

While the lawyer and Niall had their conflab, Tom and Lauren mapped out the interview strategy. Tom would lead, and Lauren would fill in the blanks. With Lauren already having met Niall, it made sense for Tom to take the bad cop role.

Fifteen minutes later, Tom knocked on the interview room door and went in, taking the seat opposite Niall. Lauren sat down beside him. It was a basic room, with a table and four chairs. Weak sunlight streamed through a single, small window that was caked with years of dust and grime. The lawyer introduced himself as Mr Stanford. When Tom asked for a first name, he was told that Mr Stanford would do nicely.

Tom started the recording device on the table. He stated the date, time and who was present, putting a little extra weight on the *Mister* part of Mr Stanford's title. With the pleasantries out of the way, he got down to business.

'We're here today, Niall, to ascertain why you lied to us during the investigation.'

Neill leaned in and opened his mouth.

'My client made an honest mistake,' Mr Stanford cut in. 'Mr Wampler was asked where he was on a specific date, and was not given the time to double check before giving an answer. He stated he was in London, when it was actually the next day he visited the capital. It's an easy mistake to make when you're being hounded by the police. The fact you've hauled him in here, and embarrassed him at his place of work over a simple mix-up, is a bit over the top.'

Tom nodded to show he had acknowledged Mr Stanford's statement, but never took his eyes off the suspect. When Stanford was done, he said, 'Niall, can you see how getting the date wrong looks suspicious.'

'No comment.'

'Did you lie about going to London because you killed someone and wrapped their body parts up as presents?'

'No comment.'

'Did you leave a present for Maddison?'

'No comment.'

'Did you leave a present for yourself?'

'No comment.'

'Did you leave the present for yourself to throw us off the scent?'

'Why would I...'

Mr Stanford tapped the table in front of Niall.

'No comment,' Niall said.

Under the desk, Tom clenched his fists in frustration, knowing the sick individual who chopped limbs from their victims and grotesquely parcelled them in wrapping paper could be sitting opposite them now. He searched Niall's features for any trace of guilt, remorse. Any emotion at all, but saw nothing. Taking a breath, Tom changed tack, though he was pretty sure it was going to be a 'no comment' interview all the way to the end. Still, he had to cover the questions, knowing they could play a part in a conviction further down the line. He made a show of checking his notes, despite knowing what he was going to say next. He glanced up at Niall, who seemed a little embarrassed at not being very helpful and smiled. He passed a sheet of paper across the table, setting it in the middle so that Niall and the lawyer could see it.

'This is a CCTV still from The Plough. You can clearly see the date and time in the bottom corner. The man you are with, Joshua Price, was dead not long after this. Probably killed hours after leaving the pub. You might have been the last person to see him alive.'

This kind of insinuation was usually enough for a suspect to spill their guts, to plead their innocence. But Niall simply sat motionless, eyes fixed on the piece of paper.

'Was this just three mates meeting up?'

Niall threw a sideways glance at the lawyer, who shook his head.

'No comment.' It was almost apologetic.

'What were you talking about?'

'No comment.'

'Was it something to do with work?'

'No comment.'

'About your trip to London? Joshua's trip to Munich?'

'No comment.'

Tom reached across the table and pointed at the third man. 'Who is the man in the suit?'

Another quick look at the lawyer, another almost imperceptible shake of the head.

'No comment.'

'Is he a friend?'

'No comment.'

'A colleague?'

'No comment.'

'Did you kill Joshua Price?' Tom asked.

'No…'

'My client has nothing more to say,' Mr Stanford said, standing up. 'You've hounded him with nothing more than baseless claims with no evidence to back them up. I expect Mr Wampler to be freed as soon as this meeting is over, as he clearly has no knowledge that can help you. I also expect you to place a call to his work, absolving him of anything that could have a lasting impact on his career.'

'We can keep him for twenty-four hours,' Lauren said coolly.

'Yes, but what will that accomplish?' Mr Stanford said, steeling his gaze. 'You've made a scene. Dragged a hardworking young man from his place of work. You've embarrassed yourself with the arrest and the subsequent questioning. There's surely no point in prolonging that.'

Tom finished the recording and clicked the device off. He stood, thanked both men for their time, and turned to go. He half expected Niall to stop him, to say he had nothing to do with any of this, but Mr Stanford had him well trained. Instead, faced with more stonewalling, Tom wrenched the door open and stalked down the hallway. At the front desk, he made plans with the DC for Niall's release, and then returned to the office, where he sat with his head in his hands.

Had he just been in a room with a sadistic murderer?

And worse – had they just let him go?

21

TOM AND LAUREN HIT school traffic as they rolled into Newcastle. They'd spent the drive discussing Deborah's impulsive actions, how Mr Stanford had run rings around them, and the chances that Niall was their killer.

Now, as they idled in traffic, Tom could feel the case eating away at him. He was still stewing over the interview – frustrated at how it went, along with his own performance. A no-comment interview wasn't unusual, they happened up and down the country every day. But he couldn't shake the feeling that Niall *wanted* to talk and was being silenced by Stanford. He considered the moral and legal implications of swinging by Niall's house, or bumping into him at his local, and posing further questions to him that way. But anything obtained would be unlawful and inadmissible in court, and the stunt would more than likely see Tom dismissed from the case.

Instead of dwelling on the failed interview, he cast his thoughts forward to the here and now. They were only minutes from the house that Maddison and Tristan shared, and he needed to be present. Tristan might have valuable information to impart.

Finally, after running a gauntlet of lollypop ladies, they pulled off the main road and into a quiet cul-de-sac. The houses here were semi-detached, closely packed around a central circle. Each house had a small garden, some of which were better maintained than others. Twinkling Christmas lights lit the windows; a few gardens had inflatable snowmen or wireframe reindeer glowing faintly in the winter gloom.

Tom pulled the car into the driveway of number 4 and climbed out. He walked to the door and knocked. While he waited, he noted that Maddison and Tristan's house did not have a tree in the window. Perhaps Tristan thought that, with his wife-to-be away on her hike, there was no point in putting one up. Maybe they planned on assembling and decorating it together when she returned. He knocked again, though the darkness inside was a clue that Tristan wasn't home. Or was … but dead.

Lauren led the way around the back of the house, accessing the garden through an unlocked gate. There was a rickety shed, an expanse of grass, and a small, patio area. Lauren rapped on the back door, and jiggled the handle, but there was no give. She shone her torch through the kitchen window, but there was no sign of Tristan, body or otherwise.

As they were about to leave, her torch raked over the ground. She drew in a sharp breath, bent down and picked something up.

'What's that?' Tom asked.

'It's one of those key holders that's meant to look like a rock.' She picked at the middle and it split, revealing a key.

'Hey presto,' Tom said, pulling the key out. 'Forensics will have our heads if there's a body in the house.'

'We'll take a peek inside, and if Tristan *is* dead in there, we'll hightail it outside and call it in.'

'Deal.'

Tom pushed the key into the lock and turned. The click seemed thunderous in the quiet gloom. He opened the door and called out, alerting Tristan to their presence.

The kitchen was tidy, with clear worktops and a small rectangular table pressed against one wall. A clock ticked loudly in the darkness. Tom crossed the kitchen to the door, and flicked the light on. He entered the living room, where a sofa faced a large wall-mounted TV. Photos lined the mantelpiece, showing Tristan and Maddison in far-flung places, beaming at the camera. The room was neat, if a little musty.

'I don't think he's been here for a while,' Lauren said. 'No man is capable of keeping a house this clean.'

'Sexist much?'

'I'm just saying. Men are very good at relying on women to give them a nudge.'

'You've been engaged, have you?'

'Well, no,' Lauren said quickly, but Tom was already laughing.

'Ready to go upstairs?'

'Yeah.'

Tom hit the switch at the bottom of the stairs, lighting the landing above. They climbed the steps, Tom calling out again in case Tristan was sleeping. He didn't want to frighten him. Though, he was almost certain Tristan was not in the house. If he had been asleep, surely all their shouting would've awoken him. If he were dead, Tom would be able to smell him by now.

Tom pushed open a door to his right, and flicked the light switch. It was the master bedroom, judging by the king-sized bed. This was messier, clothes strewn about the floor, the duvet crumpled, a mirror propped against the wall waiting to be hung.

Just as Tom suspected, no Tristan.

They backed out of the room and tried the others, but the house was empty. No sign of Tristan in either the second bedroom or the bathroom.

'Maybe he's staying with a mate while Maddy's gone,' Lauren suggested. 'She said he was a gamer. Maybe he's hanging out with a friend, playing *Football Manager* or *FIFA* or something.'

'Maybe,' Tom said, but he was unconvinced. 'Let's see if he's working late.'

They trooped down the stairs and out the back door, locking it after them and returning the key to the rock. In the car, Lauren typed his workplace into Google Maps and the disembodied voice begun to direct them. If she was right, it would only be a ten-minute journey.

Tom followed the satnav to an area called South Heaton. NW Technologies sounded like something from a Marvel film. A secret lair contained within a multi-million-pound building made of glass and exposed steel.

The real NW Technologies was a far cry from that.

At first, Tom missed the turning, having dismissed the satnav as incorrect. He travelled down the road for a while, used a roundabout to retrace his steps and then complied with the satnav's wishes.

It led them to a car park, surrounded on three sides by dilapidated red-brick buildings. An array of aged signs adorned the fronts. There was a car garage with a shuttered front, wide and tall enough to accommodate a couple of vans. There was a martial arts dojo; a carpet shop; a bathroom tile emporium and a rather manky-looking soft-play centre called Jungle Jims. Tom couldn't imagine what low ebb a parent would have to be at to resort to taking their child there.

He pulled into a space, and he and Lauren made their way to the door belonging to NW Technologies. It was the smallest unit on the lot, almost anonymous aside from the small PVC plaque beside the door, declaring their name in a blocky font. Tom pushed on the handle, and let Lauren enter first.

It opened into a cramped office, no bigger than a bedroom. A workbench at the back was covered in an array of computer paraphernalia. There were a number of slim monitors, a couple of computer towers and some gadgets Tom couldn't name. There was a small bookcase pushed against one wall, with a huge collection of manuals, seemingly stretching right back to ENIAC

– the world's first computer. There were two desks squeezed into the centre of the room.

A man in a plaid shirt was sitting behind one. Could it be?

'Tristan?' Tom said.

'Nick,' the man replied. A pair of thick-rimmed glasses magnified his eyes. His thick, grey-flecked beard spilled down the front of his shirt. Tom couldn't place the logo on his trucker hat. 'You're looking for Tristan, are you?'

'We are.'

'Join the club,' he said. 'Who are you?'

'DI Tom Stonem. This is my partner DS Rea.'

'Is Tristan in trouble?'

'No, nothing like that,' Tom said. 'We're actually looking for him to ensure his safety. When was the last time you saw him?'

Nick tapped on his keyboard and then examined the screen. 'Tristan was called out on the eleventh of December by a company called Jago Tech, in the city. It was near quitting time, so I didn't expect to see him again that day. But he didn't show up the next day, or any of the following ones. I assumed he was ill, or had quit, and never bothered to tell me.'

'You're the boss?'

'Nick Waites,' he nodded.

'Is this type of behaviour unusual?'

'Yes,' he nodded. 'Tristan is usually very reliable. He's a good worker. Good at his job and good at handling people who think they know better than him despite them calling us for help.'

'How long has he been working here?'

'Five years, maybe six.'

'And nothing like this has ever happened before?'

'He's had days off, you know? But he's always told me. This is the first time he's gone AWOL.'

Tendrils of fear crept up Tom's spine.

'Did he mention anything about Maddison being away?'

'Yeah.'

'Was he pissed off about it?'

'No, why would he be?'

'Do you have a list of companies he worked for in the days before he disappeared?'

'Disappeared?' Nick straightened up, alarmed. 'Fuck, I feel awful. When he didn't show up on the second day, I left a message on his machine telling him if he wasn't in by lunchtime, I'd have to let him go. Is he in trouble? Has something happened?'

'That's what we're trying to figure out,' Tom said. 'Look, give us a list of his activity in the last week. Call outs, home visits, wherever. If you know any of his friends, give us those details, too.'

Nick started clacking on his keyboard, and soon the printer was spewing out pages.

'I don't really know anything about his mates. Sorry.'

'Did he ever mention someone called Joshua?'

'I've heard the name, but I don't know anything about him.'

'Niall?'

'No.'

Rosanna's name drew a blank, as did the picture of the man in the suit that was with Joshua and Niall in the pub. Aside from the list of companies, they had reached a dead end.

'Did he ever go for drinks after work?'

'Occasionally we go to The Crown, but rarely. I've got two young kids who I like to get back to after a long day here. Tristan and Dane sometimes went without me.'

'Dane?'

'Our other employee.'

'Could we have his details?'

'Sure,' Nick shrugged, scribbling a number on a Post-it.

After that, he collected the pages from the printer, stuck the Post-it on the top of the stack, and handed them over. Tom took the pages and thanked Nick for his time.

'You'll keep me updated, yeah?' he said.

'We will.' Tom passed him his card, and asked if he would call should Tristan get in touch.

Nick nodded, and said, 'Do you think he's okay?'

'It's probably just a massive misunderstanding,' Tom said, with more confidence than he felt. 'We'll keep you posted.'

They left, and took a detour to Tristan's house on the way back to Haltwhistle. Tom hurried back inside, slipped both toothbrushes in an evidence bag, and then got behind the wheel again.

'I'm guessing that's for what I think it is?' Lauren said, as he passed the bag over.

'Absolutely,' he nodded. 'Let's see what his DNA tells us.'

22

TOM DROPPED LAUREN OFF at the police station. She wanted to keep trawling through the list of fired employees, and Tom's plan wouldn't require both of them.

Half an hour later, he was in Carlisle, pulling into the hospital. After paying through the nose for the pleasure of simply parking his car, he entered the building. The familiar sterile, cold, blue and white walls welcomed him as he passed reception, calling Claire to tell her he was here. She met him at the doors of the mortuary, bouncing slightly on the balls of her feet.

'This is very exciting,' she said.

'I'm just hoping it gives us an answer,' Tom replied.

They went in, the door closing behind them with a quiet whoosh.

'You're lucky you called when you did,' Claire said, leading him over to a workstation. 'We have a quiet window where we can get the ball rolling straight away. So, what have you got?'

'We know who the hand belongs to, but the foot is still a mystery, right?'

'Right.'

'Well, I'm hoping you can compare DNA from a toothbrush to the foot. If it's a match, that's a way of getting an ID, yes?'

'Right again.'

Tom slipped on a pair of latex gloves and pulled the evidence bag from his pocket. He carefully removed one of the toothbrushes,

130

the blue one with the almost crushed bristles – the one he judged to belong to Tristan.

'Can you run this against the foot?'

'I can.' She took it from him and handed it to one of the techs. Claire spoke to them briefly, then turned back to Tom. 'It'll be about an hour. Maybe two.'

'I can wait.'

'Well, I'm about to knock off for the night. Do you fancy grabbing a drink to kill a bit of time?'

Lauren's face swam unbidden into Tom's mind, a smarmy look plastered on it. He almost smiled.

Don't get carried away. She's your colleague, remember? Off limits.

'Yeah, sure,' he said.

It might take his mind off the woman he *really* wanted to see.

Claire disappeared for a while and reappeared wearing figure-hugging jeans and a flowery blouse with a denim jacket pulled over it. Tom wondered if she kept a nice set of clothing should a date materialise during her shift, or if she simply dressed well at all times. They left the hospital and walked to the city centre in ten minutes. The chill had a bite to it, so he offered her his coat, but she declined. The moon was high in the sky, and bright, though somewhat smudged by passing clouds. They ducked into one of the first bars they came to, not too far from the hospital in case an emergency called them back.

Dusk was an upmarket establishment – all exposed brickwork, moody lighting and upcycled wooden tabletops. An array of colourful bottles shimmered behind the bar like stained glass. A Christmas tree on display near the entrance was adorned with golden baubles. The sight of them now made Tom feel sick, and he couldn't help casting his gaze downwards to check for any oddly shaped parcels encased in robin wrapping paper.

A jazz track, complete with running bassline and competing brass, thrummed loudly through wall-mounted speakers. The bartenders were dressed in crisp shirts, with waistcoats and pocket squares. They looked expensive and well-groomed; Tom felt shabby in comparison, his clothes wrinkled, smelling slightly of sweat. He looked like an extra who had wandered onto the wrong film set.

The music petered off slightly as they made their way through the back, finding an empty booth near the fire escape. They slid in on opposite sides, and Tom passed a menu across the table. While he perused it, he tried not to think about what an unusual situation he found himself in: waiting for a severed foot to tell him a secret, while having a drink with a woman who Lauren had accused, half-jokingly, of fancying him.

A waiter approached, several earrings glinting in the light of a disco ball. Claire ordered a vodka martini, while Tom stuck with a Coke. The waiter tapped their orders on a tablet and then vanished.

'Whatever happened to good old pen and paper?' Tom muttered. 'Or remembering?'

'All right, Grandad,' Claire laughed. 'Surely in your line of work, progress is a good thing.'

'But not in a bar,' Tom replied. 'Can't they remember two drinks by the time they walk ten feet? I'm all for progress, but sometimes I think it's making us lazy.'

Claire chuckled, but didn't reply. She checked her phone and then returned it to her bag. For a while they chatted about the case – the evidence, the timelines, the working theories. Tom asked about how DNA testing worked, and she asked about the progress they had made, and why he thought the owner of the brush might be the owner of the foot. When they ran out of road, conversation drifted. She asked questions about his life, and the chances of him staying around once the case was done. It was asked casually, but Tom understood the subtext.

He shifted in his seat, uncomfortable, and part of him wished that he had never accepted the offer of a drink. Claire was nice

– smart, competent, pretty – but something wasn't clicking into place. Tom found himself wishing that Lauren was here instead. He pictured her across the table, unbuttoning her coat, rolling her eyes at the overpriced menu, agreeing with him about the unnecessary gadgets and making some wry comment about the bar's name sounding like a failed boy band. A warmth stirred in his chest, and it unsettled him.

He had never thought of Lauren as anything other than an excellent partner before coming to Haltwhistle. But now, in this quiet moment, he realised maybe that wasn't quite true.

The two got on like a house on fire and understood one another. He trusted her with his life – hell, she had already saved it once. He thought of how often they laughed together, the way she had pushed him playfully out of the office door the other day. He thought of her pale blue eyes, her smile, and realised that the feelings were not new – it was just the first time he was recognising them.

Fuck.

Well, they would have to stay buried, wouldn't they? He was a DI to her DS – he was her senior, her boss, her partner. There were too many lines to cross – ethical, professional, personal.

Except, lines did get crossed, didn't they? Office romances happened all the time. And, if it came to it, leaving the job to be with her would be a difficult decision, but one he might consider. He got on well with Sophie, and…

Before he could chase the thought further, Claire's voice snapped him back to reality.

'Tom?'

'Yeah?'

'You were miles away.'

'Sorry,' he said. 'What were you saying?'

'I asked about your parents.'

Explaining that he had been adopted would take too long, so he gave the short version – that his parents lived near Manchester, and he was excited to see them at Christmas. He asked about her family but found it difficult to concentrate on her answer.

It was a relief when her phone rang, and she snatched it up. She listened intently for a minute. When she spoke, her voice had changed: it was clipped and clinical. She asked some technical questions Tom couldn't hear the answers to. When she hung up, she fixed him with a grave look.

'It seems you've found your victim. The DNA matches.'

Tom felt the floor tilt, like a ship striking a wave that nearly capsized him.

Two victims. Not just Joshua Price, but Tristan Watt, too.

Tom stood up too fast, his head spinning as he muttered something vague and hurried to the toilet. He threw up in a sink – his knuckles were white on the porcelain, eyes streaming as bile burned his throat. Cold sweat coated his skin.

This couldn't be happening again. Another Christmas, another twisted killer. His chest ached, and his breath came too fast, too shallow. For a second, he wasn't in a bar – he was somewhere else. Somewhere darker. His ears buzzed like static, and he clawed at his neck, his shirt collar too tight. It was happening again. Another panic attack.

He remembered Dr Dougan's advice.

Closing his eyes, he sucked in lungfuls of air. He turned the tap, and splashed cold water on his face, gritting his teeth and counting his breaths as he did. Finally, he opened his eyes and studied himself in the mirror.

Was he up for this?

No one would blame him if he requested for Natalie to take him off the case. Or, if he handed in his notice. No one would blame him … except himself. Someone was out there, hacking limbs of young men, and he intended catch whoever it was. He couldn't live with himself if he didn't try.

Back at the booth, Claire studied him, worried, but nodded quietly when he told her that he needed to go. He could see she was disappointed, and the two walked back towards the hospital in near silence. Cold water lingered on his skin, and the freezing night stung, but he welcomed it. He needed it.

When Tom reached the car, his hands were shaking. By the time he was halfway back to Haltwhistle, he realised that he couldn't even remember if he had said goodbye to Claire.

Or called her Lauren when he did.

23

So, THE WORLD NOW *knew about poor old Tristan.*

Before heading out for a late-night hike, the figure had watched the hastily arranged press conference. That detective, Tom, looked like he had seen a ghost – pale, sweaty, tie askew – as though he'd sprinted through a nightmare and hadn't stopped to catch his breath. He had spoken about how the killer had claimed two victims. Two men who knew each other. Two men who shared a friendship group, who hung out, laughed, enjoyed a pint together, and all that bullshit.

Tom had attempted to paint a picture that the public would lap up – a tragic story to stir feelings of hurt, sadness and outrage. To make people care, to mobilise them to do their darndest to bring the perpetrator to justice.

Except, the police were chasing their tails.

Outside, the air was crisp and clean. Snowflakes swirled, soft and slow, not in droves, and probably not enough to lie, but enough to make walking at night feel like a fairytale.

Or a nightmare, considering what they were carrying.

The sack on their back shifted with each step, the contents inside thudding dully – solid, heavy, wrong. The next package. The next gift.

The first two packages had been necessary to attract the police. To get the ball rolling. From here on in, it was a game, one that they had to play. After all, Tristan and Joshua's friendship group had been extra generous in their giving this year, whether they had wanted to or not.

The figure moved through the forest like smoke, stepping over roots and skirting muddy hollows until the trees thinned and they emerged onto a winding country lane, framed by hedgerows and drystone walls. In summer, this place would be heaving with hikers and annoying families on bikes. But, for now at least, they had it all to themselves.

They followed the land for a while, and finally came to a stop in front of a grey wall, its stones worn smooth by wind, rain and time. It was neither tall, nor ornamental. The fact it remained at all was incredible. The hush of centuries thrummed within its walls, haunted by soldiers long dead. Men who had stood guard in the dark, eyes scanning the northern wilds for movement, for invaders, for anything that threatened their fragile reach.

The figure ran a gloved hand along the cold, weathered stone. They imagined the clash of swords, the shouts in Latin, the friction of men who did not belong here yet fought to claim it as their own.

This wall marked where an empire had fought tooth and nail to reach.

Beyond it was another hostel.

The figure dropped the sack carefully to the ground and loosened the drawstring at the top. The opening yawned, and they retrieved a wrapped present from within. They assessed their handiwork – the paper was pulled tight, the corners crisp. It was their best work yet.

Practice really was making perfect.

Under cover of darkness, they stole towards the hostel. In a matter of hours, or maybe days, the area surrounding Hadian's Wall would evolve from an ancient stronghold to a crime scene.

Would its public reputation change forever?

The figure didn't know, but they thought their little stunt would ensure a media frenzy once word got out. Reporters would be foaming at the mouth, jostling for the best spot, comparing their actions to that of 2,000-year-old vengeance.

Pressure would mount on the police. The public would clamour for justice. For blood. For the sick bastard behind this to be locked up. For the key to be thrown away.

Poor old Tom and his team had their work cut out.

And the best part?

They had barely begun.

24

20th December – 9:30 AM

TOM WAS GLAD TO get out of the station, even if it was currently pissing down.

After delivering the morning briefing, the place had erupted into a seething mass of energy. Officers were barking into phones like they were trying to sell shares on Wall Street, and keyboards clacked furiously as Tristan's last moments were pieced together. A call to Nick had confirmed Tristan had driven a company van, as well as the date, time and location of his final call out. With a bit of luck and a lot of digging, they'd be able to locate his body, which could offer clues as to who killed him.

Tom, for his part, was heading back east with a 'to-do' list the length of his arm. He wanted to swing by Tristan's house to see if the SOCO team had managed to unearth anything that might help with the case. After that, he'd head to his place in Durham to pick up some fresh clothes before meeting with Dr Dougan. Then, he and Lauren had scheduled a chat with Dane Higbee, the third wheel at NW Technologies. Lauren had managed to unearth some intel on Mr Higbee, and Tom wanted to see the look on his face when confronted with this news.

The rain lashed against his windscreen in thick sheets, the wipers struggling to keep up, screeching across the glass like nails on a chalkboard. Tom leaned forward, eyes squinting through the watery blur, wondering if it was the weather or the job that made everything feel so bleak.

139

He knew that Dougan would offer to take him off the case if the thought of chasing a serial killer – not that whoever was behind this could be classified as that just yet – was triggering for him. It was an offer that sounded tempting in the cold light of day, but one he knew that he probably wouldn't accept.

There was also the small matter of Lauren, and his feelings for her. He had decided, after much deliberation, to ask Dr Dougan what he thought. He could spin it that he was asking for a friend, but Dr Dougan was too long in the tooth to be fooled by that. No, if Tom wanted to chat through his options, he'd have to be honest.

Traffic was crawling, and it took longer than he'd anticipated to reach Tristan's house. The cul-de-sac looked completely different to the night before. Blue lights lit up the morning gloom, guiding him towards his destination like a lighthouse. Tom slowed at the outer cordon and showed the young officer– who now resembled a drowned rat – his ID. The officer waved him through, and Tom parked as close as he could to the scene without upsetting anyone. As he got out of the car, he could see neighbours at their windows, breath fogging the glass, curious to spot anything juicy.

And there was plenty to see. Forensic tents, police tape pulled this way and that like a spider's web, a scrum of people in polythene suits and face masks. Tom ran to the closest tent and signed in, accepting one of the white coverall suits from the officer. The rain played a symphony on the tent's roof as he slipped his suit on over his clothes. When he was ready, the officer held the flap open, and Tom ran the rest of the way as quickly as he could.

'New foot covers,' a SOCO stationed just inside Tristan's front door said. 'We don't want you bringing a load of water and muck inside with you.'

Tom slipped his foot covers off, deposited them in the bin provided and pulled his new ones on over his shoes. The SOCO nodded a thank you and allowed Tom entry.

Compared to their clandestine entry the previous night, the house felt completely different. Then, it had been silent, like the house had been holding its breath, unwilling to give up its secrets. Today, it had no choice. Every room was full. Suited teams were combing through every aspect of Tristan and Maddison's life.

In the living room, Tom stood by the fireplace and looked at a picture of the couple in front of a sunset. Tristan appeared a cheeky-chappie, his spiky hair and clean-shaven, unlined face reminiscent of a little boy in whose mouth butter wouldn't melt. Ironic, considering the stories he'd heard from both Niall and Rosanna. Maddison clung to him, a wide smile baring wine-stained teeth, a strappy vest hinting that that they were somewhere warm.

His heart sank at the thought that they hadn't yet reached Maddison. That she was likely waking up, despairing at the weather, checking her phone to find she had no reception. No umbilical cord to the outside world. One of the DCs back in Haltwhistle was ringing around all the hostels in her supposed area, but they obviously hadn't got through yet. Tom had left them specific instructions to call him once they had.

Tom surveyed the room for more clues. A cluttered bookcase beside the telly held more framed photos. Maddison in a graduation gown. Tristan with what looked like a five-a-side trophy. A picture of the two of them in a pub, arms around a third man – dark hair, square jaw, pint held aloft. Tom didn't recognise him.

'Tom.'

Tom turned to find Henry Pearson, head of the scene of crime investigation team, approaching him.

'Henry, good to see you.'

'How's Middle Earth treating you?'

'I could get used to it, you know.' Tom smirked. 'It's peaceful.'

Henry looked around the room, eyes settling on the photo Tom had just been looking at. 'Peaceful isn't the word I'd use.'

'No, but you know what I mean.'

'I do, but you're too young to retire to the Shire, my boy,' Henry said. 'You'd drive yourself round the bend.'

'Maybe,' Tom nodded. 'Anyway, before you go all Phil Spencer on me, tell me what you've found.'

'I always saw myself as more of a Kirsty, but there you go. We've found the grand total of diddly squat.'

'Nothing?'

'Nothing that we deem massively helpful. No body, no blood, no signs of a disturbance.'

'What about correspondence on his computer? Diaries? Notepads? Anything like that?'

'There is an iPad and a Mac that have been bagged and tagged and taken to the techs, but that'll be a day or two before we hear anything. There's been no threatening letters written in blood or anything yet, but we live in hope. The moment I have anything, you'll be the first to know.'

'Thanks, mate.'

'Now, if you've had your poke around, would you please vacate my crime scene. You're contaminating my aura.'

Tom chuckled. 'That aura of yours smells like Dettol and stress.'

He wanted to point out that it technically wasn't a crime scene, but knew better. Instead, he went to the outer forensic tent and called the station in Haltwhistle, but there was nothing to glean. No update on Maddison. No new leads.

Frustrated, he trudged back to his car and slammed the door harder than he needed to. As he set the satnav for Durham, he felt a surge of anger. The killer was playing with them, and the police didn't have the first fucking clue who it was or where the next present would turn up.

That needed to change.

The rain was still relentless, and as it neared the hour, Tom turned the radio down. He didn't want to hear the news, to be reminded of the lack of progress they – he – was making.

Instead, he savoured the silence.

He knew he was in danger of unravelling and hoped that a session with Dr Dougan would be the thing to reset the balance. He needed to pull it together. For Maddison. For the victims. For himself.

If it didn't, he wasn't sure what his next move would be.

* * *

Dr Dougan was in his usual chair with a familar neutral expression on his face when Tom walked in. He wore the same suit as always, and greeted Tom with the same firm handshake. It was reassuring to know that, despite whatever crazy shit was happening outside these four walls, Dr Dougan and his office remained a failsafe bubble of normality. Tom hadn't realised how much he craved that until now.

After the pleasantries, Dr Dougan leaned forward slightly, his voice gentle. 'What would you like to speak about today, Tom?'

Tom exhaled, long and slow. 'The case is getting to me. Obviously I can't go into detail, but there are two deceased and no leads. No suspects. I think it's only a matter of time before the killer strikes again, and I can feel it getting to me. I didn't think I'd be dealing with another potential serial killer so soon after … you know. Especially not at this time of year.'

'It's bringing back memories?'

Tom nodded, jaw clenched.

'Tom, I know we spoke about PTSD a while ago, and I remember you were initially quite dismissive about the label.'

'PTSD is for people who have been blown up and lived to tell the tale.'

'Post-traumatic stress disorder is not just for war veterans. Anyone who has experienced trauma can suffer from it. Tell me, do you ever have flashbacks to that moment in your kitchen?'

'Yes.'

'Do you ever have nightmares about it?'

Tom hesitated, then nodded again.

'And you've moved, haven't you? So that you don't have to be in the house where it happened.'

'Yes.'

'Have you experienced any more panic attacks?'

Tom told him about the moments before the press conference in the scout hut and in the bathroom of Dusk, where he felt like he was drowning. Dr Dougan nodded, and when Tom finished speaking, scribbled something in his notepad.

'Tom, experiencing PTSD symptoms is not a weakness.' Tom felt heat prickling the back of his neck, all the same. 'It doesn't mean you are broken, and it doesn't mean you are weak. It means you are human. To be honest, it's almost reassuring that you're experiencing this. What you went through was horrific.'

'It doesn't *feel* reassuring,' Tom said, and Dr Dougan held up an apologetic hand.

'Sorry,' he said, 'poor choice of words. What I mean is that the brain can only process so much – there are things that it simply cannot make sense of so quickly. While a year may feel like a long time for you, the events will take years, decades, or even the rest of your life to process. There is no one-size-fits-all approach when it comes to PTSD. It's okay to need help.'

'What help can I have?' Tom asked. 'I've tried your breathing exercises, and they work for a short while, but it's almost like slapping a plaster on a bullet wound. I need something more robust. With long term results.'

'Exercise is a good one.'

'I've been enjoying the outdoors,' Tom said, before telling Dr Dougan all about his morning walk, and how work has curtailed any further excursions.

'Great to hear. One walk won't change your life overnight, but I'm glad you can see the potential. I'd encourage you to keep that up. As well as exercise, I can recommend some medication.'

Tom considered that for all of a second before dismissing it. He knew drugs, even prescribed medication, had side-effects that could have implications for his job. If word spread that he was taking something for his nerves, lawyers would jump on the opportunity to bring it up, to make him look weak in front of a jury. Archie Walker would have a field day. No, even if it helped, medication was not the way forward.

'What else?' Tom asked.

'I could recommend to Natalie that she takes you off the case. I know you benefitted from some time off after the incident last year; perhaps another period of rest would do you the world of good. Or,' he added, noting Tom's expression, 'adjusting your role to more of an administrative one for a month or so. No time off, but away from the frontline. You could stay on the case, but from afar.'

'People would talk.'

'Probably,' Dr Dougan admitted, 'but people have an opinion on everything. You might be water-cooler fodder for a few days, but conversation would soon move on. Your mental health isn't worth sacrificing to avoid a few raised eyebrows.'

Tom didn't respond immediately. His thoughts wandered west, to Haltwhistle, to the hills and the crisp air, to the small but dedicated team he was growing fond of, to the precious time spent with Lauren. He knew that if he accepted a less hands-on role, he'd regret it instantly. While the presents and the lack of progress was jarring, and the thought of chasing a serial killer sometimes overwhelming, he knew he would drive himself mad keeping an eye on the case from the sidelines. He'd feel bad for abandoning Lauren, and knew that the moment he accepted, he'd be chomping at the bit to get back out there.

There was something else, too. A shot at redemption. While he had failed to see what was right in front of him last year, this time he had the chance to put things right. There were bound to be details he had overlooked, players with more skin in the game than he'd anticipated, and he felt the fire inside him being stoked up again.

'That won't be necessary,' he said in a distant, perfunctory tone. 'Talking this through has helped. Honestly. But I'm ready to crack on. I need to see this through.'

Dr Dougan regarded him for a long moment, and then nodded, accepting defeat. 'The offer stands. If at any point you feel the need to take a back seat, even if it's just for a day or two, you let me know and I can set things in motion. I'll fill Natalie in on what we've discussed.'

'Thank you.'

'Is there anything else on your mind?'

Lauren was on the tip of his tongue, but Tom shook his head instead. He knew anything he disclosed here might end up in a report. Maybe not *everything* – *but* he couldn't be sure, and that sliver of doubt was enough to keep him quiet. That part of his life – those tangled feelings – he wasn't ready to expose just yet. So, instead of mentioning Lauren and his deepening feelings for her, he thanked Dr Dougan for his time. Despite withholding this, he felt a lot better than when he entered.

Not fixed. Not whole. But *lighter.* And for now, that was enough.

25

TOM AND LAUREN KNOCKED on the door of a tapas restaurant in the shadow of St James' Park. The rain still sheeted down in relentless torrents, and Tom swore under his breath as he hammered on the door again.

Eventually, a waiter in a crisp white shirt, red bowtie and matching waistcoat answered the door. He pointed to the sign displaying the opening hours, ensuring that Tom understood that the restaurant was not yet open. In response, Tom pressed his ID against the glass, which the waiter squinted at, his eyes widening a fraction. He pulled a set of keys from his pocket, unlocked the door, and ushered them inside.

'Sorry about that,' he said. 'We're not open yet. The chefs haven't even arrived.'

The restaurant was warm and inviting, despite the fact it wasn't open. Rich with the scent of garlic, seafood and something zesty that lingered in the air from the night before, Tom felt his stomach rumble. The idea of sitting down at one of the tables with Lauren, while small plates of food were brought to them, was certainly tempting – but not why they were here.

They were here to meet Dane Higbee.

'Where is he?' Tom asked the waiter.

'Upstairs, fixing the computer.'

'Is it all right if we go up to speak to him?'

The waiter shrugged. Tom took this to mean yes, and headed for the stairs, Lauren in tow.

'Are you happy to take the lead?' he asked.

'Sure thing,' Lauren replied.

The stairs led them to the first floor, which had a short corridor and two toilet doors. Another flight, usually off-limits to the public, led them to a small landing with an office door at the top of the building. Tom pushed it open without warning.

The office was tidy and cream-coloured, with an IKEA desk, a faux-leather office chair and a couple of filing cabinets. A man was on his knees with his head under the desk, bum in the air, arsecrack exposed. He was fiddling with some leads, his eyes on a laptop, when he heard the door open and looked around.

'Dane Higbee?' Lauren asked.

'That's me. You must be Lauren? And Tim?'

'Tom.'

Tom didn't know if it was some sort of power play, but he replied like it wasn't.

'Ah, sorry about that, Tom.'

'No worries,' Tom said. 'Thanks for meeting us.'

'It's no problem. I'm just finishing up here, if that's all right, and then we can have a chat.'

Tom watched, arms folded, thinking that Dane was remarkably calm for a man about to be questioned by two detectives. Lauren may not have told him exactly why they were meeting, but he must have guessed.

Under the desk, Dane pushed a couple of leads into ports and then typed furiously on the keypad of his laptop. He waited a moment, and a pop-up appeared on his screen, which seemed to be to his liking. He smiled, closed the lid, disconnected the leads and stowed the laptop away in a case. Finally, he stood, allowing Tom to size him up for the first time.

Dane Higbee was just a shade over six feet tall, with dark hair and course stubble. His arms were toned, but his NW Technologies polo was stretched over a growing beer belly. A waxy scar in his hairline caught the light.

'What were you doing?' Lauren asked.

'The booking system has been down since last night. It just needed an update and a few bugs removing, and now it's good as gold.'

'Dane, I appreciate you meeting us today. I know you're busy, so we'll try not to keep you too long.'

'Do I need a lawyer?' he asked.

'Depends what you've got to hide,' Tom said.

Dane shot him a sharp look. 'I've got nothing to hide, mate. Now, I've got half an hour before my next appointment, so why don't we cut to the chase?'

With only one chair in the room, and everyone seemingly unwilling to be the one sitting, they found themselves stood awkwardly in a triangle. It felt like an unfunny version of the Spiderman meme.

'Dane,' Lauren started. 'As I'm sure you're aware, there have been two suspicious deaths in the past week. The first was Joshua Price and the second was Tristan Watt. No one is accusing you of anything, but currently, you are one of the only known links between the two men. Naturally, that raises some questions.'

Dane waited. When Lauren didn't say anything else, he said, 'Is that a question?'

'It's a statement,' Lauren replied. 'Can you tell us how you knew Tristan?'

'Tristan and I have been working together for a couple of weeks, since I started at NW Tech.'

'How well do you know him?'

'Not well,' he said. 'I mean, when we were in the office together, we chatted and were becoming friendly. He seemed like a nice dude, but a lot of the time is spent on call outs, so we weren't exactly tight, you know?'

'Did he seem worried about anything?'

'Like I said, I didn't really know him, so I have nothing to compare it to. He was quite a quiet dude, but I don't know if that's because he had something on his mind or if he was just shy.'

'Did he talk about Maddison?'

'That's his missus, yeah? The one doing the walk?'

'That's the one.'

'Not really,' he said. 'He told me about the walk, but not much else. We went for a couple of beers and things like that, but we mainly talked about the job and football.'

'He didn't say if he was unhappy with her, or anything?'

Dane regarded Lauren as if she had two heads, and then raised an eyebrow at Tom.

'Clearly she's never been down the pub with lads, has she?' He looked back at Lauren. 'We're not known for our conversation skills. I've had mates that I've known all my life that I know very little about. I couldn't tell you much beyond their favourite beer or Newcastle player.'

'Don't you think that's a bit sad?'

'Just the way it is,' Dane shrugged.

'Did Tristan ever say anything negative about Nick?'

'Usual moaning you hear in every office. Boss expecting too much from us, pushing us too hard and what have you. To be honest, I just listened. I'm pleased to have nabbed a job so quickly after leaving my last, and don't want to fuck it up by whinging behind Nick's back.'

'Leaving?' Tom said.

'What's that?'

'You said leaving your last job, but you didn't exactly leave of your own accord, did you?'

Something dangerous flashed in Dane's eyes. 'Well, I was let go. Happy?'

'And you didn't seem too pleased about it,' Lauren said, taking over. She reached into her bag and pulled out a folder. From it, she retrieved a piece of paper which she passed to Dane.

'Do you know what those are, Dane?' she asked.

'I do. And I know how it looks.'

'How *does* it look?' Lauren pressed.

Dane sighed. 'Like I had some sort of vendetta against my old boss.'

'Joshua Price, now dead.'

'Like I said,' Dane shrugged. 'I know how it looks.'

'You were pretty vitriolic against Mr Price and his company, Silver Skies.'

'I'd just been let go. I was upset. Angry. I ranted on Facebook, got it out of my system and then moved on with my life.'

'Did you ever take anything? Or do anything to lose them money?'

'No.'

'A batch of insulin went missing, do you know anything about that?'

'Why would I?'

'So you didn't steal anything, or act out any of the threats you posted online for everyone to see?'

Dane shook his head. 'I did not.'

'Tell us about Joshua.'

'I don't want to speak ill of the dead, but he was a twat. He was handed the company from his old man, didn't do a fucking thing to earn his place, and swanned around like the world owed him more. He didn't have the first clue about the business, yet meddled in things he didn't understand. Believe you me, I wasn't the only one he pissed off.'

'Oh yeah?'

'Yeah. Honestly, I was pissed I got fired, but I probably would've walked anyway. He got on everyone's nerves, even his number two. The fights they were having sounded like an old married couple.'

'That's Duncan MacMaster you're referring to?'

'Yes.'

'There was animosity there?' Lauren prompted.

'Like I said, Joshua had no idea how to run the company. Duncan had lived and breathed it for years, and then this uppity arsehole comes in and starts making changes to suppliers and distributors. The insulin probably went walkabout due to his ineptitude. Then, when all that backfired, he starts laying people off to cover his arse. That's when me and a load of others were given the heave-ho. Like I said, he made a load of people unhappy, but I reckon Duncan hated him more than anyone.'

'He didn't post online abuse.'

'No, he didn't,' Dane admitted. 'And I've told you that I'm sorry I ever did that. It was childish.'

'Mr Higbee, can you tell us where you were on the evenings of the fourteenth and fifteenth December?'

'I'd have to check my calendar, but I reckon I was at home. Aside from going for an after-work drink, I don't go out much. Money is tight, you see.'

'And, if you were at home on those dates, would anyone be able to vouch for you?'

'I'm single, sadly, and I've not had my end away in a while, so I'd have been alone.'

'Doesn't look great, does it?' Tom said.

'It might not look great to you, but it doesn't mean anything to me,' Dane replied. 'I know what you're implying – that I had something to do with the murders, but I didn't. I haven't killed anyone.'

'Well, to be sure, we're going to need you to drop off any tech you own at the police station in Haltwhistle.'

'Now, hang on a minute,' said Dane, his voice hitching, 'that's fucking miles away.'

'And we'll need it in the next twenty-four hours,' Tom continued, as though he hadn't been interrupted, 'otherwise we'll come to your house with blue lights flashing and the sirens blaring. Your neighbours get to enjoy a free show, and you have the pleasure of becoming the talk of the town. Do I make myself clear?'

Dane held Tom's stare for an eternity, before nodding.

'Right. Well unless you have something else to accuse me of, I better be off to my next appointment.'

Dane scooped up his belongings and left the room without a backwards glance. They heard his heavy footsteps on the stairs, and then the dramatic slam of the front door.

Tom glanced at Lauren. 'Whoever he's off to help next has my sympathies.'

Lauren smiled. 'He seems like the kind of guy who has to try very hard to keep his emotions in check. It'll be interesting to see if there was any communication between him and Joshua, or anyone else at Silver Skies for that matter.'

'His comment about Duncan and Joshua arguing was interesting.'

'Definite motive,' Lauren agreed. 'If what he said was true. I reckon it's worth putting in another appearance at Silver Skies, cranking up the heat and chatting to people on the floor.'

'Agreed. Let's get ourselves back to Haltwhistle for the day, see if anyone has been able to contact Maddison.'

They left the restaurant and jogged through the rain, dodging the deep puddles that had pooled on the pavement. Back in the car, Tom turned the heating up and waited for the windscreen to clear.

'Do you fancy a bite to eat tonight?' he asked, as he pulled out of the car park.

'Sounds good to me. There's an Italian on the high street that Deborah recommended.'

'Could be interesting,' Tom laughed, noting a fluttering in his gut, 'if it's coming from her.'

Comforted by the thought that he wouldn't be spending the evening alone, Tom pumped up the radio, surprising Lauren by singing along to Coldplay's Christmas Lights. When it finished and he had lapsed back into silence, he briefly considered admitting his feelings to Lauren during dinner, but decided it was better to wait until the case was over.

If it would blow up in his face – best to do it on home turf.

26

TOM'S FIRST SURPRISE CAME when he stepped inside La Tavola di Nonna.

The Italian restaurant was on the main street, nestled between a charity shop that could do with a lick of paint and a colourful florists. Inside, the lighting was a warm golden hue, with flickering candles on every table and strings of tiny bulbs stretched lazily across the ceiling like vines. The tables were draped with red and white checkered tablecloths, the air thick with the scent of freshly baked bread, garlic and a tangy tomato sauce. The faint twang of an instrumental guitar weaved its way through the hum of conversation and the clinking of glasses. A traditional Norway Spruce Christmas tree was mounted by the bar, a shimmering star perched on top.

Tom stood awkwardly at the 'Wait here' sign for a few minutes, hands in his coat pockets, until a waiter in a black apron spotted him and made his way over.

'Good evening, sir,' he said. 'Do you have a booking?'

'I think my friend booked a table. It'll be under Lauren Rea.'

The waiter tapped at an iPad. 'Table for three?'

Tom frowned. 'I thought it was just the two of us.'

'It says here three, sir.'

'Okay. Maybe another colleague is coming along. Thanks.'

He followed the waiter through a maze of tables to one tucked in the back corner, half-hidden behind a faux-Doric pillar. It offered the perfect view of the open kitchen, where chefs moved like performers, tossing dough and plating up as though they were taking part in an improvised dance.

Tom slid into the chair and nodded when the waiter offered a drink.

'I'll just have a water for now, if that's all right? And then order properly when the others come.'

The waiter nodded and then toddled off. Alone, he glanced towards the entrance, wondering who the third seat was for. Maybe Deborah had caught wind that some of the team were dining at her favourite Italian and invited herself. Maybe Martin saw it as a chance to tag along, to get to know the hired help better. It was hard to know, and neither prospect thrilled him.

The truth was far worse than both scenarios combined.

The bell above the door chimed, and Lauren walked in, her face thunderous. A man with a thick neck and biceps the width of Tom's thighs trailed a few steps behind. Lauren trudged to the table without waiting for a waiter to show her the way.

'You okay?' Tom asked.

'Not really,' she muttered, before adding quickly, 'I was going to tell you in my own time.'

'Tell me what?'

Before she could answer, the man joined them. Lauren yanked a chair out and threw herself into it, while Tom stood to greet the mystery man. He extended a hand to the visitor, and had his fingers crushed to the bone for his troubles.

'Nice to finally meet you, Tom,' he said.

'Ah, I'm afraid you have me at a disadvantage, mate,' Tom replied, before shooting a look at Lauren.

'Tom,' she said, exhaling sharply, 'this is Ben. My fiancé.'

Tom felt his head expand and contract. Heard a faint rushing in his ears.

'Your … *what*?'

'I'm going to nip to the toilet,' Ben said cheerfully, and wandered off in the direction of the toilets.

'You're getting married?' Tom said, sinking into his own seat, attempting to disguise his horror with a feeble laugh.

'I'm sorry I didn't tell you. I haven't told *anyone* at work, so don't feel too put out.' She smiled at Tom, and when he didn't return it, she continued. 'We've been seeing each other for about ten months, and he asked me to marry him a few weeks ago. It's so new, and then we were put on this case and I didn't want to … I don't know. I just wasn't ready to tell anyone.'

She fiddled with her napkin, avoiding his eye.

'Fair play,' Tom said. 'Far be it for me to be giving relationship advice, but – isn't getting engaged after ten months a bit quick?'

'Maybe,' she shrugged. 'When he asked, it felt right, but…'

'But?'

Tom followed Lauren's gaze and saw Ben emerge from the toilet. She said quickly, 'I know this whole situation is fucking weird, but please just go along with it and then I'll tell you more tomorrow.'

He nodded, as Ben squeezed past the pillar and sat down beside Lauren. Now a trio, the waiter approached, took their drink orders, and handed out menus. Tom held his up, and let his eyes roam over it, though he was taking nothing in, his mind occupied instead by what he'd just been told.

His gaze flicked to her fingers, and he saw that she wasn't wearing an engagement ring. Maybe this was because it was new and he hadn't given her one yet, or maybe he had and she wasn't wearing it because she wasn't as committed. Or, maybe she hadn't wanted to let Tom know. He still wouldn't have known, had Ben not forced her hand.

His stomach churned.

Fiancé.

That word landed like a brick to the back of the head. He knew he was being foolish. She had never expressed an interest in him, and he hadn't in her. The feelings he had for her – which he couldn't deny anymore – were new, or newly-discovered, at least. He couldn't blame her for going about her life. Even so, he couldn't help but feel blindsided. He'd thought they were close, but perhaps he had misread the situation completely.

The waiter returned, and Tom ordered a lasagne without really thinking about it. Without his menu as a shield, conversation became unavoidable. Ben filled the silence, talking about his gym, his lifting schedule and PBs, how Lauren and he met.

'And now we're trying to plan a wedding,' he said, nudging Lauren playfully. She didn't respond. 'Though, getting this one to commit to *anything* will be a Christmas miracle. Honestly, I thought most girls dreamed of organising their big day, but Lauren treats it like we're arranging an appointment at the dentist.'

Lauren flushed. 'It's not that. I'm just so busy at the minute…'

'I know, babe,' Ben said, 'I was joking.'

Lauren managed a brittle smile, while Ben took a swig of his water, seemingly unaware he'd pissed off his fiancée. Thankfully, the icy silence that followed was broken by the arrival of food. They ate in a mostly tense silence. Forks scraped against plates, conversation from other tables washed over them, and when the waiter came to collect their plates, the offer of a dessert menu was batted away with a resounding no. The bill arrived, which Ben insisted on paying, and they stood to leave.

Outside, the air was cool, but the heavy rain from earlier had thankfully thinned to a fine drizzle. Ben and Tom shared an awkward bro hug, and Lauren shot him a look. Apologetic? Regretful? Something else Tom couldn't quite understand?

'See you tomorrow,' she said, quietly.

Tom nodded and then turned and walked in the opposite direction. His thoughts were a jumbled mess. He didn't know what was worse – that she hadn't told him, or that she hadn't wanted to.

Back at his flat, he lay on his bed and stared at the ceiling. He considered the implications.

Eventually, he decided there were none. Lauren was getting married. His burgeoning feelings would have to be quashed. It was as simple as that.

After all, there was a murderer to catch, and truthfully? He could do without the distraction.

27

LAUREN SAT THROUGH THE briefing, studying Tom as he recapped their progress, before doling out jobs. Deborah and a couple of DCs were allocated to Silver Skies, to interview those still working there and cast another eye over Joshua's office, after the initial search yielded nothing. Two officers were assigned to comb through Dane Higbee's tech (which he had dropped off late the previous evening). Anyone spare was assigned to the dead, in hopes of kicking something loose that they hadn't already uncovered. That meant finding links, tenuous though they may be, and interviewing anyone they deemed of interest, on the off-chance they could provide information.

'You and I,' Tom told Lauren, when the room had mostly emptied, 'are going back to Newcastle.'

'What for?'

'We've got a pub lunch booked at The Plough.'

'Where Joshua, Niall and the mystery man met?'

'The very same.'

If he was annoyed at her for blindsiding him the night before, he was hiding it remarkably well. She'd braced herself for a frosty, hurt or even angry reception, but he seemed to be in a good mood, though perhaps there was a dash of the 'me thinks the lady doth protest too much' in his performance. It reminded her of Ross from *Friends* insisting he was *fine* – while clearly being the opposite.

Regardless, they left the station together, hurrying through another relentless downpour to his car.

'The weather is bloody awful, isn't it?' he said, unlocking the door as he went.

Lauren glanced at the grey skies as she flung the door open. 'Doesn't look like it's clearing anytime soon, either.'

'Hopefully it keeps our killer off the streets.'

The small talk grated. It was too polite, too pedestrian for her to handle.

'Tom,' she said, once they'd pulled out of the car park. 'Look, I'm really sorry that you had to find out about Ben and me the way you did. I—'

'It's fine,' he cut in.

'No, it's not fine.' She took a deep breath. 'You're talking to me about the weather like we're a pair of octogenarians sitting in a care home. It's weird. Just let me say my piece, and then we can move on. Please.'

'Okay.'

'Truth is, while I've been over this way on the case, I've mostly been ignoring Ben because I want to give my full concentration to the investigation. When I got back last night, he was there at the guesthouse.' She internally winced at the memory. 'I think he felt he was being romantic and charming, but it pissed me off. I'd told him that I wanted to give my all without distractions, and he hadn't listened. Anyway, I told him we had plans, and he insisted on coming along. He wanted to meet you.' She paused, wondering how Tom felt about this revelation. 'I told him no one knew about us, and he said now was the perfect chance to announce our engagement.' She sighed, her gaze focused out the window. 'I should've told you about Ben, because we're friends. But, as you know, I'm quite private. So I wanted to keep the professional and personal parts of my life separate.'

'Understandable.' His voice sounded clipped.

'There's also…' She hesitated, and he cast her a sideways glance. 'Go on.'

'I shouldn't be saying this, really, but I've been thinking that…' She circled her hand. 'Everything is happening too quickly. I've only known him ten months, and I only said yes to the engagement because I was swept up in the moment. But now – I don't know. Truth is, I'm having doubts.' She looked to him with pleading eyes. 'Please don't repeat this to anyone.'

'Your secret is safe with me,' he said, without missing a beat. 'Time doesn't mean anything, though. My parents got engaged after five months and have been happy together for decades. Maybe if you give it a chance…'

Despite herself, she felt a shiver of disappointment that Tom endorsed her engagement. Then quickly dismissed the feeling.

'Maybe. But honestly, I've had doubts for a while. Him turning up last night uninvited and unannounced was just the tip of the iceberg. I think…' Lauren trailed off. She didn't know how to finish the sentence, wasn't sure what she wanted to say.

Or maybe was afraid to admit it out loud.

'Well, if you ever want to talk about it,' he said, finally.

'Thanks.'

The heavy rain didn't let up once the entire drive. They arrived a few minutes before The Plough opened, so waited in the car, taking in all they could through the sheets of water that cascaded down the windscreen.

The pub was just outside the city centre, tucked just off a busy A-road. The building was old and a little down at the heels, but charming enough with its red brick exterior and bay windows. There were posters in the window advertising events long gone – a tribute to Bon Jovi, a local darts final, 80s karaoke. A series of faded stickers clung to the glass showing that the pub had broadcast Premier League football from seasons past. A chalkboard sign outside advertised a weekly quiz night with cash prizes, and a steak night on Thursdays.

A wreath of holly and pinecones hung on its oak door.

'Football from a decade ago and a ribeye,' Tom said. 'What more could you want?'

'Is that because it's been ten years since Man United won anything?'

'Oh, that *is* harsh,' Tom said, putting a hand to his heart – slipping into their familiar routine, despite everything. 'You really know how to cut to the quick of me.'

'You walked right into it,' Lauren laughed. 'And look, the landlord's opening and sparing your blushes, so let's get moving.'

They ran through the rain towards the door. Stepping inside, Lauren was greeted with that strange déjà vu that came from seeing a place in person after watching it on grainy CCTV. Her eyes went straight to the table – the one Joshua, Niall, and the suited man had claimed. It was empty now, wiped spick and span under harsh overhead lights. On video, the pub had looked poky and dim. In reality, it was spacious, with a long bar trailing one wall and a scattering of sturdy wooden tables across the floor. A darts board hung at the back beside a postage-stamp stage that barely had room for a duo and a mic stand.

Tom introduced himself to the barman – a tall, broad-shouldered man with a friendly face and the kind of presence that implied he could throw someone out without breaking a sweat. They shook hands, and then he nodded a hello to Lauren, who was a few steps back.

'How can I help you?' he asked.

'We're wondering if you could give us a hand in identifying someone,' Tom said.

'I can try.'

Tom pulled a printout from his pocket, unfolded it and set it on the bar. He lifted the page off the bar and scrutinised it.

'Your colleague was in not so long ago to get this.'

Deborah.

'And she didn't ask who they were?'

'No. She was quite keen to get going as soon as I gave it to her.'

Tom tapped the image, his finger hovering over Niall.

'We know who this man is. But we're not so sure of the other two.'

Clever tactic, Lauren thought. If the barman told a lie about Joshua, then they could call him out on it.

'I only know this guy,' he said, pointing at the suited man. 'The other two, I'd not seen before that night, and I haven't seen since. His name is Freddie. He's a regular.'

'Surname?'

'Sutherland.'

'What do you know about him?'

'He owns a garage that sells second-hand cars,' he said. 'I know he likes a Carlsberg and supports Sunderland, but beyond that, not much.'

After a few more dead-end questions and the news that the chef wasn't arriving until four, they retreated to the car. Lauren had that excited feeling in her gut that they had found a new direction to pursue the case. The name *Freddie Sutherland* rang a faint bell. She called Gateshead station. Natalie picked up.

'Freddie Sutherland,' Natalie repeated the name over the loud-speaker, 'has a record. Five years ago, during lockdown, he was arrested on suspicion of domestic violence. His girlfriend at the time didn't want to press charges, so the whole thing was dropped. Freddie spent a night in the cells and was then released. There's been nothing since. Why? Does he link to your case?'

Lauren relayed what they knew about him so far, which didn't amount to much. After ending the call, she googled his name. The top result was a link to his car dealership, which she clicked on. The website was fairly professional, with well-taken photos of the cars on offer, alongside descriptions, the number of miles they'd done, and the prices, which seemed fair.

She clicked on the 'Meet the Team' tab. Four men, all of whom seemed to be in their late thirties or early forties. None of them were smiling, creating an unapproachable vibe.

Freddie's photograph in particular looked like a mugshot. His hair was cropped short, his beard shaped to his jaw. His cheeks were sunken, his eyes sallow, and he was staring down the lens like he wanted to hurt whoever was wielding the camera. Maybe Lauren was projecting – letting the domestic-violence incident cloud her thoughts. Maybe she wasn't. Either way, she was sure they were about to deal with someone rather unpleasant.

'Shall we go see him?' she asked.

'After lunch,' Tom replied. 'I promised you a pub lunch and I want to be known as a man of my word.'

He started the engine and pulled out of the car park.

28

AFTER WOLFING DOWN a couple of sausage rolls and packets of Quavers hastily bought from a roadside Greggs, Tom and Lauren pulled into the gravel-strewn car park of Sutherland's Motors.

The forecourt stretched ahead of them, cluttered with used cars arranged in precise rows, as if trying to project a fabricated sense of order. The vehicles stood like weary soldiers – some polished and hopeful, others bearing the battle scars of long service: rust flaking around wheelarches, sun-faded paintwork, alloys scuffed and dented by careless owners.

A salesman hovered beside a blue Nissan Micra, gesturing animatedly to a middle-aged couple. Though too far away to catch his pitch, his exaggerated arm movements and constant nodding made it easy to fill in the blanks. He was laying it on thick. Across the lot stood a battered Portakabin, evidently serving as the site office. Its windows were smeared with grime and cobwebs, and one of the steps leading to the entrance was held together with gaffer tape. If the company's website had projected a façade of professionalism, the reality shattered that illusion.

Tom imagined Freddie Sutherland – or one of his greasy henchmen – running dodgy dealings straight out of *Matilda*: sawdust in the gearbox, tampered odometers, bumpers held on with *super* Super Glue. In his mind, Tom pictured Freddie as the

166

Danny DeVito character, small and smug, but when he stepped out of the office, Tom saw that he was only half right.

Fredde was tall – more than six foot – with a suit worn smooth at the knees and elbows. Five o'clock shadow clung to his hollow cheeks, his hair retreating from his temples. He looked like a man who'd once taken pride in his appearance but now only dressed the part out of habit. Still, there was something preening about him, something in the way he carried himself that suggested a man acutely possessed of his own importance. Even from across the forecourt, Tom could make out the distrust in Freddie's eyes as he surveyed them. Clearly, he'd clocked that Tom and Lauren were not here to test drive a Fiat 500.

As they set off towards him, Lauren turned to Tom.

'There's something I've been wondering,' she said.

'Go on.'

'It's already the twenty-first of December. What if our killer is planning something big for Christmas Day? To round off the holiday season – and their murder spree – in style?'

It was a thought that had crossed Tom's mind, too.

Before he could respond, his phone buzzed in his pocket.

He briefly stopped in his tracks to answer and listened to the information relayed. He asked for the details to be texted to him, and then hung up.

'What's up?' Lauren asked.

'They've found where Maddison is staying. A hostel in Kirk Yetholm.'

Tom opened up the Maps app, tapped in the location, and showed Lauren the screen.

'It's in bloody Scotland.'

She glanced at it and then rolled her eyes. 'It's hardly the Highlands. It's only just across the border.'

'How do you want to play it?'

She deliberated. 'How about I talk to Mr Sutherland here, and you go and try to catch Maddison. You can swing by and pick me up later, or I can get a lift back to Haltwhistle with Phil or someone else from the station.'

Tom turned towards Freddie again. 'Are you sure you're going to be okay with him on your own?'

'I'll be fine. Are you going to be okay telling Maddison her fiancé is dead?'

'I'll manage. Keep in touch, all right?'

'Yeah, you too,' Lauren said. 'Good luck. Drive safe.'

Tom headed back to his car and entered the address into the satnav. As the route loaded, he glanced in the rearview mirror one last time at Lauren, and then pulled away. Soon, the city gave way to open countryside – fields stitched with dry-stone walls and the occasional tumbledown barn. The skies were the colour of pewter, with low, heavy clouds threatening rain.

What if the killer really was planning something on Christmas Day? What if they didn't catch them in time? Time was ticking: only four days left.

He could not, *would* not allow the Christmas List Killer situation to repeat itself.

Even with such concerns weighing heavy on his mind, his thoughts drifted, unbidden, to the night before.

He'd convinced himself that Lauren was off-limits. That whatever feelings he had for her were redundant because of her engagement to Ben. But then, she'd hit him with the unexpected confession that she wasn't entirely happy. In fact, it sounded like a break up was imminent. It still probably meant nothing. He didn't know if she even felt anything romantic towards him – just because she was breaking up with her fiancé didn't mean she'd automatically wind up in his arms. But still, the odds just increased that she might. That was the thing with hope: it was stubborn, and easy to cling on to when you shouldn't.

He pushed thoughts of Lauren aside for now, and considered the task at hand. Maddison was about to receive news that would tear her world apart. She was so close to completing her long-distance walk, a personal journey that clearly meant the world to her – and here was Tom about to stain the memory with the worst news.

He ruminated on his job, and wondered if it would have taken its toll on him regardless of the trauma suffered last year. There were limits to what a human being could endure, and policing felt like a war of attrition. In a world filled with drug dealers, rapists, murderers, predators and victims, surely one's cup could only contain so much before overflowing. He sighed as he crossed from one country into another, Scotland welcoming him with grey skies and near-darkness, despite it being just after 3 p.m.

The landscape grew wilder. He passed through sleepy villages and wound his way down narrow country lanes, sometimes having to nose the car into hedges to let oncoming traffic squeeze by.

Eventually, he reached the hostel.

It looked like an old Victorian school, sturdy walls with tall, arched windows streaked with condensation. The building was nestled between rolling hills, flanked by skeletal trees shivering in the wind. Moss grew thick on the stone lintels, and the slate roof bore the weathered stains of a hundred winters.

He pulled into the small car park, let the engine idle, and waited for a moment, drawing a breath deep into his lungs and exhaling slowly. When he felt a little more grounded, he got out, gravel crunching under his boots as he made his way towards the front. A simple wooden sign to the side of the door displayed the name of the hostel; he knew he was in the right place. Someone had perched a fir tree behind it, but hadn't bothered to adorn the branches with decorations.

Inside felt cosier than the establishment where he'd met Maddison before. There was carpet for a start, as well as heating that blasted you upon crossing the threshold, though there was an odd smell. No one was at reception, so Tom skulked around to see if he could find anyone, noting green tinsel strewn across the mantel.

There was a living room, though Tom supposed it wasn't called that, even though with a crackling fire, a television and a couple of sofas that sagged with use, that's what it resembled. Off to the side was a games room, complete with a ping-pong table, a selection of scuffed board games and even a PlayStation 4 hooked up to a small TV. In the canteen, a few hikers in fleece tops and thermal leggings chatted over steaming mugs, but Maddison was not among them.

After he'd completed his loop, he arrived back at reception, where a young man was now behind the desk. He looked about twenty, with a scruffy beard and a mop of curly ginger hair tucked under a beanie. His name tag said 'Shay'.

'What's the smell, mate?' Tom asked.

'I don't know,' Shay admitted. 'Someone suggested that it might be the tree beginning to rot. It only has to hold out for another four days, so I'm reluctant to take it down. Anyway, can I help you there, mate?'

'I'm looking for Maddison Cassidy. Has she checked in?'

'Who are you?' Shay asked. 'I can't just give out that information. I could get in trouble.'

'Well done for being security conscious,' Tom said, before showing him his police ID.

Shay's eyes widened, as though mentally conjuring a million questions. Instead, he tapped on the keyboard and looked at the screen. 'Room four. But she's not here.'

Tom frowned. 'What do you mean?'

'She checked in, went to her room, and went straight back out again.'

'With all her gear?'

170

'Aye.'

'Any idea where she was off to?'

'Sorry, pal,' he said, shaking his head. 'There's loads of routes and trails to take around here. She could be on any one of them.'

'Do you mind if I wait for her?'

'No worries at all, pal, no worries. There's food through there and there's a fire over that way,' he said, gesticulating with two sweeping motions like a flight attendant.

The fire was calling. Tom nodded his thanks and started towards the living room, but something caught his eye near the door.

He hadn't fully noticed the Christmas tree on his first jaunt around the hostel. It was a cheap plastic one with fibreoptic lights that glowed faintly, decked with red and silver baubles and draped with gold tinsel. On the ground below were a smattering of presents. Most bore the same rectangular shape, as if someone had popped to a shoe shop and asked for some boxes wrapped in the same green and red striped paper. The smell was stronger here, one he knew too well.

Tom kneeled, slipped on a pair of gloves and gently moved some of the presents. As he shifted a box, an oddly shaped gift stood out – oblong, wrapped in red paper patterned with robins. Tom's chest squeezed tight. He recognised that pattern.

Unearthed, the stink of decay and death was overwhelming. He reached for the gift tag, his fingers shaking as he seized it.

The tag read: *For Rosanna.*

'Get everyone out,' Tom said to Shay, over his shoulder. 'This is now a crime scene.'

29

It was working.

The faint slackness in his movements, the colour draining from his cheeks, the way he pushed through each day with a brittle smile – all of it told them the plan was unfolding exactly as it should. What they were doing was almost tender in a way. No explosions, no spectacle. A slow undoing, impossible to halt.

Every morning, they pictured the rot tightening its grip, weaving itself deeper into his body. He probably didn't even know that he was inching closer to death with every breath.

They had chosen their timing with care. Measured the dose, weighed the days. And they knew – with absolute certainty – that by Christmas he would be gone. A perfect ending to a season he had ruined.

'Dead by Christmas,' they whispered into the quiet, the words as sweet as a carol on their tongue.

There was no stopping it now. The clock was ticking, and he carried the means of his own destruction inside him.

The plan was a success, and the figure allowed themselves, just for a moment, to savour the triumph.

He would rue the day he ever started this.

30

IT TOOK THE FIRST tranche of officers around forty minutes to arrive, forensics a little longer.

Tom had waited at the entrance all that time, motionless, his eyes fixed on the treeline that fringed the hills and the ancient wall once built to keep out Barbarians. He couldn't shake the feeling that someone – *the* someone behind all this – was out there, hidden behind pine trunks and wreathed in shadows, watching him. Maybe even smiling at the chaos they had caused.

With every passing minute, he itched to go back inside, to tear away the wrapping paper and confirm what he feared. However, he knew that forensics would make him regret it if he did. Instead, he stood still as a statue, while his stomach roiled and bile climbed his throat at the thought of the present. The smell – thick, metallic, and sickly sweet – seemed to have embedded itself in his nostrils, though that could just be his imagination playing tricks.

When the first officers finally arrived, Tom issued orders as soon as their boots touched the ground. One was to guard the entrance and another was to position himself at the fire escape around the back. A third was stationed at the car park entrance. Within minutes, an inner and outer cordon had been established with blue tape flapping in the wind like a warning.

When more officers arrived, he tasked them with taking a roll call of who was staying here currently and then interviewing them. The hikers had been dispatched to what was essentially a glorified garden shed – cold, draughty, and reeking of damp. Tom felt a flicker of guilt, but there was no room for comfort in a murder investigation.

When the forensics vans finally pulled up, Tom's chest tightened. Anticipation. Dread. Fear. The last two 'gifts' had been bad enough. Maddison had received a foot. Niall, a hand with a finger missing. If his suspicions were true, Rosanna's parcel would be the worst of them all.

The SOCO team jumped out of their vans and immediately began unpacking equipment, snapping on gloves and zipping themselves into white suits. Tom briefed them on the situation as clearly and as succinctly as he could, laying out what he knew – or thought he knew – and what he suspected was wrapped up beneath the tree.

A crime-scene photographer and a videographer followed him inside, the latter already narrating the beginnings of the investigation for the official record. As they entered the dim interior, the stench intensified. It smacked into them like a wall – sour, organic, unmistakably human. Tom was impressed that the videographer was able to keep the disgust out of his voice.

They approached the tree, the package still there, grotesquely festive. The photographer took methodical shots from every angle, making sure to capture every last detail. They radioed for the head SOCO to join them and waited a few minutes until he appeared.

The honours were left to Tom.

He crouched beside the present, heart hammering. His fingers hovered for a second before he pinched a fold of the wrapping paper and gave it a gentle tug. The paper tore with a soft rip – an almost delicate sound in the heavy silence. Emboldened, he tore away more.

And just as he thought, the paper fell away to reveal a human head, severed at the neck.

For a sickening moment, the world fell away, before it lurched back into focus again.

It belonged to a woman who had once been beautiful, but was no longer. Now, her features were waxen and slack, her skin a dull grey with a slight greenish hue. Decomposition hadn't started in earnest yet, but it was on its way. Her eyes were closed. Her hair, tied into a short ponytail, gave her a strangely practical appearance, like someone who'd anticipated a busy day at work, instead of death. Aside from where the head had been severed, there was no blood and no bruising.

Tom could've been backstage at Madame Tussauds, looking at an eerily-lifelike prototype of their next waxwork. Except this head had weight. Presence. It was undoubtedly real.

'What kind of sick bastard…' Tom heard the photographer mutter from behind, before catching himself, seemingly realising that the videographer's camera was still running.

Tom didn't speak. Instead, he followed the photographer's instructions, turning the head this way and that so that the camera could capture it from every angle. When the photographer was done, Tom gave a small nod, and the head was carefully bagged and sealed.

'No obvious sign of what caused the death,' the SOCO said, crouching beside him as he bagged up the wrapping paper separately. 'I can't see any impact marks or lacerations. It's not apparent what killed her.'

'Maybe the rest of the body tells the story,' Tom replied quietly. 'Stab wounds, gunshot to the heart, blunt-force trauma, torture – who knows.'

'I'll put a rush on it,' the SOCO said, rising. 'Is this definitely connected to the investigation you're working on?'

'Without a doubt.'

'I'll get this to Carlisle Hospital as a matter of priority. I'll flag it so the pathologist knows to get it to the top of the list and ask them to send you the results as soon as they possibly can.'

'Appreciate it,' Tom nodded. 'Thanks, mate.'

The SOCO left. So, too, did the photographer and the videographer, to make sure the chain of evidence was preserved. With them gone, silence returned – disturbed only by the flicker of emergency lights and the low hum of a generator somewhere outside. Tom stayed hunkered down beside the tree, fairy lights still flashing on and off, the smell of death lingering.

His phone rang and he retrieved it from his pocket.

He was glad to see the name onscreen.

'Hi Lauren,' Tom said.

'Hey,' she replied. 'How did it go?'

'Maddison had already been and gone.'

'Bollocks,' she muttered. 'A wasted trip, then, all the way to Scotland for nothing.'

'I wouldn't say that.'

He told her what they'd found instead.

The humour drained from her voice.

* * *

Tom had barely stepped back into the station in Haltwhistle when Lauren enveloped him in a hug. His heart thudded in his ribcage.

'You're all right,' she murmured into his chest.

He let out a slow, weary breath, and nodded.

'For now,' he said into her hair.

They pulled apart, her hands lingering for a beat too long on his shoulders, as if double-checking he hadn't cracked under the pressure.

'Come on, then,' she said, tilting her head towards the inner sanctum of the station. 'Tell me all about it.'

As they walked down the corridor towards the office, he filled her in on all that had happened. The discovery of the head and the rushed post-mortem. How he had left the local officers in charge of the search for Maddison, and how Rosanna was being summoned for questioning.

'All we can do now,' Tom said, sinking into this chair, 'is wait.'

Lauren gave a curt nod, then said, 'Well, while you were playing horror show in the woods, I had a fun little chat with Freddie Sutherland.'

He raised an eyebrow. 'Define fun.'

She chuckled and reached for her laptop. 'He was all charm at first, as you'd expect from a car dealer. He offered me a drink, gave the Portakabin a quick tidy while I had my tea, all that jazz. I think he thought he might be able to flog me something if he really made an effort.'

She clicked play on a recording and let him hear a snippet. Freddie's syrupy tone made Tom grimace.

'He sounds like a game-show host.'

'And not a very good one at that. More a rerun on Dave than primetime BBC. Let me fast forward a bit...'

She scrubbed through the audio, checking it at various points before letting a short section play. A nasty edge had crept into Freddie's voice, the gloss stripped away and his tone beneath clipped. Such was the change, it was as if he'd left the room and let one of his colleagues take his place.

'As soon as I pushed,' Lauren said, 'he got defensive. Like he'd practised being friendly but hadn't rehearsed what happened if the shit hit the fan.'

As the interview ended, Tom leaned back in his chair and asked Lauren what her read of the situation was.

'Well, he claims that he knows Joshua solely as a client. Apparently, he had recently sold Joshua a Renault Clio, but he wouldn't tell me how much for. I've applied for a warrant so that we can dig into his financials, although maybe Rosanna will be able to help with that if she's coming in today.'

Lauren took a swig from her water bottle before continuing.

'When I asked why he had been for a pint with Joshua and Niall, he claimed Joshua had invited him out. I asked if that was common practice during a transaction for a new car. He said it was unusual, but Joshua had seemed like "a good guy to know."'

'I wonder if that translates to he knew Joshua was loaded,' Tom said. 'And what about Niall? Also a good guy to know?'

'He claims he didn't know him. Said Joshua and Niall were already at the pub when he arrived. First time he'd ever clapped eyes on the bloke. But they got along well, apparently.'

Tom shook his head slowly. 'It's just such a weird situation, isn't it? A sudden pub session with a random bloke who buys a car and a stranger, in the midst of a couple of murders.'

'Suspicious as hell, yeah. Someone in that odd little triangle is hiding something. That's why I didn't just stop at Freddie – I've also applied for financial warrants for Niall and Joshua, too. Their bank records, phone activity, all of it. Let's see if money or messages tell us what they won't.'

'Good work today,' he said, earning him a smile.

For a while, they worked side by side, mostly in silence, with only the clatter of keys filling the office. Nobody joined the police for the paperwork, but it was a crucial part of the jigsaw. Every name, every date, every gut feeling – they had to be logged, or risk slipping through the cracks. When the case reached court, these were the foundations that would hopefully secure a conviction and bring the victims' families justice.

Tom received a text from his mum:

```
No test results yet. I assume you're still
busy, but we hope you're still coming home
on Christmas Eve? We'd love to see you.
```

He replied, thanking her for the update, and telling her he hoped to have the case sewn up by then.

They were almost finished when Martin arrived in the doorway, brandishing a takeaway bag. The rich scent of curry filled the room, making Tom's stomach rumble and his mouth salivate.

'I imagine it's going to be a late night,' Martin said, as he set the bag down on the table between them. 'Least I could do.'

They thanked him, and dug in gratefully. The lamb bhuna was delicious, and Tom had to force himself to slow down to avoid indigestion. As he was wiping up the last remnants of sauce with a chunk of naan bread, a message came through on his phone.

'Rosanna's here,' he said to Lauren.

'Well, then,' she replied, setting down her fork. 'Let's see what she has to say for herself.'

31

A DC HAD ALREADY settled Rosanna in the interview room and brought her a cup of water. Tom and Lauren had been preparing to enter when the warrants arrived. Instead of going straight in, they spent the next thirty minutes combing through Joshua's financial records. The Clio transaction leapt out, along with a few other inconsistencies they marked for later. When they were ready, they rose and proceeded to the interview room.

Since they had last seen Rosanna, she had undergone quite the transformation. There were heavy shadows under her eyes, and the clothes she was wearing seemed to dwarf her. Her collarbones were sharp against the fabric of her blouse. Tom guessed she hadn't eaten properly in days. Clearly the death of her husband had hit her hard. She didn't smile as Tom and Lauren sat down in the seats opposite her.

'Hi again, Rosanna,' Tom said. 'Thanks for coming in.'

She scoffed. 'It's not like I was given much of a choice.'

'Well, we still appreciate it. I believe that our colleague already checked and you've declined a lawyer.'

'Why would I need a lawyer?' she asked, rolling her eyes. 'I'm the fucking victim in all of this. Or have you forgotten that?'

'We have to ask, regardless,' Lauren said, kindly. 'If you're happy to proceed, we'll get started.'

180

Rosanna gave a stiff nod. Lauren turned on the recording device, stating the date, time, who was present and the purpose of the interview.

To begin, Tom slid a photo across the table, showing Joshua, Niall and Freddie sitting around a table in The Plough.

'Do you know this man?' he asked, pointing at the car salesman.

Rosanna leaned in, eyes narrowed as she studied the picture. After a beat, she shook her head.

'For the tape please, Rosanna,' Tom prompted.

'No, I don't know him,' she said. 'I've never seen him before in my life.'

'His name is Freddie Sutherland. He sells cars in Newcastle.'

'Good for him,' she said as she shrugged, though Tom could see she was interested.

'Do you have any idea why Joshua would have been meeting with him?'

'No.'

'We have reason to believe that Joshua bought a car from him recently. A Renault Clio.' Tom pushed a second sheet in front of her, this one a screengrab from Joshua's online banking account, the transaction highlighted bright yellow. 'Fifteen thousand seems a little steep for an eighteen plate Clio, wouldn't you say?'

'I'm not a car salesman. I don't know anything about them.'

'Well, we had a quick look, and they go for anywhere between four and ten grand. Tops. What I want to know is why he was buying it, when he has a perfectly good Range Rover sitting in his driveway.'

'Had,' she said.

'Pardon me?'

'Had a perfectly good Range Rover sitting in his driveway.' She regarded him with cloudy eyes. 'He's dead, remember? He doesn't have anything anymore.'

Tom paused, giving Rosanna a minute. Then he said, 'Sorry. I should've considered my words more carefully. But we need your help on this. Rosanna, can you think why he'd be buying an old Clio?'

'No.' Some of her resistance crumbled, and she stopped speaking in short sentences. 'He was obsessed with cars. He always had the latest *Top Gear* on and had magazines all over the house, folded down at pages of cars he wanted to test drive. I have no idea why he'd be buying a Clio. And an old one, at that.'

'Did he mention needing a second car?' Tom asked. 'A cheaper runaround, or anything like that?'

'No. And if he was in the market for something, it wouldn't be a Clio and it wouldn't be second-hand.'

'Could he have been buying it for Niall?'

Her brow twitched, suspicion crossing her features. 'Why would he do that?'

'Well, that's what we're trying to figure out,' Tom said. 'They were drinking together. Maybe Niall had asked him for a favour.'

'He never mentioned anything like that to me. Now, is that it? Can I go now?'

She made to leave, her chair screeching against the floor.

'Actually,' Lauren said, 'there's something else.'

'What now?' she said, clearly impatient to get going.

'Today, we found another parcel with another body part inside. This one was addressed to you.'

For a moment, she sat stock-still, as though she hadn't been able to process the words. Tom put it down to grief and gave her a moment. Sure enough, her reaction came. Her lips parted and her eyes widened in silent terror. She looked like she might be sick. Trembling slightly, she sat down again and gripped her plastic cup. Some of the water sloshed over the side, though she didn't seem to notice.

'What do you mean?' she asked. 'Where? W-why me?'

'We don't know, but we're hoping you can help with that.' Tom fetched a third piece of paper from the file, but before passing it across, warned her that it wasn't the most pleasant thing she'd see that day. Tom had chosen the least gruesome picture that he could, but at the end of the day, it *was* still a picture of a decapitated head. He could see Rosanna steel herself as she accepted the sheet with shaking fingers.

Rosanna stared at it. For a second, her body locked up, her breath held. Then the reaction came in waves – her hand flew to her mouth, and she doubled forward, moaning.

'Jesus Christ!' she uttered, as she took in the horror.

More tears came. The ink ran as her teardrops pitter-pattered onto the page, further distorting the terrible image. Tom gently retrieved the sheet before it could cause more distress.

They waited, letting her cry. Lauren pushed a packet of tissues across the table, and Rosanna took them wordlessly. She blew her nose several times, and then sat back in her chair, her eyes red and puffy, exhaustion washing over her.

Tom leaned in gently. 'Do you want to take a break?'

'No,' she whispered. 'I just want to go home.'

'And we'll try and make that happen as soon as we can. I need to know, do you recognise her?'

'Yes,' she said quietly, before clearing her throat. 'Her name is Evie Kirkby. She's one of Joshua's colleagues.'

Tom and Lauren exchanged a knowing look. There was something in her voice and in her body language that suggested there was more to the story than simply knowing her name. Tom knew that the best way to let this play out was to sit silently and wait for Rosanna to fill in the blanks. For a while, it seemed like his plan was doomed to fail. Rosanna simply sat there, staring at the wall, glassy-eyed. But then, she roused, and said, quietly:

'I know how this is going to make me look, all right? But I swear I had nothing to do with any of this. I couldn't. I'm not a killer. Fuck, I even make a little sugary drink for tired bees in summer. I'm not… I couldn't… I couldn't do any of this.'

'Just tell us what you know,' Lauren said, soothingly.

'For a while, I suspected that Joshua and Evie were sleeping together.'

'Did you ever confront Joshua about it?'

'I never had proof,' she shrugged. 'I'd check his phone when he was in the shower, and his emails if he ever left his work laptop lying about. Nothing. But I just *knew*. Or thought I did. You know that feeling?'

'What did Joshua do to make you suspect he was having an affair with Evie?'

'I'd seen them on work dos – Christmas dinners, conferences, that kind of thing. They'd always find their way to each other. It was the body language, the way they looked at each other. Flirty. Like teenagers. When he said he had business trips … I started wondering if he was staying at hers.'

'Did Evie have a partner?'

'I don't think so.'

'Can you think why her head might have been addressed to you?'

'I have no idea!' she yelped. 'Fuck, it's such a mess. But between this and Joshua's finger being cut off, it's like someone wants it to look like I did it. Like I'm some kind of fucking monster.'

When neither Tom nor Lauren spoke, she went on, frantic now.

'I've been with my parents ever since you told me about Joshua. I've not left their house once, except to go to the shops, but that was for an hour in the middle of the day. Otherwise, I've been cooped up in their house like a fucking prisoner. They'll tell you that, they will. Ask them. Ask my sister. She's been around to

184

visit, and she's been texting me about going out for a drink but I just can't face leaving their house. I'll show you. I'll give my phone so you can check. I've got nothing to hide.'

'Thanks, Rosanna. We appreciate your cooperation. We just have a few more questions—'

Before he could finish his sentence, there was a quiet knock at the door. A DC poked his head in and motioned for Tom to come with him. Tom nodded and turned back to the table.

'Interview paused at…' He checked his watch. 'Nine-nineteen p.m.'

Lauren pressed the pause button.

'I'll be right back,' Tom said, rising to his feet.

Outside, the DC told him that Claire had been in touch to request a callback. The results of the post-mortem were in.

Tom walked quickly to the office and called her. When she answered, her voice was clipped. Not cold, exactly, but cool enough that he sensed a shift between them. Perhaps she hadn't appreciated the speed with which he'd left their sort-of date the other night. Or calling her by the wrong name.

'The full report will be with you first thing,' she said, 'but the headlines are that there's significant cerebral oedema – swelling of the brain – but no blunt-force trauma to the skull. Possible causes of death are therefore cardiac arrest or suffocation. Poisoning or a drug overdose can also cause swelling on the brain, but the blood tests I ran ruled out those possibilities. Ultimately, without the actual body, there's not much more I can do.'

'Thanks, Claire. That's really helpful.'

She offered a stiff goodbye and hung up.

Tom returned to the interview room and restarted the recording device.

'Interview resumed at nine twenty-six p.m. As I was saying before we were interrupted, Rosanna, we just have one or two more questions. Can you think of anyone who would've wanted to harm Evie?'

'No, I barely knew her. More to the point, I have no idea why someone would send me a fucking head.' On the verge of more tears, she stopped. A moment later, she said, 'Can I ask you a question?'

'Of course,' Tom replied.

'If it was meant for me, why wasn't it sent to my house? Why leave it at some hostel two hours away?'

It was a very good question – one neither he nor Lauren knew the answer to.

32

TOM HADN'T SLEPT. NOT properly. His mind had whirled all night long, turning over fragments of the case – the severed head, the endless false leads, the spiderweb of connections that refused to form a coherent pattern. His head felt claggy and disturbed.

So, he'd gone out early and taken to the hills. The rising sun soothed his soul, as did the sodden pathways and the scent of wet bark and damp moss. As he squelched along, he forced himself not to think – just to move. To breathe. To simply 'be' in the moment. Each step, each inhale, was a small rebellion against the noise in his head. This was the new and improved meditation. Dr Dougan would be proud.

After a shower and some breakfast at his flat, he arrived at the station feeling … not rested, exactly, but revitalised, despite the pitiful few hours of sleep he'd managed.

The same could not be said for those who were already there. The energy was depleted, those at the business end of a nightshift sagging and ready to leave. Even those who had just arrived, Deborah among them, seemed a little out of sorts, like their energy had been smothered before it even sparked. Tom knew that as the SIO on the case it was his job to rally the troops, to guide them out of the labyrinthine maze they found themselves in.

With that in mind, he'd wiped the whiteboard clean. Every theory, every scrap of assumption or conjecture – gone. If they were going to find the truth in this mess, they needed clarity. A full reset.

After coffee had been poured and mince pies had been claimed, the briefing room filled. Tom gave them a few minutes to say good morning and catch up before he approached the front of the room.

'Morning, everyone,' he said, and the room quietened, all eyes turning to him. 'Lots to go through today, starting with Evie Kirkby.'

He lifted a photo of her from the table and pinned it to the centre of the whiteboard. It was a picture he'd extracted from her Facebook profile page – her in a bar in Tenerife. Her plaited hair trailed down her back, her mouth open wide, presumably mid-laugh. She wore a green vest top and looked to be having the time of her life. It was from a couple of years ago, but Tom had chosen it on purpose. He hoped that seeing a vibrant young woman in the prime of her life might subconsciously fuel his team's motivation. Not that he doubted their capabilities, but sometimes that was the extra boost needed when an investigation stalled.

'Evie Kirkby was twenty-nine years old when she was killed. I'm sure most of you know by now, but her head was found wrapped under a tree in a hostel at Kirk Yetholm. I spoke to a psychologist first thing this morning and she believes that Evie could have been the primary target all along. That the others were practice, or mere pawns in the game.'

'Why does she think that?' Deborah asked.

'She thinks that, since the hand and the foot were not immediately identifiable, they could have belonged to anyone. It didn't matter – all that did was make us chase our tails for a bit. But Evie? Leaving her head, unmistakable and intentionally placed? That was a message. A deliberate escalation.'

'Do you agree with her?'

Tom deliberated for a moment and then shook his head.

'No, I don't. I think each of the three victims have been chosen carefully. They knew each other. They're connected. That's not coincidence.'

'But if she's right,' Deborah pressed, 'why does she think Evie matters more than the others?'

'Because she is a psychologist, not a police officer,' Tom said. 'She's trying to see things from the killer's perspective, rather than ours. She might be right when she says that Evie was always the intended target, but I stand by the Harry Bosch motto: everybody counts or nobody counts. Evie, Joshua and Tristan have left behind parents, brothers, sisters, partners. Their deaths mean something to someone, and to us. Today, though, we *are* going to start with Evie and explore the pathways we can take.'

He reached for two more photos – Joshua and Tristan – and stuck them beside Evie's. Around them, he drew a large bubble and the word 'Victims'. Underneath, he stuck three more pictures: Maddison, Niall and Rosanna. Inside this bubble, he wrote the words 'Gift Recipients'.

'These six people are inexorably linked. Three dead, three intended recipients. Why them?'

A pause stretched on. Some looked around, others stared dead ahead, waiting for someone to take up the questions. Eventually, Lauren did.

'Could it be some sort of sick Secret Santa?'

Heads turned.

Tom gestured for her to go on.

'Well, it just reminds me of that game. You know? Everyone pulls a name out of a hat and has a certain amount of money to spend. Could the three recipients each be behind one of the deaths? Could they each have killed someone and then delivered the body part as proof they'd done it?'

It sounded a little far-fetched, but not implausible; Tom was certainly not willing to rule it out at this stage. He wrote Secret

Santa at the top right-hand side of the board under the heading 'Motives'.

'Anything else?'

Deborah spoke up.

'I like that idea,' she said. 'And there is a plausible motive, isn't there? Rosanna believed that Joshua and Evie were having an affair. That's been a reason for murder since time began. She could easily have killed Evie, and then delivered the head to herself to throw us off the scent.'

'But Joshua is dead,' a DC pointed out. 'If Rosanna killed him, what was the point of killing Evie, too?'

'Maybe Evie had a suspicion that Rosanna did it, so she killed her to make sure no one ever spoke up against her.'

'Maybe,' Tom said, folding his arms. 'However, we've checked Rosanna's alibi, and she seems to be telling us the truth. Since Joshua's death, she's been at her parents' house. She left for an hour or two here and there, but certainly not enough time to travel the length and breadth of the country killing, lopping off limbs and delivering them throughout Northumbria. She's barely left her room, according to the dad.'

'What about at nighttime?' Deborah shot back. 'Have her parents stayed up all night with her, guarding the door?'

'Well, no,' Tom admitted.

'And if she's barely left her room,' Deborah pressed on, 'she could be killing at night and sleeping in the day. Her parents think she's grieving, and are leaving her to it, when really she's sleeping off an all-nighter where she's been chopping arms, legs and heads off people.'

It was well-reasoned, so Tom added 'Affair' to motives.

Lauren leaned forward, energised now. 'The presents are all being delivered near where Maddison is, right? Regardless of whose name is on the gift tag.'

'Correct.'

'And her fiancé was one of those killed... What if she delivered the first present to herself, made a song and dance about it, got us to believe she was the victim, and then carried along the Pennine Way, murdering as she went and dropping presents for us to find in her wake?'

Tom cast his mind back to that first interview, Maddison white as a sheet, hands trembling, but defiant. He didn't see her as the killer, and said as much. Tom recognised the delight of a challenge in Lauren's eyes.

'Her and Niall used to date—'

'In high school,' Tom said, knowing it sounded thin.

'Yeah, but some flames never die, do they? What happens if one of them, or both, never forgot about the other? Niall is a single man who has lied about where he was during one of the murders. Caught on camera, no less, with one of the victims—'

'But not Maddison's fiancé.'

'Not the fiancé, granted,' Lauren said. 'But still one of the victims. What happens if Maddison, Niall, or both of them together orchestrated the killing of Tristan so they could be together? Maybe Niall did the killing, and Maddison did the hiding.'

'Maddison claimed she was happy with Tristan,' Tom pointed out. 'She'd borrowed money from Joshua to pay for the wedding. Why would she kill him?'

'Desperate people do desperate things,' Lauren shot back. 'Maybe she and Tristan argued about the money. Maybe Tristan was the one to force her to borrow money in the first place, and she wanted out. Maybe she borrowed the money, killed Joshua so she wouldn't have to pay it back and then killed Tristan so she wouldn't have to marry him. Now, she's sitting on fifteen grand and no one is going to be asking a grieving woman for that back anytime soon. Maybe her plan is to disappear into the sunset with the money, never to be seen again.'

There was a murmur of agreement to Lauren's finely-crafted argument. Tom added money to the list of motives, and then stepped back from the board. It was messier now than ever, and they were no closer to finding a path to the truth. Still, it had been good to hash it out, uncover what people were thinking and why, and while they might not have cleaved any suspects from the list, it was still a worthwhile exercise.

'Don't forget our pal Freddie,' Lauren said.

Tom reached for the last photo. 'For those of you that don't know, this is Freddie Sutherland. He's a car salesman, who was in the middle of selling Joshua a Renault Clio at an overinflated price. Rosanna has no knowledge of the sale, and as a rich man and a car snob, we don't think the car sale was legit. It's possible Joshua was paying Freddie off for something else, but we don't know what. It's something we'll be looking into as a matter of urgency. To complicate matters further, Freddie, Joshua and Niall were captured on CCTV in a Newcastle pub shortly before Joshua's death. He is definitely a person of interest.'

The final picture Tom fixed to the board showed the three gift tags that had been fastened to the presents.

'We've had a handwriting expert assess these,' he said. 'The expert is almost certain that they were written by the same person. He thinks that the author may have a tremor – there are certain bits circled in red that he has pointed out for us. It could be that they were nervous or cold when writing, which may cause a temporary shiver, but it may be attributed to a longer-term illness. Something to keep in mind, or to keep a watch out for when interviewing.'

He ended the meeting with good news. Dane Higbee had been cleared, on account of a deep dive into his laptop. He also had been able to rule out Duncan MacMaster from Silver Skies, after some sterling work by Deborah.

After that, he divvied out jobs again. There was CCTV to watch, doors to knock on, various hostels along the Pennine Way to visit, on the off-chance someone had encountered Maddison and saw her acting strangely.

He would take the hardest jobs himself.

He had to tell Maddison her fiancé was dead.

And then he had to face Niall: as it stood, still their most likely killer.

33

TOM WAS BURIED IN a case file, flipping through witness statements, when the phone rang. He snatched it up without looking. *A fresh lead? Lauren? Dad's test results?*

'Tom, it's Deborah.'

'Is everything okay?'

'Did you know that Maddison owns her own flat?'

He frowned. 'What do you mean?'

'She and Tristan had moved in together, but she hasn't managed to sell her old place yet. It's still on the market, but I've spoken to the estate agents and there hasn't been a viewing in a couple of weeks. Between you and me, they think she valued it too high.'

'Great work,' Tom said, rising from his seat, car keys already in hand. 'Send me the address. I'm on my way.'

With Lauren elsewhere for the day, he travelled alone. The drive was a silent one, filled only with the restless spiralling of his thoughts. The whiteboard loomed in his mind – names, timelines, motives – but none of it lined up. Without more data, it was impossible to make headway. Maybe something in Maddison's flat would give him just what he needed.

The block of flats was situated in the city centre, its modern façade facing the murky waters of the Tyne, the iconic bridge rising in the background. A sad, browning fir tree was perched outside the communal door. *Tis the season, indeed*. He couldn't escape it.

Tom parked in the small car park, climbed out, and spotted a man in a suit huddled by the door to keep warm. As he got closer, the man held out a hand, which Tom shook.

'Tom, is it? Your colleague called ahead. I'm Stuart, the estate agent.'

Stuart led him inside, through the reception foyer towards a lift. As they ascended, Tom received the full sales pitch – square footage, river views, communal garden – though he hadn't asked for it. Mercifully, the lift pinged and the doors opened onto the fourth floor. Tom followed Stuart down a short corridor, until the estate agent stopped at one of the doors, slotted a key into the lock, and pushed the door open with a flourish. His face immediately fell at the fetid stench that greeted them.

'What the hell is that?' Stuart asked, recoiling.

'That,' Tom said, his voice grim, 'is the smell of rotting flesh.'

He knew that the forensic team would be unhappy with him entering the flat, but he didn't really have a choice. He needed to know what was causing the smell, and if there was anyone in there who was hurt – or worse. He ventured inside, leaving the estate agent in the hallway with his hand clamped over his mouth, his complexion drained of colour.

The door closed behind Tom, leaving him in a dim hallway with three doors branching off. Tom followed his nose to the door facing him and opened it into an open-plan living space. The room was long and narrow, with a kitchen at one end and a living space at the other, separated by a small circular dining table. The kitchen was tidy and clean, the living room neat and utilitarian, with a boxy sofa facing a TV, and a bookcase pushed against the wall. It was to this that his nose led him.

The bookcase was mostly empty. Those that remained were popular titles – *Twilight, Harry Potter, the Chronicles of Narnia*. As well as books, there were several trinkets – a metal ornament of the Eiffel Tower, a carved marble depiction of the Taj Mahal, a pebble worn smooth on one side.

Glaringly out of place was the severed finger, blackened and bloated, a gold ring at its base. This close, the smell was overpowering, and Tom felt his stomach churn.

He took a couple of quick photos, before calling the forensic team. They assured him that they wouldn't be long and asked him to vacate the scene immediately. Tom told them he knew the drill, before hanging up. At the door, he took one last pointed look at the finger. Whoever had left it there hadn't done so by accident.

It was a message.

A trophy.

Or both.

Tom stepped back into the hallway, grateful the stench was feebler out here. Stuart was waiting, leaning against the wall, some of the colour returned to his cheeks. He was on the phone.

'Hang up right now,' Tom barked. Stuart disconnected the call immediately, slipping the phone into his jacket pocket.

'I was only calling the office,' he replied.

'If this gets out before we let the press know,' Tom said, ignoring his last comment, 'I'm holding you personally responsible. I can't imagine a night or two in a cell would do much for your career.'

Stuart assured Tom he would keep schtum, but Tom had heard that excuse before.

'I'll be holding onto the key for a little while, if that's all right. Forensics will be here soon, and it would be better if you weren't here when they do.'

Stuart didn't argue. He all but sprinted to the lift. Tom called after him, 'Keep your phone on. We'll have more questions.'

Stuart didn't look back as the lift doors slid shut.

True to their word, the first wave of SOCOs arrived not long after. They sealed off the corridor and got to work inside the flat.

Tom was issued a plastic suit and was permitted to stand just inside the inner cordon. Watching the action unfold around him, he felt like a football player on the subs bench, waiting, knowing there was nothing he could do until he was given the nod.

Eventually, he was granted permission to join them in the inner sanctum. He returned to the living room where Iain, head SOCO, was studying the finger sealed inside a clear evidence bag.

'You think it's your guy?' he asked.

'I hope so,' Tom nodded. 'I'd hate to think there are other hands with missing fingers floating about out there.'

'I'll get it sent to the hospital for testing, but I'd bet my mortgage on it,' he said, before stepping towards the door. Before leaving, he stopped and said, 'There's a phone in the bedroom you should see.'

Tom followed him out of the living room and entered the bedroom. The room was the definition of a box room, big enough only for a single bed and a wardrobe. There were no personal flourishes in here. The windowsill and the handles of the wardrobe were covered in a fine layer of dust – clearly she, or any prospective buyers, hadn't been here in some time. Tom surmised that Maddison had already moved most of her stuff into Tristan's house, and these were the final dregs of her past life.

On the bed lay the phone, already encased in an evidence bag. It was an old Motorola, the type that looked like a relic from the early 2000s. It was a cheap handset, and Tom had seen thousands of them during his time on the force. In an age of expensive smartphones, this type of small cheap plastic phone meant only one thing – it was a burner.

Tom could feel his heartbeat quicken as he lifted the bag and navigated the menu towards the contacts.

There was only one number stored there.

Joshua's.

Why would Maddison have a phone with only Joshua's number in it? Tom thought as he tried to find the messages. When he did, there were only two text messages to be found. Both were sent from this phone to Joshua's:

```
Joshy, please don't tell Tristan what
happened!!! Xx
```

Then, a day later:

```
If you tell, I'll tell.
```

That was the sum total of the conversation. There was no reply, no hints at the aftermath, and no further messages from Maddison to check if Joshua had received the messages.

Tom checked the call log, but there had never been any outgoing or incoming calls. Or, if there had, they'd been wiped. All the phone contained were those two messages: one desperate and pleading message, the other verging on vengeful.

He set the phone back down on the bed. Jaw clenched, he berated himself.

Lauren had pegged Maddison right from the start, but he'd always waved that suspicion away. Even this morning, he'd not been convinced by Lauren's argument that Maddison could be behind this. He'd cast her as the victim, had been taken in by her fragility, the shock, the tears – while Lauren had questioned why she was continuing to walk the Pennine Way even after finding a severed human foot. If Lauren was right, which was looking increasingly likely, Maddison had nothing to fear from continuing on her merry way because she *was* the danger.

A knot of shame twisted in his gut. If he'd just listened to his partner, perhaps Joshua and Evie need not have died. He felt the crushing weight of responsibility for the two deaths. Again, he'd failed to protect the people who needed him most. Just like last year. Just like Seth had said. The weight of the words, and the memory, hit him like a hammer. He remembered Seth's face, remembered the vitriol with which he'd spat his insults.

Tom's face burned, and his legs felt like they'd been dipped in lead. The walls felt like they were closing in on him, so he turned and left, the abruptness of his movement catching the SOCOs by surprise, though he barely noticed. He took the stairs two at a time, stepped out into the cool air, and stood in the car park feeling the breeze tickle his bare skin for a few minutes. He waited for the surging anger to pass.

He fetched his phone and saw that he had a missed call from Lauren.

The sight of her name extinguished his rage in an instant.

He called her back, ready to tell her about the developments in Maddison's flat. But when she answered, all he could hear was the deafening swirl of wind.

'Hello?' he said.

'Tom. Can you hear me?' Her voice was muffled, lost in the roar.

'Just about,' he replied. 'Are you okay?'

'I need you,' she said. 'I know where Maddison is.'

34

TOM FOLLOWED THE SATNAV deep into the Pennines, the roads narrowing with each passing mile, flanked by wild moorland and dry-stone walls. For once, the rain had relented, and a rare, brittle calm had settled over the hills. The sky stretched out, cobalt and cloudless, and despite it being a little after three o'clock, the setting sun bled orange along the horizon. It might have been beautiful – serene, even – if Tom hadn't been silently unravelling.

The rhythmic thud of tyres on uneven tarmac was the only sound inside the car, apart from the loop of self-recrimination in his head. He should've backed Lauren's judgement from the start. Try as he might, he couldn't stop Seth's taunts continuing to circle.

He was pleased, then, when he spotted his partner's car in a lay-by, flanked by two marked units. He passed by, travelling a little further down the road to find another lay-by he could park in. Despite the blue skies, the cold was biting, the wind finding a way through his thick coat.

He hopped the stile and began the slow trudge across water-logged grass, boots squelching as he went. The field rose toward a rocky escarpment, rugged and severe. Rainwater glistened on the lichen-covered rock, which loomed ten metres high, jagged at the top like broken teeth.

And there – just visible at the edge of the roof – stood Maddison, her figure ghostlike against the dying light.

Tom joined Lauren, who stood with two younger officers, one of whom was trying to calm Maddison down.

'What's happening?' Tom said, when he reached Lauren.

'Are you okay?' she said, in reply. 'You look dreadful.'

'A real confidence booster,' he joked. 'Just what I needed.'

'I'm serious, Tom.'

He gave a tired smile. 'I'm okay. It's just been a day and a half so far. I'll tell you about it later. What have we got here?'

Lauren motioned upwards. 'Maddison phoned nine-nine-nine. She gave her name and location, and said she needed help. I arrived to find her standing on the edge, but so far it's been hard getting anything out of her. She's been threatening to jump if we come any closer.'

'How long has she been up there?'

'Not sure. We've been here for an hour or so, and she was here before us. I've asked her what she wants, how we can help her, but she just keeps saying she's going to jump. That she wants to die.'

Tom narrowed his eyes at the ledge. 'If she was going to jump, she'd have done it by now.'

'Or she's building up the courage' Lauren replied. 'I think we have to tread carefully.'

Tom nodded grimly. He stepped forward, craning his neck to see her better. The sun was in his eyes. Maddison was nothing but a silhouette. A gust of wind roared, lifting her hair like smoke.

'Maddison,' he called when the wind died down, 'this is Tom.'

Her reply came quickly, shrill and manic. 'Go away!'

Instantly, she screamed, telling him she was going to jump if he came one step closer. Her voice echoed down the rockface. Loose scree broke free near her feet, cascading down the slope in a shower of pebbles.

'Okay, Maddison,' Tom called, raising a placating hand. 'I'm staying put, all right?'

He paused, choosing his words carefully. He knew one misplaced syllable could tip her over the edge, metaphorically and literally, but he had to get her down; had to put an end to this Mexican standoff.

'Maddison, I'm guessing by now you've heard about Tristan. I'm truly sorry. We wanted to be the ones to tell you, to make sure you were okay, to get you the support you needed.' He waited for a reply, but none came.

'I know you had big plans,' he continued. 'I know you pictured a life together, and I know you're probably feeling like you don't want to face tomorrow. But I can assure you, the world is a better place with you in it.'

A beat. Then, from above: 'No, it's not.'

Tom took another step, slower this time, and waited for another threat, but there was only silence.

'It really is, Maddison. And I'm not just saying that to get you down from the ledge. You have a lot to live for. We need you to come down, to help us with catching who did it. Only you can do that for us.'

A raven shrieked overhead, its wings slicing the sky. More scree crumbled and fell. Maddison shifted – Tom saw her feet move slightly away from the drop.

'You think you know what I'm going through?' she shouted. 'You don't. You've got no idea.'

'I do,' he called back. 'I know what it feels like to lose someone close, and…' His chest fluttered, the words faltering on his lips as he became acutely aware that Lauren could hear each one. He steeled his resolve. 'And it nearly killed me.' Lauren stirred at his side. 'But things do get better. I promise they do. Now, can we send someone up to help you down?'

There was another vast stretch of silence, before her reply eventually came.

'Yes.'

Tom turned quickly, nodding to the officers. 'Go. Now.'

The two younger men started up the ridge, scrabbling over the loose rock, searching for foot and hand holds that would take their weight. Tom watched their progress, with one eye on Maddison.

Lauren moved beside Tom, voice low. 'Are you lining up a transfer as a negotiator?'

'I only told her what she needed to hear,' he said, eyes still on the ledge.

'No, it was more than that. It was honest and human.'

'Heroic, some might say,' Tom said, breaking a smile.

'Well, let's not go too far,' she said, and they smirked.

The officers reached the summit. They spoke softly to Maddison. One led her gently by the arm while the other removed the backpack slung over her shoulder. She didn't resist. Together, they escorted her down the slope, slow and steady.

Tom's breath caught when he saw her properly. She looked skeletal. Her cheeks were sunken, her skin drawn taut across bone. Dark circles hollowed her eyes. Her hiking clothes draped from her gaunt frame, giving her the appearance of a child playing dressing-up.

She approached them and smiled at Tom like he was her saviour. Then, he spoke.

'Maddison Cassidy, I'm arresting you on the suspicion of murder. You don't have to—'

Her smile vanished, twisted into rage. 'You bastard!' she spat, pulling against the officer holding her. 'You lying, smug *bastard*!'

Tom finished the arrest while she fought, but she was too weak to do much more than flail. The officer cuffed her wrists and led her away towards the car, her shouting continuing, calling Tom all the names under the sun.

'Still think you're a hero?' Lauren said to Tom, who chuckled.

'She doesn't,' he said, with a wry grin. 'I can't imagine she's going to want to say much to me back at the station.'

'Let's find out,' Lauren said. 'Race you back.'

* * *

Tom stopped for petrol on the way. As he filled the tank, his thoughts drifted – inevitably – to Lauren. Her words from earlier still echoed in his mind: the praise, the smile, the gentle touch on his shoulder. It probably meant nothing – she was kind to everyone – but still, it sparked a flicker of hope in him. Hope that maybe, just maybe, she'd change her mind.

As crazy as it was to consider … could she really end her engagement and choose him instead?

The pump clicked off. As he replaced the nozzle, his phone rang. He pulled it from his coat pocket and checked the screen.

Mum.

His stomach dropped.

'Is everything okay with Dad?' he asked as he made his way across the forecourt.

'He's okay. I was actually calling about you.'

'Really?' That certainly caught him off guard.

There was a moment of silence, and then she said, 'Tom, have you seen *The Sun* today?'

'The paper?'

'Yes.'

'No. Why?'

Another moment of hesitation, and then, 'Maybe I shouldn't have brought it up, but there's a short article about the investigation, and … well, it's mainly about you, and it's not very flattering. I just wanted to let you know in case anyone says anything.'

He forced a laugh. 'It's *The Sun*, Mum. I'm probably in there next to Bigfoot and a woman who married a ghost.'

'Okay, son. As long as you're all right. Are you still coming down?'

After promising his mum he was fine and that he would be, and ignoring the tendrils of doubt creeping in, he hung up and walked into the petrol-station shop. The smell of cheap coffee and day-old pasties in a nearby fridge made his stomach roil.

The Pogue's 'Fairytale of New York' was blasting out through an overhead speaker.

The newspaper rack stood just inside the door. The main headline screamed about migrant crossings, the kind of manu-factured fury that prompted pub conversations and stoked radio call-ins. Above it, three smaller headlines ran side by side – one on who would be top of the Premier League at Christmas, one on trans rights, and the last: **CHRISTMAS CURSE FOR DI STONEM.**

His stomach tightened further. He picked up a copy, paid for it along with his petrol and then retreated to the car. He pulled away from the pump, but didn't join the A-road. Instead, he pulled over into a bay at the edge of the forecourt, parked beneath a flickering overhead light, and opened the paper with shaking hands.

The headline was repeated here, bold and unapologetic. Beneath it was a photograph of him from last year pinning a journalist to a wall outside Gateshead police station. Tearing his eyes away from the photo, he started on the article.

CHRISTMAS CURSE FOR DI STONEM

Another holiday season, another body count – should DI Tom Stonem still be leading investigations?
By Archie Walker

Newcastle-Upon-Tyne

For most, Christmas brings music, mince pies and cherished moments with family. For DI Tom Stonem, it seems to bring something far more sinister: murder.

The embattled detective, who transferred to Gateshead following what police sources once called 'commendable service' in Manchester, has once again found himself at the centre of a high-profile homicide investigation – his second Christmas running.

Last year, Stonem's name was tied to the infamous *Christmas List Killer* case, a grisly affair that left multiple people dead, including a sitting MP and a young woman described by many as 'full of promise'. Stonem himself narrowly escaped with his life, but his reputation has been under scrutiny ever since.

Now, just twelve months later, he's back in the spotlight for all the wrong reasons. With three people already confirmed dead and no arrests made, frustration is mounting in the hunt for the culprit that has been dubbed The Christmas Tree Killer. His most recent press conference offered little in the way of answers and even less reassurance.

The question now being asked in police circles – and loudly on the streets – is – **Why is Tom Stonem still in the job?**

'If he did excel in the North West, why not send him back there?' one Newcastle resident quipped when asked about the case. It's a sentiment being echoed more widely as confidence in Stonem's leadership continues to erode.

If this were football, some say, he'd be benched. If it were politics, he'd be impeached. And yet, here he remains – at the helm of another chaotic investigation with no suspect in custody and more grieving families desperate for answers.

A spokesperson for Haltwhistle Police Station declined to comment when approached.

As the holiday season unfolds, and the body count rises, many are wondering: how many more chances can one detective get before someone steps in?

When he finished, he read it again, just to make sure it was real.

Tom stared at the page for a long time, though his vision was blurry and tunnelled. He'd endured criticism in the past, but this wasn't criticism, this was just plain nasty. He tried to reason: that Archie didn't know what he was talking about, that it was a team effort and simply unfair that he had been singled out. But it didn't work.

By the time he reached the bottom of the page, his pulse hammered in his ears. He tried to blink the sting from his eyes but the tears kept spilling down his cheeks. His breath caught, then came in gasps – too shallow, too fast.

His fingers went numb. The paper slid from his lap. His chest tightened, like a fist clenched around his heart. He tried to breathe deeply, to slow down, but the air wouldn't come.

Panic surged.

Fumbling with the door, he stumbled out of the car and crouched beside it, leaning against the cold metal, head between his knees. His breaths came in ragged bursts, fogging in the freezing air. He was vaguely aware of a couple nearby staring, but their concern didn't register. Nothing did. Just the pounding of his heart. The roar in his ears. The shame.

He didn't know how long he stayed like that.

He thought the walking was helping. But maybe he was kidding himself.

Maybe the panic attacks were getting worse.

Eventually, his breathing began to steady. The trembling subsided enough for him to crawl back into the driver's seat. He shut the door but didn't turn the key. He sat there, motionless, surrounded by the soft crackle of cooling metal and the rustle of wind against the car.

He didn't want to go back to the station – not now, not after that. The idea of walking into the briefing room, of pretending to be in control while people whispered behind his back, made him feel nauseous all over again. He didn't want to go to his flat, either.

His fingers began to dial Dr Dougan's number before he talked himself out of it.

So he stayed put, sitting in the car as the light faded, letting the night envelop him.

35

LAUREN FOUND OUT ABOUT the article when she got back to the station. A copy of the paper was lying on the table in the office – open on the spread that damned Tom's performance. Her stomach lurched, and she immediately tried to call Tom. Then again. And again. Each time, it went straight to voicemail.

She stared at her phone a moment longer, thumb hovering, torn between calling a patrol unit to track him down or letting him have the space he clearly wanted. In the end, she resisted. Tom would resurface when he was ready. He always did.

Trying to focus, she sat at her desk and pulled up her notes for the next interview. Maddison was waiting next door. The clock was ticking, and this conversation – what Lauren asked, how she framed those questions – might determine the trajectory of the whole case.

Her phone buzzed.

Ben.

She hit mute and slid it away without looking. They hadn't spoken properly since his visit to Haltwhistle, and if she was honest, she didn't know where they stood anymore. He was kind. Dependable. Safe. But he didn't make her laugh the way Tom did. With him, it was easy – too easy sometimes. She'd catch him watching her when he thought she wasn't looking. There was something between them ... Maybe. But she didn't know what to do with it, and now wasn't the time.

She pushed thoughts of men and feelings out of her mind, knowing that for the next couple of hours, Maddison was the most important person in the world. She ran through her questions again, made sure she had all the evidence she needed, and then stood.

Outside the interview room, she took a deep breath and then pushed the door open. Maddison was slumped behind the desk, her eyes puffy and red. She was chewing on the sleeve of her hoodie and looked thoroughly defeated. Lauren sat down opposite her, started the recording, and recited the formalities.

'I just want to check, you're sure you don't want a lawyer present,' Lauren said.

'I don't need one,' Maddison said curtly. 'I've not done anything.'

'Very well.' Lauren said. 'Before we start, I just want to confirm that the doctor has checked you out. He told me you were okay to be interviewed.'

'He has.'

Lauren opened her notepad. 'Let's start from the beginning. How did you find out about Tristan's death?'

'I saw it in a newspaper,' Maddison said, voice low. 'I'd checked into a hostel and was hanging out in the common room. There was a paper on the table, and I picked it up. The story was on the front page, and I freaked.'

'I'm sorry you've had to go through that,' Lauren said, softening. 'Maddison, I'm going to be really straight with you. We've been to your flat and found some things. Of course, we'll give you a chance to explain, but I have to say, the situation isn't looking good for you.'

'What things?' she asked.

'We'll get to that. First, I need you to tell me about your relationship with Tristan, and I want you to be as honest as you can be.'

Maddison puffed out her cheeks, and said, 'Tristan was … he was a great guy. He was funny and caring when he wanted to be. I loved him. But there were times when he could be really controlling. It put a lot of strain on our relationship, and in the spirit of being truthful, I don't know if I actually wanted to marry him. We actually planned a secret Christmas wedding, but I postponed it last minute. Something he held as a grudge ever since. But there is no way I would ever have killed him just to get out of it altogether. I swear to God. I'd have told him if I didn't want to go through with the wedding. He might've been upset, but he'd have respected that.'

Lauren nodded slowly. 'What sort of controlling behaviour are we talking about?'

'He used to check my phone,' Maddison said, frowning. 'He told me he didn't. But if I ever left it out somewhere while I showered or was working out, it would be in a slightly different place. Or an app I rarely checked was open. Things like that. I wasn't imagining it.'

Lauren scribbled that down, and said, 'Anything else?'

'He'd sometimes comment on my clothes. He'd tell me that my skirt was too short, or that I was showing a bit too much boob. He'd tell me I looked like I was asking for attention. Sometimes I changed, sometimes I didn't. He accused me of cheating a couple of times, but that was mostly when he'd had a few drinks.'

Lauren kept a cool head, despite the news of Tristan's clearly controlling behaviour.

'Were these suspicions warranted?'

For a while, Maddison sat in silence and her gaze dropped to her lap. Lauren gave her the time she needed, and was rewarded when she said, 'I made a mistake.'

'What kind of mistake?'

'I slept with someone. It only happened once.'

'Who with?'

'Niall.'

'Just to confirm for the tape, are you saying you slept with Niall Wampler, your high school boyfriend?'

'Yes,' she said, nodding.

'When was this?'

'November,' Maddison said.

'And how did that come about?'

'It was at an event Rosanna organised for a charity that her aunt helps out with. It was a silent auction at this beautiful hotel on the coast that overlooked the sea, and we all had to wear fancy dresses and tuxedos. Tristan couldn't make it,' Maddison shrugged, 'but I didn't want to let Rosanna down, so I went alone. They sat me at a table with other loners, one of which happened to be Niall.'

'Who you hadn't seen since school?'

'Yeah. It was totally awkward at the start. But, after a few drinks we started reminiscing about old friends, things that happened when we were teenagers, and then we eventually talked about our relationship. It felt like ancient history, but he remembered little details that clearly meant a lot to him. It was so sweet. Tristan had been a dick to me the previous couple of days, trying to make me feel bad for going without him, saying my dress made me look like a slag and things like that. Niall's little bit of sweetness just made me melt. I guess I was vulnerable. I told him which room I was staying in and said if he wanted to revisit the past, he knew where to find me.'

Lauren scribbled some more notes, and then asked, 'Did you have sex that night?'

'Yes.'

'Did it happen again?'

'No. I woke up in the morning with an awful hangover and full of regret. Niall was there beside me, snoring up a storm. I tried to pack my stuff quietly and planned to get out before he woke up, but I dropped a book and he jumped out of bed like there was a fire. After that I had no choice but to go to breakfast with him. Well, I went first and then he came down ten minutes later, but Joshua kept looking over at us with this look in his eye.'

'You think he knew?'

'I'm not sure. The day after, I bought a cheap phone to text him on. He and Niall occasionally met through work, and I figured Niall might let it slip, so asked Josh to keep it to himself, but he never replied. I just had to hope he would.'

'You threatened him.'

'I just wanted to make sure he was listening.'

'Why didn't you just text him on your own phone?'

Maddison looked incredulous. 'Obviously, I was worried Tristan would look through it, see the message and then want to know what I was on about. He always had a way of finding things.'

'And you kept this phone at your flat?'

'Yes,' Maddison said.

'You should have told us about the flat, Maddison. It could have helped with our enquiries.'

'I didn't think it was important. It's up for sale, and I don't spend any time there anymore.'

'Someone has been there recently,' Lauren said. 'We found a couple of things of note when we searched the premises.'

Maddison looked genuinely confused. Then, her face crumpled. She brought her hands to her face as great, wracking sobs came.

Lauren waited a moment for the crying to subside, and then asked, 'Why that reaction?'

'It's all too much. I swear I haven't done anything. But it feels like someone's setting me up. That's why I wanted to end it all today. It's all too much. After spending the night with Niall, Tristan got worse – he was more possessive than ever, and paranoid.'

With good reason, Lauren thought.

'I don't think he knew,' Maddison continued, 'but maybe he suspected. That's why I decided to go hiking. I needed space. To make him see I wouldn't be controlled. To figure out what I wanted.'

She sniffed hard, wiping some tears away.

'And now he's dead,' she whispered. 'I loved him. I really did love him. No one deserves to die like that. I'm just so scared. When I saw that fucking wrapping paper in the hostel at Kirk Yetholm, I freaked. I checked in and went straight back out again. I wanted to go somewhere no one could find me. I thought I could wild camp, but I could barely do one night. It was freezing, and I didn't want to die out there. I need someone to help me. I need you to help me.'

Lauren swallowed. What came next would feel like she was kicking Maddison while she was down, but it was her job to ask the difficult questions and deliver monstrous news.

'Maddison,' she said. 'I need to let you know that we found Joshua's ring finger in your flat.'

Maddison's eyes widened. 'What the fuck?'

Lauren tried to assess the reaction, but it seemed genuine. Shock, revulsion, horror.

'Do you know how it got there?' Lauren asked.

'No!' she wailed. 'I promise. I've not been there in weeks. I didn't … I couldn't…'

'Does anyone else have keys?' Lauren pressed.

'Umm… The estate agent has two sets, and my parents have one, but they live miles away. Rosanna has a key from a time she watered my plants for me, but other than that, no.'

'Tristan?'

'No.'

'Could he, or anyone else, have made a copy without your knowledge?'

'I don't know…'

Maddison looked moments away from passing out through exhaustion. Her skin had turned a dull grey, and she was trembling. Lauren decided to pause the interview for now.

'Maddison, I'm going to let you have some rest. You'll spend the night in the cells while we investigate further, and we may need to speak to you at some point in the next few hours. Someone will be along soon to take you. Try to get some sleep, okay?'

She clicked off the recording device, gave Maddison a nod and then left. Outside the door, she stood with her back against the wall, considering the interview. The evidence was stacking up: a one-night stand with an old flame, a burner phone with a pleading text and then a threat to a dead man, a dead fiancé and a finger in her flat.

None of it looked good.

And yet, in Lauren's opinion, Maddison seemed more broken than guilty.

She puffed out her cheeks, anticipating a long night ahead. She pulled out her phone, hoping that Tom might've called while she was interviewing, but there was only a text from Ben, saying he was playing poker with the lads tonight.

She locked the screen without replying and got back to work.

36

While Lauren interviewed Maddison, Tom had remained in the forecourt, sitting motionless in his locked car, the engine off. His meditation of sorts was broken only by a sharp knock on the passenger side window. A young man with a branded uniform had peered through the fogged glass, making an okay sign with his thumb and forefinger. A startled Tom had nodded and started the engine in reply, driving off without so much as a backward glance.

He'd driven through the darkness, phone off, wandering, and wondering without a clear destination. He couldn't face the station, nor his colleagues. Haltwhistle was out of the question. Yearning solitude above all, he had driven to Durham, its now familiar streets offering solace. He spent the night in his own bed, cocooned in a dreamless sleep that barely scratched the surface of his exhaustion or paranoia.

Upon waking the next morning, he realised people were worried. When he finally turned his phone on, it buzzed and chimed with a variety of missed calls from Lauren, as well as from Martin, Dr Dougan and Natalie, who had left a number of voicemails. Her tone had morphed from concerned to curt and increasingly firm. He decided to call her back first. She answered on the first ring.

'Tom,' she said. 'Thank God. Are you all right?'

'I'm fine,' he said. 'I'm assuming you've seen the newspaper?'

216

'Yes.'

'I needed space.'

'Needing space is fine, but next time, let someone know first. You scared the hell out of everyone.'

'I know. I'm sorry.'

'You're seeing Dr Dougan this morning. No arguments.'

She hung up before he could respond.

Two hours later, he exited the therapist's high street office with a cocktail of feelings vying for attention. Dr Dougan had expressed regret that their sessions together did not seem to be enough for Tom, and encouraged him to see a GP, with the view of receiving SSRI treatment. Selective Serotonin Reuptake Inhibitors, Tom was told, were antidepressant medications used to treat a variety of mental health conditions, including depression, anxiety disorders, and OCD. Tom had nodded, said he understood, and accepted a leaflet with the clinical detachment of a man who didn't want to discuss feelings any longer.

He told himself he'd look into it. But not yet. He wasn't sure if the SSRIs had side effects, but he didn't want them to impair his judgement or performance when the case was ongoing. He'd look into it when the killer had been caught.

Sheltering in an alcove next to the Waterstones, he checked his phone and discovered Lauren had sent through some emails. He opened his inbox and saw that she had attached the financial transactions of Niall Wampler and Freddie Sutherland. Scanning the documents, he saw they were too long to make sense of via a small phone screen, so he phoned her instead.

'Hi,' he said sheepishly when she answered. He was glad to speak with her.

'Good to hear from you,' she said, warmth radiating from her voice. 'Are you okay?'

'Yeah, fine,' he said. 'I just needed…'

'I know,' she said. 'Everyone here is saying that Archie Walker is a massive dickhead.'

'He's had it in for me since last year.'

'I know. Some people hold a grudge. Look, Tom, I know saying "don't worry about it" is easier said than done, but if I can help in any way, just let me know.'

'Thanks.'

'Did you get my emails?'

'I did,' Tom said. 'The PDFs are a little tricky to make out on my phone. Can you give me the headlines?'

'The headline is that Niall is in deep and has some questions to answer. I'll give you a proper rundown when you get here, but do you fancy swinging by Niall's work on your way back and bringing him in?'

'I'd be delighted,' he said. 'See you soon.'

'Be safe,' she said, before hanging up.

Be safe... It was probably simple concern for a colleague.

A little over three hours later, Tom strode into Haltwhistle police station with Niall Wampler handcuffed at his side. The man looked smaller than usual – less cocky, more contained, like a deflated balloon. A DC led him away to the interview room. Tom followed for a few paces, then turned into the office. Before he could say a word, Lauren was out of her chair, pulling him into one of her signature hugs. He hugged her back tightly, grateful for her support.

She pulled away slowly, her face mere inches from his. It felt natural.

That was when Martin chose to walk in, clapping Tom on the back and declaring loudly that Archie Walker, the author of the newspaper article, was a bloody bellend. Tom appreciated his show of support, but not his timing. He managed a feeble laugh and listened to the DCI waffle on as Lauren slunk away to her desk, where a small mountain of paper was waiting. When Martin finally said his goodbye, Tom crossed the office and sat beside Lauren, nodding at the highlighted documents in front of her.

'Been busy?'

'Just a smidge,' she said. 'Wait until you see what I've got.'

For a while, she talked him through her findings. The financial documents were covered in luminous green and yellow highlighter markings. Some of the pages had a corner turned down; others had scribbled notes in the margins. Lauren had clearly been through this with a fine-tooth comb, spending hours making absolutely certain that every detail, finding and question was covered. They had a lot of ammunition to take to their interview with Niall – and even more when the time came to confront Freddie again.

After forging a plan of attack, and checking it a couple of times for chinks in the armour, they made their way to the interview room.

Niall was behind the desk, a different animal to Maddison. Where she had been morose and haunted, Niall sat with his legs crossed, fingers steepled like he owned the place. It seemed some of his natural confidence had returned.

'We hear you've decided against a lawyer this time,' Tom said.

'That's right,' Niall replied. 'If he'd let me speak last time, I'm confident I wouldn't be here now. I have nothing to hide.'

Lauren handled the formalities with the recording device, and Tom began. He spread out several pieces of highlighted paper across the table, and asked Niall to take a look. Niall spent a few cursory seconds checking over the papers and then leaned back in his chair.

'Can you confirm for the tape that what we are showing you are your financial records?'

'I can.'

'And you agree that we haven't altered them in any way?'

Niall scooched forward again, scrutinising them in slightly more detail. Then he agreed that everything looked in order.

'I'm going to summarise for the tape,' Tom said. 'Niall, we believe that your spending is erratic, and your management of money is poor. You've got multiple credit cards, two of which are maxed out and the other one is near its limit. The overdraft in your current account is the highest your account permits, and it seems that when you get paid, it barely makes a dent in your debt. You're spending beyond your means. Would you agree?'

Niall flashed them a winning smile. 'What can I say? I'm a man of expensive tastes.'

'I can see that,' Tom said, nodding. 'In fact, so expensive that on November fifteenth, a large cash deposit landed in your account from an untraceable account. Care to explain?'

'I've taken out a loan.'

'From who?'

'No comment.'

'Are you in trouble?' Lauren asked. 'Has someone come looking for money you owe?'

'No comment.'

'Taking out a loan isn't illegal,' she said. 'And nothing in your spending suggests criminal activity, so you needn't worry on that front. We'd just like to know where you borrowed from.'

'And I'd prefer to keep that to myself.'

'Did you borrow the money from Freddie Sutherland?' Tom asked.

'Like I said—'

'You'd rather keep it to yourself, we know,' Tom interrupted, and then leaned forward like he was ushering Niall into his circle of trust. 'It's just we've had a look at Freddie's accounts, too, and we suspect him of being a loan shark as well as a car salesman. We can't prove this yet, and the amount you received does not line up with the accounts of his we've been able to access, but we believe he has hidden accounts that we're still to find. But, rest assured, we will. If he has anything to do with the murders, and it turns out you borrowed money from him and wouldn't tell us, that makes you look complicit.'

Niall didn't reply.

'Very well,' Tom said, trying to sound like he wasn't bothered either way, 'we'll move on.'

He made a show of shuffling through papers, and as he was about to speak, Niall said, 'All right. Yes, I borrowed the money from Freddie.'

'Oh yeah?'

'Yes. I took out a loan with an extortionate interest rate, but I needed the money. I missed my first payment, and Freddie sent me a message reminding me the interest would only increase. When I missed the second, he sent some lads around to scare me. He told me the third reminder wouldn't be quite so friendly.'

'And yet you don't have broken bones or a black eye,' Tom noted, 'so you must've found a way to pay.'

'Joshua bailed me out.'

'Is that what the three of you were meeting about in the pub?'

Niall nodded.

'And now Joshua is dead,' Tom continued. 'Did you kill him so you wouldn't have to pay him back?'

'What?' Niall said. 'No, nothing like that. Jesus.'

'Let's consider further evidence,' Tom said. 'We spoke to Maddison, and we know you had sex during a charity event.'

'Technically, it was after the charity event,' Niall said, 'but, yes. We had sex.'

'Even though you knew she had a fiancé?'

'She propositioned me,' he shrugged, looking like the cat who'd got the cream. 'And I was glad she did. I loved her at school. I was gutted when we broke up, and I always thought we might get together again someday. When I heard she was coming to the event, I was chuffed. And then I found out Tristan wasn't coming, and I couldn't believe my luck. We had the chance to reconnect without her arsehole fiancé there. It felt like a sign. One thing led to another, and we slept together.'

'Why didn't you tell us?'

Niall shrugged again. 'I thought it would look bad.'

'It looks worse keeping it from us.' Tom said. 'Would you still like it to be more than a one-night thing?'

'I would.'

'But you deny killing Tristan?'

'Of course,' Niall jabbed the table surface, insistent. 'I said I'd *like* it to be more than a one-night thing, not that I was willing to murder a rival. It's not a fucking Shakespeare play.'

'But you hated him,' Tom said. 'He bullied you at school.'

'He made my life hell.'

'Did you ever try and take revenge on him?'

'No.'

'You're sure about that?'

'One hundred per cent,' Niall said, a confident grin on his face.

Tom pulled a stapled stack of papers from his folder and slid them across the table.

'Recognise these?'

As Niall leafed through the documents, Tom watched as Niall's shoulders deflated and the bravado all but disappeared. Eventually, Niall set the papers down and looked at Tom defiantly.

'Do you know what these are?' Tom asked, giving him the chance to explain himself.

'I ... I...'

'I'll explain for the recording device,' Tom said, 'shall I? These, Niall, are online communications between yourself and Tristan. Except it's not you and Tristan, but rather a host of fake personas you created. To threaten him. Harass him. Catfish him. For years.'

'I didn't—'

'You did,' Tom said, 'our tech team have been busy beavering away, tracing them all back to you. It seems your computer's security settings aren't what you hoped they'd be. Explain to me why you did this.'

Niall looked torn, like an MP caught in a compromising line of questioning and knowing there was little wriggle room left. After weighing it up, he said, 'As I've said, I hated Tristan for bullying me. After leaving school, I set up some fake accounts and tried to scare him. I tried seducing him in the hope he'd come and try and fuck one of the people I made up, and I could take the evidence back to Maddison. She'd see what an arsehole he was, and see me as her saviour.'

'So it was all to try and win Maddison back?'

'It was to show her she was with the wrong person.'

'Okay,' said Tom, 'let's get this straight. You borrowed money from a loan shark, and couldn't make the repayments. Joshua bailed you out and was murdered soon after. Ten years ago, Tristan took your girlfriend and bullied you. Over several years, you harassed him online. Then, you slept with his fiancée and a short time later, he was murdered, too. I have to say, mate, it isn't looking good for you.'

'No,' Niall snapped, his flat palm slamming the table. 'You're twisting what I said. You're setting me up for something I didn't do.'

He continued in this vein for some time, until Lauren cut across him to state the interview was ending. She informed him he'd be led back to a holding cell, though neglected to mention that the love of his life was only a few metres away. She told him he'd be kept a little longer while they made some further inquiries, and then left him in the capable hands of a DC.

When they were alone, Tom asked, 'What do you think?'

'I think he should've brought his fancy-pants lawyer,' she said. 'Without him, I think Niall has dug himself a very deep hole.'

37

TOM AWOKE AFTER ANOTHER poor night's sleep. His mind kept flitting back to the interviews of Maddison and Niall, his subconscious attempting to make sense of them. He kept replaying their words, tone, body language – scanning for inconsistencies, some fracture in their story. But there didn't seem to be any. Now, Tom had nothing to show for his sleepless nights except dark rings under his eyes and a new depth of tiredness.

He sighed and perched on the edge of the bed, staring blankly at the wall. It was moments like this he wished he drank coffee. A jolt of caffeine might be just the thing to force him back to life. Instead, he pulled himself to his feet and shuffled to the window. Maybe a walk would help – a stretch of the legs and the cold air on his skin might shake the fog from his mind. Dr Dougan would certainly approve.

But nature had other plans.

When he pulled the curtains open, rain lashed against the window, rivulets running down the glass – not as seasonal as snow, and relentless this year. Beyond, the sky was a slab of unmoving grey, and the forecast – judging by the wind rattling the pane – was unlikely to improve. With a groan of resignation, he made some toast, showered, and gathered his things for the day.

At the station, the mood had shifted slightly. The grim under-current that had settled over the team still lingered, but there was

224

an edge of forced cheer threaded through it. A few of the DCs
had swapped shirts for Christmas jumpers, and someone had set
the radio to a channel dedicated to festive music. George Michael's
voice filled the room, crooning about lost love, while Deborah
moaned loudly about being eliminated from 'Whamageddon'.

Tom didn't bother asking what the hell she meant. He
suspected it would only make him feel older than he already did.

Instead, he made his way to the office and found Lauren with
headphones on, scribbling on a notepad. When she saw him,
she paused whatever she was listening to and slipped her headphones off.

'Happy Christmas Eve Eve,' she said.

Which reminded him that he'd need to call back Mum to
confirm plans. His mind drifted to Christmas Day – him, a
hundred or so miles away in Manchester; Lauren hanging out
with Ben. It didn't seem fair.

'Is that a thing?' Tom asked. When Lauren nodded, he said,
'In that case, you too. What are you up to?'

She gave a tired smile. 'I was just relistening to the interviews
with Maddison and Niall.'

'Anything?'

'Nothing is jumping out,' she said, shaking her head. 'But it
has to be one of them, right?'

'It feels that way,' Tom said, taking the chair beside her. 'Both
of them have a motive to kill Tristan, though I'm not sure about
Joshua and Evie.'

'Both received money from Joshua,' Lauren said, tapping her
pen. 'And money, sex, power – that's your holy trinity for motive.'

'True, but why Evie?'

'Yeah, that's the one where it all falls down, isn't it?'

Before they could ruminate further, Tom's phone rang. He
answered, and the head of the search party tasked with finding
the bodies of Evie, Joshua and Tristan introduced himself.

'Anything?' Tom asked without preamble.

'No, sir,' came the reply. 'Not yet. There are other things we can try, but as it's Christmas Eve tomorrow, everyone is due to down tools. We'll start again after Boxing Day. That all right?'

'Looks like it's going to have to be,' Tom said. 'Let me know when you're back at it.'

He hung up and relayed the update to Lauren, who uttered a frustrated sigh.

'What next?' she asked, her lips pursed.

'I'll listen in to the interviews with you,' he said, 'to see if anything jumps out.'

Lauren shimmied her chair across, and handed a pair of head-phones to Tom, who pulled them over his ears. Lauren hit play, and for a while, they listened. Occasionally, she wrote something in her notepad, but really there was nothing to be gleaned from the second listen.

'I guess we let them stew for a few days, if we can get them,' Lauren said when it was over, 'and see if something shakes loose over Christmas.'

'Good plan.'

'When are you leaving?' she asked, leaning back in her chair.

'This afternoon,' Tom said. 'You?'

'Tomorrow morning, first thing.'

'Want to grab some lunch?'

'Always.'

They grabbed their coats and made their way along the high street, the rain heavy as ever. Bonnie's café was bustling, filled with couples lunching and locals holding hot chocolates while hiding from the storm. They managed to snag one of the last remaining tables and ordered a sausage bap each. Tom would miss Haltwhistle when the time came, and Bonnie's famous sausage baps was one of the main reasons why.

'What are your Christmas plans?' Lauren asked, when they'd finished eating.

'It'll be low key. Dad is still waiting for test results, and they've started fostering again, so they have a seven-year-old whose experiencing his first Christmas in Manchester. So I'll try to make it special. I remember what it was like. What about you?'

'I'll be spending it with my parents, Sophie and … Ben,' she said, though the last name came out frosty. Tom didn't press it.

'I'm not sure I'll be able to get into the spirit,' Tom admitted with a grimace. 'I really wanted the case signed, sealed and delivered before Christmas Day, but that doesn't look like it's happening. I don't think I'll be able to shrug it off for a few days, knowing the killer is out there, potentially with something big planned for Christmas Day.'

'I feel the same,' she said, 'but we need some downtime, otherwise we'd go stir crazy. We don't even know if something will happen. He or she could be in custody, so just try to relax. Is your plan to come back on the twenty-seventh?'

'Yeah, maybe Boxing Day if I can swing it. Though I'm not sure how well that would go down.'

'Not well?' Lauren guessed, her brow etched with concern. 'Try to enjoy your time with your dad. Help your mum out, too. Be a good boy.'

They laughed as one of the waiters came to clear their table. Once the plates were gone, Tom reached under the table. He pulled a carrier bag from his rucksack and slid it across the table.

'What's this then, officer?' Lauren asked, eyebrow cocked while affecting a Cockney accent.

'Just a little something,' he shrugged.

Lauren opened the bag and retrieved a piece of A4 paper from inside. She studied it for a moment, and then she smiled, a rosy hue tinting her cheeks.

'I can't believe you remembered,' she said quietly.

'Well, I remember you telling me about how you listened to the CD so much you wore it down.'

'I told you that a year ago,' she said.

'Everyone has an album that shapes them,' he shrugged. 'Mine is *Enema of the State* by blink-182 – an absolute classic. Yours stuck with me because I thought it was a terrible choice.'

'Oi! Don't act like you're John bloody Peel,' she laughed.

'They're playing it in full,' Tom told her, 'but it's not until April, so you've got a while to wait. Sorry about that.'

She feigned shock, pressing a hand to her chest. 'You mean you couldn't alter their tour schedule to make it sooner for me?' She raised a brow. 'In that case, I don't know why you bothered.'

Tom laughed, and she said, 'Honestly, this is amazing,'

Then, she reached into her handbag and pulled out an envelope, handing it across to him.

'You didn't have to—' Tom began

'*You* didn't have to,' she reminded, handing it over.

Inside was a gift voucher for an outdoors shop, with enough credit to buy some decent hiking gear.

'I know it's not as good as gig tickets for a playthrough of the greatest album ever made,' she said, beaming, 'but I can see how much getting out into the great outdoors is helping you, so thought you could get yourself a big coat or waterproof trousers or something to—'

'It's perfect,' he said, meaning it. He was touched she'd paid such close attention.

For a few minutes, they basked in contented silence. Rain beat steadily against the window, fogging the glass. Somewhere behind them, plates clinked and people laughed while discussing Christmas plans. Then, Tom's phone rang. When he answered, Martin told him he was permitting everyone to go home early on account of the worsening weather. Tom and Lauren were free to set sail when they were ready. He wished them both a merry Christmas, and then signed off.

'Well, that's us done,' Tom said, slipping the phone away.

But the thought of parting from Lauren sapped some of his seasonal cheer.

They stood, paid the bill at the counter and then zipped up their coats before leaving the café. As they made their way to their cars, they dodged puddles and used shop awnings as cover where they could.

'It's funny how neither of us wrapped our presents,' Lauren said, unlocking her car.

'I couldn't bear to buy a roll of paper. After – you know.'

'Yeah. Me neither,' she said.

They took a step towards each other and hugged. Tom didn't want to let go, but a loud clap of thunder overhead, followed by a flash of lightning forced him to.

'Safe travels for tomorrow,' he said, as Lauren opened her car door. 'Keep in touch. Let me know when you get home safe.'

'You too,' she said. 'I'm praying to all the gods that the M6 isn't a nightmare for you.'

'Pray there aren't any more killings, too, while you're at it,' he said, forcing a smile.

Lauren gave a small wave. 'Merry Christmas, Tom.'

38

THE WEATHER WAS DREADFUL – sheets of freezing rain lashed at Tom's windscreen as sleet peppered the edges, blurring his view. He wasn't the only one crawling through the country to make it home for Christmas, either. Every A-road and motorway was choked with the same weary pilgrimage, with only the distant, flickering hope of a joyful Christmas keeping everyone going.

By the time he hit a standstill near Lancaster services, due to a particularly nasty collision (if the radio reports were anything to go by), his jaw was tight from clenching and his hands ached from gripping the wheel. The brake lights stretching ahead looked endless, like a river of red on a road to nowhere.

He thought of Chris Rea and that bloody song – how it somehow romanticised this exact hell: tailbacks, ice and unfounded optimism. *I'm driving home for Christmas,* the singer crooned, as if crawling along the M6 in a freezing downpour was an act of magic, not misery. And the bit about the freeway? Tom snorted. Rea was from bloody Middlesbrough.

When he finally made it back to his parents' house in Hazel Grove, a small town not far from Manchester, he was ready to call it a day.

But he knew that was the last thing he could do.

He hadn't seen them in a while, so he would have to put on a brave face for them. He stopped at the end of their street, turned the ignition off, and completed some of Dr Dougan's breathing exercises. Then, he drove slowly down the street, marvelling at the flashing reindeer, the inflatable Santas swaying in the wind, the synchronised light shows in the sash windows. It looked like a scene from an over-the-top Christmas movie, one where, despite everything, it all comes good in the end.

He pulled into the driveway, and the front door opened as it always did before he could turn the engine off, as though his mum had been watching from the hall since breakfast. He grabbed his bags from the boot and walked up the gravel path. The smell hit him as he stepped inside – warm spices, pine needles, and something roasting in the oven. The hallway was a burst of festive chaos: garlands on the banister, a talking snowman by the radiator, a homemade wreath on every door.

'It's good to see you, son,' his mum said, wrapping him in a tight hug before producing a tray as if from thin air. 'Mince pie?'

'Go on then,' he said, accepting one. It was warm, flaky, and almost good enough to forget the journey. 'Homemade?'

'Of course,' she said, pride in her voice.

'How's Dad?'

'He's doing okay,' she said, ushering him out of the porch. 'Come on, love. Let's get you warm.'

If Tom thought the hall was festive, it paled in comparison to the rest of the house. In the living room, a choir sang softly from a speaker in the corner. Somewhere, a timer buzzed, and his mum ran off to see what she needed to do next. The fire crackled gently in the hearth, throwing amber light across the walls, and a selection box lay half-eaten on the coffee table. The room smelled of cinnamon and furniture polish, and the tree in the corner was a towering pine draped with tinsel and glittering baubles. Underneath it was a riot of colour – presents in every size and shape. The red and green wrapping paper, festooned with bows, made Tom feel sick.

'I thought you might go a bit easier on the decorations this year,' Tom said, half-smiling.

'We were going to,' Tom's dad said, in way of hello, 'but then little Danny came to us, and we wanted to make his first year here unforgettable. He's such a sweet little lad. Reminds me of you.'

He wondered when he would meet his new 'brother'. Tom admired his parents taking on another foster child at their age. They'd given him everything he could possibly want. He figured that maybe they wanted to recapture the magic shared when Tom was Danny's age.

'God help him,' Tom said, and his dad laughed. 'Is he still up?'

'No, he was trying to stay awake, but his little eyes were drooping while he was watching *Gladiators*. He wanted to meet you, but we told him you could have breakfast together.'

'How are you doing?' Tom said, sitting down in his favoured chair.

Dad seesawed his hand. 'Not too bad,' he said. 'It's the waiting that's the worst. All that worry and it could end up being nothing.'

Tom felt his throat constrict. *Nothing* was what they all hoped for. 'Yeah, I hear you.'

'How's the case?'

Tom sighed and told him – about the loose ends, the dead ends, and the mounting frustration that came with leaving it all behind for a few days.

'Charming,' his dad said with a dry laugh.

'I don't mean it like that,' Tom said, smiling. 'It's lovely to be here and to see you both. I just wish I was arriving with someone in cuffs, you know?'

'I don't think your mum would have appreciated that. Although, with the size of turkey she's ordered, she might be grateful of an extra mouth.'

After that, they lapsed into silence, the quiet between them filled by the opening scenes of a Christmas film playing on the TV. His dad nodded off by the first advert break. His mum floated in and out of the room with snacks, drinks, and the gentle efficiency of someone who never truly mastered the art of relaxing.

Tom tried to stay present. Tried not to look at the mountain of gifts under the tree or picture Evie's severed head nestled among the boxes. But the thought wouldn't ease up. All he could see was rotten flesh and exposed bone. His chest tightened.

Tom stood, waking his dad as he did.

'I'm off to bed,' Tom said.

'Grand,' his dad nodded. And then, 'You're okay with Danny being here, aren't you?'

'Of course.'

'I know it's strange, getting used to another member of the family. But we never see you these days, as it is. I might not be around for much longer.'

'Dad...'

'No point avoiding it. I know the job is tough and you have to give it your all. But we do miss you, son. We want Danny to get to know you. For you to be a good influence on the boy.'

Thoughts of Seth swam unbidden into his head.

'It's not that I don't want to visit,' he said, as he thought of Dr Dougan's words: *a work-life balance is key. Not just for yourself, but those around you, too.*

'We know. But you're always welcome.'

'I know.'

'Danny's almost as good at football as you.'

'That wouldn't surprise me,' Tom laughed. 'The last time I kicked a ball I think I tore my hammy.'

'You'll have to play with us sometime. Me. You. Danny.'

'I'd like that.'

'Promise?'

'Promise.'

He bent down and kissed his dad on the forehead, called a goodnight to his mum and then escaped upstairs.

39

THE SOUND OF A loud American accent jolted Tom awake in the early morning gloom. He blinked at his watch.

5:47.

Great.

He lay still for a few minutes, trying to quieten his mind, hoping for sleep to return. No such luck. Eventually, he got dressed and padded downstairs.

The source of the noise was unmistakable – two overly energetic YouTubers yelling over each other about secret rooms they were installing in a vast mansion Tom was sure couldn't actually belong to two twenty-somethings who looked like they hadn't shaved a day in their life. In the living room, Danny was curled up on the sofa under a tartan blanket, wide-eyed and utterly transfixed.

'Do you mind turning it down a notch?' Tom asked.

Danny nodded, and pressed on the remote, the chatter dying down.

Able to hear himself think, Tom introduced himself.

'Hello. I'm Tom – the adult son, all grown up and moved out – so you won't have to worry about me hogging the remote.'

The boy nodded again, shy. He had big eyes and an uncertain expression, and he reminded Tom of himself after his first placement – like someone not believing where they were, simply waiting for something to go wrong so they would be turfed out.

234

His accent was from Yorkshire, his favourite team was Leeds, and after a little coaxing, he asked Tom if they could play football together later.

'I'd love that. I think Dad might be up for a game, too,' Tom said. 'Do you want some breakfast?'

'Sure.'

Danny turned the TV off and followed Tom to the kitchen.

'What would you like?' Tom asked.

'Toast with jam, but I have to do my injection first,' Danny said, as Tom opened the bread bin.

'What injection?'

'Insulin. I have diabetes. Can you change the cartridge in my pen, please?'

Tom paused, surprised, but nodded. 'Where's your stuff?'

'The cartridges are in the fridge. The pen is up in that cabinet,' he said, pointing.

Tom grabbed the pen and opened the fridge. From a slip of blister packs, he fetched a vial and slotted it inside the pen under Danny's supervision. He screwed a needle to the end, and asked Danny if he could do the injection himself.

'Mum usually does it for me.'

Tom's heart melted at the mention of Mum, and he offered to do the injection in her stead. Danny lifted his T-shirt, flinched slightly as the small needle pierced the skin of his stomach, but didn't complain or call out.

'I have to wait twenty minutes now,' he said. 'Can I watch TV again?'

'Of course,' Tom said. 'Let me know when you want me to start making toast.'

While Danny retreated to the living room for more YouTube, the diabetic paraphernalia snagged something in Tom's mind. Maddison had mentioned that Tristan suffered from the auto-immune disease.

He left the kitchen and bolted upstairs. In his room, he yanked his laptop from his bag and navigated to the forensic report of Tristan's house. He scanned the contents and was surprised to see that there was no insulin listed. In fact, there was no medication listed at all.

Perhaps he had simply ran out, or it hadn't been noted down by one of the forensic team. Either way … something wasn't right.

He checked the time. It was too early to call anyone to verify, but he made a note to do so later.

Another detail of the forensic report caught his eye. Tristan's was the only body part severed while the victim was alive. Tom sat back, heart thumping. Of the three, Tristan had suffered the most.

Was that deliberate?

Was Tristan the key to unlocking this thing?

Jiggling his leg, he knew that he had to head north again. He had that feeling, that honed instinct screaming that he was on to something, and he also knew that spending three days stewing on it one hundred and fifty miles away would drive not just he, but his family crazy.

He repacked his stuff and went downstairs. His mum was awake and frying bacon. He explained that he had to go, assuring her that he would be back as soon as he could, though it probably wouldn't be in time for Christmas.

She looked disappointed, but didn't try to stop him. Though, she did insist that he stay long enough for one of her famously good bacon sandwiches.

'That'll set you up for the day,' she said, sliding a sandwich that looked more like a doorstop onto his plate. He ate quickly and then stood to hug her goodbye.

'Tell Dad I'll see him soon,' he said, pecking her cheek, before making his way to the living room.

There, he knelt beside Danny, who was munching a slice of toast.

'I've got to head back to work. But I'll be back in a few days. We'll play football next time, yeah?' Just as he'd promised to Dad.

'Okay.'

The sight of Danny, snuggled under the blanket trying not to show his disappointment was almost too much for Tom to bear. He thought about abandoning his plan to head North, but only for a moment. If he could catch the killer, there'd be plenty of time for football in the garden in the days to come.

Tom ruffled his hair and hurried to the car, the light show of the street now seeming less like a celebration and more like a fever dream he needed to wake from. Fast.

40

LAUREN WOKE TO A flurry of notifications – several unread messages from Ben and a missed call from Tom. She rubbed her eyes and called Tom back immediately.

He answered on the second ring, his voice low but urgent. 'I'm heading back. I think I've found something – a proper lead.'

Lauren sat up, alert. 'What kind of lead?'

'I'll explain in person. Just wanted to keep you in the loop,' he said. 'I don't expect you to stay, by the way. I know it's Christmas Eve.'

She glanced at the time. 'I can spare a few hours before heading home.'

'Appreciate it, but if you need to go, go, and I can catch you up later.'

When the call ended, she tried to FaceTime Sophie, but the screen barely had time to load before a knock sounded at the door. She froze, her stomach tightening. Peering through the peephole, she sighed.

Ben.

'Fuck,' she muttered under her breath, before pulling the door open.

'Hi,' he said, brushing past her into the room. 'Figured it was easier to drive an hour to see you than wait for a reply.'

Lauren puffed out her cheeks and closed the door behind her.

'Sorry,' she said, annoyed at herself for already being on the defensive. 'I've just been—'

'Flat out. Yeah, I figured.' His voice was clipped. 'I thought as much, that's why I'm here. To make sure you come home for Christmas.'

She frowned. 'What do you mean?'

'I mean, I thought you might be so caught up in this case that you forgot what day it is.'

'Of course I didn't forget,' she said. 'I have a daughter who I imagine is very excited for Santa's visit.'

'Oh, so you remember she exists then?'

She stared at him. 'What the fuck does that mean?'

'Nothing,' he said, with a dismissive shrug and nonchalant pout.

'No, you said it, so tell me what you mean?'

'I didn't come here for a fight.' He held up his hands and tried a disarming smile.

It didn't work.

'Well, you've just gone and started one,' she shot back. 'You're clearly implying something, so go on – spell it out for me.'

He dithered. 'It's just…' he trailed off, then looked her dead in the eye. 'Sophie misses you. And I didn't want you to forget what really matters.'

'I'm tracking down a killer,' Lauren snapped, her voice rising, finger jabbing the air. 'But I will *always* have time for my family.'

'Good, then we don't have a problem.'

The air crackled between them, tension humming like a live wire. Before Lauren could speak, her phone began to ring. Ben reached for it before she could react, scooping it up from the dresser.

'Loverboy,' he said, his finger hovering over the green button.

'Ben, don't—' she said sharply, but he already had.

'Look, Tom,' he said, coldly. 'It's barely gone seven, and you're calling my fiancée. It's weird, mate, and it really needs to stop.'

He ended the call without waiting for a reply and tossed the phone onto the bed. Lauren stared at him, stunned.

'That's my boss.'

'Exactly,' he said. 'He shouldn't be calling you at all hours, making demands of you.'

'That's the job, Ben. We don't get to clock off because it's inconvenient.'

'Not on Christmas Eve, Lauren. Surely you can see how fucked that is.'

'I think it's fucked that there is a killer on the loose. I think it's fucked that Tom had a lead and you don't expect us to follow it up.'

'Us?' he snapped. 'You just said you were coming home.'

'I *am* coming home,' she said, exasperated. 'I'll be there this evening.'

'What about now?'

'I'm waiting for Tom to get here to help him out.'

'Jesus.'

'Jesus what, Ben?' she scolded. 'It's my job. It's what I'm paid to do. You knew what I did when you met me. You knew the demands. If this is hard for you now, what happens next year? Or in five years? Ten?'

He didn't answer right away. His shoulders sagged slightly. 'I'm just trying to see you. That's all. I came here to make sure you're okay.'

'And I'm grateful. But both times you've come, you've ended up making ultimatums. If you can't understand that Tom is my boss and that he is well within his rights to phone me when new information comes to light, I really don't see how things can continue. In fact –'*here it goes*, she thought, taking a breath '– I've not been happy for a while. I think we got caught up in the idea of us – how fast it all happened. But I don't think this is working.'

Panic flashed in his eyes. 'Don't say that—'

'I didn't want to say it like this,' she went on. 'But you've pushed me into a corner. Twice now.'

He took a tentative step toward her, his arms raised like he was going to hug her, but his line of sight drifted to the dresser.

'Who are Keane?'

'A band I like.'

'And who got you these?' he asked, an air of inevitability in his voice.

'Tom,' Lauren said defiantly.

His jaw twitched. 'And you got him something, too, I suppose?'

'It's not a crime to buy your friend a gift.'

'You told me he was your boss. Now he's your friend?'

'You can be friends with the people you work with.'

There followed a bitter silence, which Lauren broke by saying she needed to leave. Without a backwards glance, she slipped past him and reached for the door handle.

'Lauren, wait—'

'Don't be here when I get back,' she said, not turning around. 'Please.'

And with that, she was gone, the door clicking shut behind her.

Already phoning Tom.

41

AFTER ALL THE TIME he'd spent brushing off Dr Dougal's warnings about work-life balance, it was ironic that following that very advice was the key to potentially breaking the case. Days of chasing dead ends and driving himself to exhaustion had yielded nothing. But the moment he went home, saw his family, and finally met Danny – that was when the clue he'd been hunting revealed itself.

Tom eased Tristan's front door shut, the latch clicking softly. A quick sweep of every cupboard and fridge drawer in both this house and Maddison's flat had confirmed it: no insulin anywhere. The frigid air nipped at his cheeks as he turned to Lauren, breath misting in the cold. He tried not to dwell on the way her fiancé had dismissed him so coldly.

'What does this mean?' Lauren asked, stuffing gloved hands into her coat pockets.

'I don't know yet,' Tom said, turning his collar up against the wind. 'But our next stop might give us something solid.'

Thirty-five minutes later, they were hunched on narrow plastic chairs in Mellor GP Surgery, a Victorian grey-brick building that smelled faintly of disinfectant and stale coffee. Fluorescent tubes buzzed overhead and a dusty, ceiling fan rotated lazily. To combat the outside cold, the heating had been cranked to full blast. Sweat pooled on Tom's brow and ran down his back. The receptionist – a woman with a tight bun and tighter expression – kept glancing

242

at the clock above her desk, then at Tom and Lauren, as though they were single-handedly delaying her glass of mulled wine on Christmas Eve.

Two elderly patients occupied the far corner: a silver-haired woman hacking into a floral handkerchief and a stooped man cradling his wrist, every small movement accompanied by a low groan.

Despite their war wounds, neither of them were the saddest people in the room. Tom had noticed that Lauren was in a sombre mood, but hadn't wanted to question her about it while they had been rushing around searching for answers against the clock. Now, with a chance to finally catch a breather, Tom broached the subject.

'Are you okay?' he asked.

She sighed. 'I broke up with Ben this morning.'

He felt a weight lift from his chest, but knew he couldn't show his relief.

She went on to tell him all about Ben's second surprise visit to Haltwhistle, his insinuation that she might forget Christmas and her daughter, and the final row that had broken them apart. Tom winced at the part about the gig tickets, and offered apologies at the end of the telling, which Lauren shrugged off.

'Best finding out now that he's a bit of a cockwomble than after walking down the aisle.'

Before Tom could reply, one of the surgery doors opened. A woman in her late thirties stepped out, white coat tugged over a teal jumper. She had tortoiseshell glasses and a pen tucked into her dark curls. A stethoscope hung around her neck, just like in the movies. She swept a glance around the waiting area and called Tom's name.

Tom stood; Lauren followed. Dr Priya Sharma introduced herself with a brisk nod and led them down a short corridor lined with posters showing how to wash your hands properly, and what to do if the symptoms of a stroke should rear their head. Her room was small but tidy – a couple of toys for kids, an anatomical foot model, a framed watercolour of Alnwick Castle above the desk. Rain pattered the window, turning the afternoon sky the colour of pewter.

'How can I help you?' she asked.

'You're Tristan Watt's doctor, yes?'

'I am.'

'My name is Tom Stonem, and this is Lauren Rea. We're detectives. We just need information about Tristan's medication.'

'That's not something I can help with,' she said. 'GDPR.'

'I know that this isn't a usual request,' Tom said. 'I could go to the court and get a warrant and all that, but we believe that Tristan may be in trouble. His life may be in danger.'

He didn't tell her that Tristan was most likely already dead, and he was simply acting on a wild hunch. The doctor looked like she was sizing up the situation. Clearly having Tristan's life in her hands was too much to bear.

'Normally, if someone came asking about another patient, I'd tell them to sling their hook, okay?'

'Okay.'

'But, since you're the police and withholding information could endanger other lives, I'm going to make an exception,' she said. 'As long as you can promise me this is not going to come back and bite me on the arse.'

'I promise,' Tom said.

'What do you need to know?'

'Tristan is diabetic, yes?'

'Type one.'

'And that requires insulin, yes.'

'Yes.' Dr Sharma clacked on the keyboard of her computer, and angled the screen slightly away. 'Tristan uses NovoRapid for his bolus, and Abasaglar for his basal.'

The word 'NovoRapid' was familiar – it was the same type of insulin that had gone missing from Silver Skies.

'What does that mean?' he asked.

'You bolus for meals roughly twenty minutes before eating to combat the blood sugar spike in the hours that follow. The basal acts like a background dose; it keeps you steady.'

'What would happen if he didn't take any?'

'He runs the risk of diabetic ketoacidosis.'

'Which is?'

'DKA is when your blood sugars go too high and stay there. Diabetics use insulin to bring their blood sugars down, as the pancreas can't do it automatically like a non-diabetic person. If it remains too high, ketones start to develop and turn the blood acidic.'

'Which can lead to complications?'

'Exactly,' Dr Sharma said. She launched into a concise lecture on diabetic ketoacidosis – weight loss, ketones, coma, death – punctuating each grim point with quick side-glances to be sure he was following.

'What about feet?' he asked, when she finished.

She looked at him, puzzled. 'Yes, it can affect foot health. Well, long spells of poorly controlled diabetes can, not DKAs directly.'

'What happens?'

'Poor control can lead to reduced blood flow. Cuts and ulcers that would normally heal quickly don't, and if you don't get them seen to, they can become infected. Serious cases lead to amputation, but it's unusual. It can also cause nerve damage which reduces sensation in the feet, increasing the risk of unnoticed injuries or pressure sores.'

Her matter-of-fact tone could have been mistaken for coldness, but Tom recognised the calm of a doctor who'd had to break worse news at 3 a.m.

'What is Tristan's control like?' Lauren asked.

She consulted the screen again.

'In the years that followed his diagnosis, at the age of twenty-one, his control was rocky. That's not unusual for students who don't want to let their diagnosis rule their lives. After a couple of years, he started to attend courses which helped. He attended his check-ups and his eye screenings, but did have various appointments at the foot clinic.'

'Did he have to get something amputated?'

'No, nothing like that. It says here he had swelling and red toes. The nurse thought he might have a touch of neuropathy. Nerve damage,' she added, noting Tom's blankness. 'She advised regular check-ups, as well as thermal socks and leggings for the colder months. Now, can I ask what this is about?'

'Tristan is missing, possibly already dead. We've just been to his house, and there's no insulin in his fridge, or at his partner's. That's where you're supposed to keep it, right?'

'Yes.'

She turned to the computer for a third time. Tom saw her eyebrows raise slightly as she reviewed information onscreen.

'I can see that he ordered more insulin than usual. It was signed off by my colleague two weeks ago. The amount he ordered would probably do him for a couple of months.'

'Is it unusual to order that much?'

'People who work abroad, or who are planning a cruise or something like that might stockpile if they aren't going to be able to get to the pharmacy. Most tend to order what they need and then top up when the time comes.'

'Does it say why Tristan wanted more than usual?'

'No.'

Tom exchanged a look with Lauren, and said, 'Thank you. This has been incredibly helpful.'

Outside, the late-afternoon sky was as dark as ink. The surgery's security light flicked on, haloing them in sharp white. It illuminated a plastic, perfunctory Christmas tree with glued-on baubles. Wind funnelled down the narrow street, driving sleety rain sideways.

They huddled in an alcove while Tom called Martin. A delivery van splashed past, spraying icy water over his shoes; Tom was cursing the driver when Martin picked up. After promising that the swearing was not aimed at the DCI, Tom asked for an immediate passport check on Tristan. While he waited, Lauren watched him, rain catching on her eyelashes.

A few moments later, Martin confirmed that his passport had not been used since the summer. Tom thanked him and hung up before Martin asked him to share his hunch.

'What are you thinking here?' Lauren raised her voice over the howl of the wind. 'That Tristan is alive?'

'Possibly,' Tom said. 'The amount of insulin is bothering me. It feels to me like he planned to lie low for a while and needed a stockpile. Why would he order so much if he didn't plan on using it?'

'That's like saying why would someone spend a hundred grand on a car before getting hit by a bus the next day. Maybe he ordered the amount to see him through the Christmas holidays, and then someone killed him.'

'Maybe,' Tom nodded.

'But you don't think so.'

'I don't know what I think. My gut is telling me he's still alive. Disappearing the day after collecting the insulin just seems too much of a coincidence, and you know I don't believe in those.'

'You think he's holed up somewhere without a foot?'

'I think the killer might be keeping him alive somewhere,' Tom said. 'Maybe the others were distractions. Maybe Tristan was the one they wanted to punish most.'

'That's a lot of maybes.' Lauren blew out a breath, mist swirling. 'So, what's the plan?'

In answer, Tom pulled his phone out again and called HQ. He asked for every available member of the search team to mobilise: he wanted boots on the ground, helicopters in the air. He wanted the north of England scoured with search dogs and thermal imaging to try to find Tristan.

A beat of silence on the line, then: 'Isn't he presumed dead, sir?'

'That's what I want you to confirm,' Tom said. 'Because if Tristan Watt is breathing, he's the key we're missing.'

When he hung up, Lauren asked, 'Now what?'

'It's Christmas Eve. Now, you go home to your daughter. I'm going to go back to my flat and wait.'

42

Christmas Day

THE FIGURE COLLAPSED ONTO *the sofa with a theatrical groan, limbs splayed. Gone were the hiking boots, crusted with mud; gone were the waterproof trousers and the headtorch that had been their faithful companion in the dark. Now they were dressed for a very different kind of expedition – one that involved carbs and comfort. A novelty Christmas jumper, its knitted reindeer lopsided from a botched wash, clung to their frame. They wore tartan pyjama bottoms and fluffy slippers on their feet.*

They knew their plan was all but ready. And in a couple of hours, it would be finished.

The turkey had been basted and shoved into the oven hours earlier, its aroma now curling its way into the living room, mixing with the pine of the Christmas tree and the cinnamon-scented candles. The television guide lay open on the coffee table, circles scrawled around seasonal staples and nostalgic reruns in black pen. A bottle of champagne sat half-empty on the counter, the cork discarded beside it, a flute of Buck's Fizz bubbling on the side table, the sparkling glass catching the glow of the fairy lights strung up around the room.

The figure grabbed the remote and pressed the power button, expecting the cheerful DreamWorks logo to bounce onto the screen to signify the beginning of Shrek. *But instead of a green ogre and a wisecracking donkey, they were met with the sombre tones of a BBC news jingle and the equally joyless face of a newsreader in a deep-purple blazer.*

249

The figure stared at the screen, confused and mildly irritated. Their first thought was the usual one: some nobody celebrity had selfishly gone and died. Nothing quite ruined a Christmas special like a national mourning broadcast. They hovered their thumb over the remote, ready to switch to ITV's rerun of Oliver!, *when something stopped them.*

A name.

Tristan.

It hit like a slap. Their thumb froze mid-click, and they slowly lowered the remote and leaned forward, pulse quickening, a wave of white-hot fury threatening to engulf them. On screen, the newsreader continued, her smug voice inflected with the carefully rehearsed seriousness reserved for national emergencies.

The screen cut to footage of a windswept field at dawn, the horizon blurred by mist and the orange haze of the rising sun. A thick-set man in a wax jacket stood awkwardly in front of a dilapidated barn. His hair was greying, his sideburns unkempt, and he kept glancing just to the side of the camera, as if looking for permission to speak.

'Well, it was a surprise,' he said, scratching the back of his head as if to emphasise his point. 'I saw the police appeal, y'know, asking folk to check barns and such. Figured I'd have a look. Well, actually, the wife told me I should.' He prattled on, like a stupid, ignorant fool who happened to stumble upon a goldmine. 'I didn't think… I didn't expect much. Anyway, me and Bonnie … that's my dog, not my wife, took a walk down, and there he was. This lad, behind a hay bale in the barn. No foot.'

The footage changed again to a live broadcast. A much more glamorous reporter was in the same field, standing in front of the same barn. Her scarf flapped in the wind, but her expression was composed.

'What do we know so far?' the newsreader asked from the studio.

The reporter remained silent for a few seconds, the message seemingly delayed in getting to her.

Eventually, she said, 'Good morning, Becky. Well, as you know, yesterday, police investigating the suspected murders of Evie Kirkby, Joshua Price and Tristan Watt issued a public appeal for people across the north to search outbuildings, fields, barns – anywhere that someone might be hidden. It turns out that plea paid off. Mr Beckett, the farmer we just heard from, discovered Tristan Watt alive in his barn, just outside Lanercost, not far from Haltwhistle. We understand he is in a critical condition. He has lost a foot, and one of the paramedics said he couldn't understand how Tristan was still alive. He is due to be airlifted to hospital soon. Police have not released further details at this time, but we'll have more updates as they come.'

The figure didn't wait for more. They turned the television off in disgust with a sharp press of their thumb, and stood up, pacing, deliberating the discovery.

They began muttering to themselves, half-formed thoughts, swear words that blistered in the air like smoke from a fresh burn. The once mouth-watering smell of the turkey was now cloying, and more than once, the figure retched.

This couldn't be happening.

They swore – loudly now – a single, vicious word hurled into the world, cursing it for its unpredictability.

Once the heat of their anger began to simmer, it was replaced with a cold, creeping dread.

Their throat dried.

Their hands trembled.

If only they knew the sorry, twisted truth. That the true grand plan … was not theirs at all.

The champagne bubbles in the Buck's Fizz looked suddenly sinister, mocking. The figure swiped at it with a hand, sending the glass spiralling through the air and colliding with the wall where it smashed into pieces.

Thoughts came in a jumbled tangle. Was Tristan even conscious? Was he capable of communication?

And if so... would he talk?

All the panic condensed into one thought, one question that played over and over, louder and louder, like a record stuck on repeat. **What happens now?**

43

JUST AFTER MR BECKETT had discovered Tristan in his barn, Tom's phone rang, jolting him from a fitful sleep. He answered without hesitation, his voice groggy with sleep. He listened carefully without speaking, thanked the caller when they had run out of information and then threw himself out of bed.

Half an hour later, his car skidded to a halt in a lay-by near Mr Beckett's farm. He jumped out, the air a shocking cold after the luxury of the car's heating, and ran to the outer cordon. The place was already crawling with bodies: uniformed officers and forensics in white coveralls, vehicle headlights cutting through the grey light of early morning. A convoy of SOCO vans cluttered the narrow lane leading to the property, their rear lights flashing dimly in the gloom. Deep tyre tracks zigzagged through the mud on the verge, left by an ambulance now parked outside the barn. Its blue lights strobed across the corrugated metal walls, painting them in eerie pulses of electric blue.

Tom slipped into a suit, signed in at the perimeter and made his way down the lane. As he walked, he couldn't help but wish Lauren were beside him. Newly single, fiancé-free Lauren. But he hadn't wanted to disturb her. By now, Sophie would be knee-deep in wrapping paper, shrieking with excitement at whatever Santa had delivered. Tom could almost hear it.

Ahead, the barn loomed – a hulking timber structure with painted metal panels, the roof sagging under decades of harsh

253

northern weather. The smell hit him before the sight of anything inside: manure, damp hay, and something far worse – a sweet, fetid rot that clung to the back of his throat.

Outside the barn, he caught a paramedic just as they were updating a colleague.

'How's he doing?' Tom asked.

'Rough,' the paramedic replied, nodding towards the interior. 'You obviously know he's missing a foot, but he's dehydrated and showing signs of infection, too. We think he'll live, but it's touch and go.'

Tom thanked him, and ducked under the police tape stretched across the open doors

Inside, the barn was dim, lit by a single industrial lamp clipped to a post near the door. Dust particles danced in the shaft of yellow light. The place felt cavernous. Cobwebs hung from the rafters like tattered curtains. Rusted tools, probably generations old, were still nailed to the walls. A battered ladder lay across the straw-covered floorboards, and feed sacks were slumped in the corners like dead bodies. In one of those corners, a cluster of SOCOs waited silently, eyes flicking between the medics and the man sprawled on the ground, waiting for the paramedics to finish so they could spring into action.

Tom stepped carefully over the barn floor, rounding a stack of hay bales.

Tristan was behind them, sprawled on the floor, his arms and legs splayed as though he'd been dropped from the rafters and left to lie where he landed.

His skin was waxy, almost blue in places, stretched tight over gaunt cheekbones. His hair was longer than in the photos Tom had seen in his home, streaked with straw and cobwebs, strands of it fanned out across the filthy floor. He looked like something dragged from a tomb. Tom's mind flashed to the moles, strung up on the farmer's fence.

Paramedics knelt either side of him, working fast. Cannulas were inserted into both of Tristan's hands. Someone was cleaning the exposed end of his leg. Tristan was panting feebly, apparently unaware of their efforts. Tom glanced at the leg: it wasn't the ragged wound Tom had been expecting. There was a roll of dirty bandages to the paramedic's side, presumably pulled off Tristan's stump so that she could investigate. The stump had been stitched, though the flesh was mottled and discoloured. Presumably, whoever had cut the foot off had treated the wound, and then left Tristan to look after it, judging by the empty bottle of disinfectant that had rolled next to one of the hay bales. Perhaps, he thought, as his health had faltered, he became unable to clean it, and it had become infected.

It turned Tom's stomach.

For one terrifying moment, he felt the usual telltale signs: chest tightening, breath hitching – but he managed to resist the panic attack. Remembered Dr Dougan's exercises.

He regained composure.

'Give us a minute,' one of the paramedics said, before turning back to Tristan.

Tom watched them work, and then a paramedic stood, ushering him backwards a few steps.

'What do you want to know?' she said.

'Had he been taking insulin?' Tom asked.

'We think so. We've tested his blood sugars, and everything is in range. There are empty vials in his pocket, and a pen with a half-empty cartridge. The little display on the end of his pen shows that he injected a basal dose last night.'

'Doesn't insulin go off?'

'It's usually good out of the fridge for about a month.'

'So he's been looking after himself?'

'As best as he can,' she shrugged. 'Though it doesn't seem to be working as it should. Yes, his bloods are in range, but he's very ill. He hasn't spoken yet – just looked at us and nodded when we asked him his name.'

'What's he been eating?'

'We don't know. Like I said, all he's done is nod once.'

'Can I take a shot at him?'

'You can,' the paramedic said. 'But go easy. He's obviously badly injured and dehydrated. We don't know if there are further internal injuries or anything like that, so don't push too hard.'

Tom nodded and edged closer, giving the paramedics space. As he passed the leg wound again, he tried not to look. The infection smelled like a visit to the tip at the height of summer.

As Tom hunkered down beside Tristan, he noted that the prone man's eyes had not wavered once, save for a slow blink every ten seconds or so. He had not tracked Tom's movements at all, simply lying there like a waxwork. Only the rise and fall of his chest and the twitch of a vein in his neck betrayed the fact he was alive.

'Tristan,' Tom began, quietly, as if trying to rouse a child gently from sleep.

Nothing.

He repeated the name, louder this time. Tristan's eyelids fluttered, and the pupils moved sluggishly to Tom's face. It was awful to watch – like some kind of automaton creaking into life. Tom tried not to let emotion flicker on his face, instead offering a faint smile of encouragement.

'Tristan, my name is Tom. I'm a detective. Can you hear me?'

The slightest of nods.

'I want to find out what happened to you. I want to know who did this to you. Can you help me?'

At that, something changed. Tom noticed that Tristan's hands began to tremble. Gently at first, but then violently, the cannulas threatening to become untethered from the skin. His whole body shook, convulsing. He retched noiselessly, and tears spilled down his cheeks. He screamed, then, a banshee wail that reverberated around the metallic interior of the barn.

It was one of the worst noises Tom had ever heard.

A paramedic acted quickly, grabbing a bag of clear liquid from their pack and hooking it up to one of the lines entering Tristan's hand. After a further minute of flailing, Tristan became still and fell silent, his body slack, like a puppet with its strings cut.

Tom looked enquiringly at the paramedic.

'Droperidol,' they said. 'It's a sedative.'

'I told you to take it easy,' the first paramedic said.

'I was—'Tom started but was cut off by Tristan raising a hand and groping at Tom's sleeve. His lips were moving, but no sound was coming out. It looked like it was taking an enormous amount of effort.

'Closer…' Tristan rasped.

Tom leaned in, his ear mere inches away from Tristan's cracked lips, heart pounding.

'Maddison…'

'She's safe,' Tom nodded, hoping the good news would soothe Tristan. Instead, Tristan's eyes widened, and he shook his head.

'She did this to me,' he croaked. 'Her and Niall. They did this to me.'

44

THE STATION WAS ALMOST deserted, running on a skeleton staff of officers and admin assistants who either had no plans for Christmas Day or had volunteered to escape them, and take advantage of the extra pay. There were no festive tunes echoing through the corridors, no mince pies or tinsel – just the heavy quiet of a place that had seen too much in the past ten days.

It seemed, though, that since the boss was away, the thermostat was fair game – the station was boiling, the heat hitting Tom the moment he crossed the threshold, making his winter coat instantly unbearable. He unzipped it as he passed the front desk and made his way down the corridor.

As he walked towards the office, he considered calling Lauren. It didn't sit right, keeping her out of this, not when things were moving fast. The next few hours were pivotal in the case: things could tip one way or the other, and he thought she'd want to be part of that. But it was Christmas Day, and Ben's words echoed in his head. Even if they'd broken up – he had a point about personal boundaries. He flip-flopped on the decision a couple of times, before deciding to leave her to it.

Instead, he called on Deborah and a pair of DCs who happened to be in his vicinity. He explained the development, and impressed upon them how important these interviews were. Maddison and Niall were still in custody, thankfully, but the time was ticking before they would have to be released.

'So, you want a confession?' Deborah said, her arms folded.

Tom shook his head. 'I doubt either of them are going to tell us they did it, but I want to put Tristan's claims to them and see what they say. If they can't explain his accusation, it'll be enough to take to the CPS tomorrow.'

'You think they'll go for murder?' asked one of the DCs.

Tom still couldn't believe that a pair who presented as relatively normal, despite the odd flare-up or two, would be capable of such sick, depraved actions. But he knew by now that psychopathy came in all shapes and sizes.

'They should,' he replied. 'Tristan says Maddison and Niall were responsible for everything: Evie, Joshua, and what happened to him. It's our job to prove or disprove that. Let's throw everything we've got at them, see what sticks. Deborah, you take Niall, and I'll take Maddison.'

Deborah nodded and stood, beckoning one of the DCs to follow her. Tom signalled to the other – a young man with close-cropped blonde hair, barely out of his probation period – and headed down the corridor towards the interview rooms.

Deborah took the door on the left, Tom the one on the right.

Inside, Maddison looked like she'd aged five years overnight. Her skin had a pallid hue under the harsh fluorescent lights, her hair limp and tangled, her clothes creased from a sleepless night in a cell. Her eyes were fixed on a smear on the tabletop, wide and unblinking.

By contrast, her solicitor looked like she had strolled off a red carpet, her expensive navy suit and silk blouse a contrast to Maddison's grey garb, her hair perfectly coiffed. She sat at a slight angle to Maddison, so that she was in her eyeline, presumably so she could give her client non-verbal signals in case the interview took a turn for the worse.

Tom and the DC sat down, said hello to Maddison and thanked the solicitor for coming.

'The interview is being recorded,' he said. 'Standard procedure.'

He pressed the button on the machine. The red light blinked to life.

'Maddison, there's been a development overnight. We're eager to hear your side of it.'

'What is it?' she asked, her voice papery.

Tom held off for a moment, letting the tension build. Then, he dropped the bombshell.

'Tristan is alive.'

She stared at him, the words bouncing off her like static.

'Alive?' she looked at him incredulously, and with the faintest trace of hope. But that could easily be an act.

'That's right.'

'What do you mean?' she said. 'No, that can't be right. I saw… I was *given* his foot. In the forest. You *told* me it was his. It was all over the bloody news.'

Tom nodded. 'And yet, early this morning, we found him – barely alive – in a barn less than ten miles from here. It's the best break we've had in the case – like finding Lazarus.'

She shook her head. 'No. No, that's not possible.'

'He's missing part of his leg,' Tom continued. 'And he was just about able to talk to me at the scene. He says you and Niall were responsible for what happened to him. And, I assume if you did that to him, you were also responsible for the murders of Evie Kirkby and Joshua Price.'

Maddison sat, a thousand-yard look on her face, similar to images Tom had seen of shell-shocked soldiers in World War One. He imagined there was a lot to process – not only was her fiancé actually alive, but he was levelling horrific accusations at her.

'Maddison. Do you have anything to counteract Tristan's accusations?'

'He's really alive?' she whispered.

'He's really alive. And he's talking. So now it's your turn. Did you have any involvement in what happened to him?'

'How can he be alive?' she asked in a shrill, pleading tone. 'How could he survive having his fucking foot cut off?'

'Look, Maddison—'

'I can't believe it.' She looked like she wanted to rise, to pace, to escape. Her solicitor clamped a hand on Maddison's arm. While it might have been a caring gesture, it looked calculated and impersonal. The fingers lingered for a second, before withdrawing again.

'Maddison,' Tom said, gently but firmly, 'did you kill Evie Kirkby?'

'No.'

'Did you kill Joshua Price?'

'No,' she repeated, sharper this time. 'And I didn't lay a fucking finger on Tristan. I don't know what this is, some elaborate story he's concocted, but I didn't do *any* of it.'

The solicitor looked like she was going to seize her client's arm again, but Maddison pulled it away, hugging it around herself instead.

'I don't want to see him ever again. He's trying to destroy my life, has been for ages now.'

'Did you attack him because of his controlling behaviour?'

'I didn't do anything to him.'

'Was it to be with Niall? To get him out of the way?'

'No.'

'Was it—'

She lurched forward suddenly, as if the table between them no longer existed. 'You're not listening! I *left* to get away from him. I went hiking to put miles between us. I didn't want to see him, or talk to him, or … or *be* with him anymore.'

Tom decided to change tack.

'Then let's talk about Joshua. You messaged him...' He made a show of looking through his notes. '...Twice. Once begging him to keep quiet, and another time basically threatening him. Why?'

'I thought he might tell Tristan about the one-night stand with Niall,' she muttered. 'I didn't want that. Not with everything already so tense.'

'Did you meet with him?'

'No.'

'Did you kill him to keep him quiet?'

'No!' Her voice cracked. 'I knew about the affair with Evie. I saw them kiss at the charity do. I figured that made us even – mutually assured destruction. I thought if I hinted that I knew, he'd stay quiet, too. That's all. He had more to lose than me – his business reputation, his perfect wife, his massive house. Yes, I messaged him, but that's as far as it went.'

'You didn't follow up? You didn't threaten to expose him?'

'I just hoped he'd keep his mouth shut,' she said. 'I never saw him again.'

Tom leaned back. 'Maddison, I have to say this isn't looking great for you.'

The solicitor cut in. 'I disagree. You have no physical evidence. No witnesses. Just an allegation from someone who, by your own admission, has suffered severe trauma and is not in a fit state to be trusted. All you really have are empty accusations and conjecture.'

'What I have is a victim missing a foot, found dying in a barn, who says that his fiancée and her bit on the side tried to kill him. Do you think he's lying?'

'He is,' Maddison said.

'So what, then?' Tom asked. 'He's framing you? You think he chopped off his own foot to get back at you?'

'I wouldn't put it past him,' she muttered, a small, brittle laugh escaping her lips. 'He's fucked in the head.'

'Right,' Tom said. 'Let's assume for a second you're telling the truth. Who *did* do this? Niall?'

'I don't know.'

'Someone trying to frame you? Someone with access to your messages, your location, your life?'

'I said I don't know!' she cried. 'I just want this to stop. I don't want to see him. I don't want to *ever* see him again.'

'That may not be up to you. But I'll tell you what is: the truth. We're going to speak to Tristan again once he's received treatment. I imagine he'll be pretty open to giving his version of events. Are you sure you don't have anything else to tell me?'

Maddison simply shook her head.

The solicitor stood, smoothing her skirt. 'My client has a matter of hours left in here. I suggest you find some evidence to back up your claims, or let her go.'

'We've already applied for a further twenty-four hours,' Tom said. 'There's no doubt in my mind that your client is guilty of two counts of murder, and one of attempted murder. And I plan to prove it before the day is out.'

45

THE OFFICE STANK OF microwaved food.

Someone – well-meaning, no doubt – had thought it might raise morale to serve a makeshift Christmas dinner for the team. Unfortunately, no amount of tinsel or seasonal cheer could mask the sad reality of congealed stuffing, slippery carrots and rubbery cocktail sausages cooked in a machine designed to reheat soup, not feed a murder squad. Even so, Tom appreciated the gesture. He balanced his paper plate on one knee, poking at a gluey heap of instant mash with the end of a plastic fork.

Someone had even made him a hot chocolate, knowing he didn't drink tea or coffee. It was a sweet gesture, one that made him think they saw him as part of the team, rather than an interloper. Sadly, like the food, it was substandard, worlds apart from the Velvetiser-perfect versions he prepared at home (which reminded him: must phone home to wish Mum, Dad and Danny merry Christmas.) But, he drank it anyway, keen to show his appreciation for their thoughtfulness.

Deborah strolled into the room and sat down in the chair beside Tom.

So apparently her Christmas plans had been scuppered, too. Not that he could envision Deborah pulling crackers and wearing a novelty paper hat round the dinner table.

'Not having anything to eat?' he asked, noting her empty hands.

'No. It smells like shit.'

The sentence was delivered in her usual deadpan, without a trace of a smile, and Tom wondered if Deborah was actually some sort of comic genius who was missing her calling on the stage. Before he had time to say anything else, the door opened and Lauren strode in, cheeks flushed from the cold.

'What are you doing here?' Tom asked, springing to his feet.

'You found a footless man in a barn and I had to find out from the *news*,' she said, pulling off her coat. 'Come on!'

'I thought—'

'I know what you thought,' she said, softening. 'And I appreciate it. But this is too big. I couldn't stay away.'

'What about Sophie?'

'She's playing with the iPad Granny got her. I left her with a mountain of chocolate coins and a blanket fort. She barely even glanced up when I said I'd be back in a few hours.'

'We were just about to go through the interviews,' Deborah said. 'So you've arrived just in time.'

'Do you want a plate before we get started?' Tom asked, holding up his own.

Lauren took one look and recoiled slightly, her nose wrinkling. 'Absolutely not. Let's crack on. I want to know everything.'

Tom went first.

'Maddison's sticking to her story. She says she didn't kill Evie or Joshua. Says she never laid a hand on Tristan. But she *did* admit to knowing about the affair between Joshua and Evie – and she blackmailed Joshua to keep him from exposing her one-night stand with Niall.'

Deborah picked up from there. 'Niall is singing from a similar hymn sheet. He also claims that he didn't lay a finger on anyone, let alone kill anyone or chop any feet off. He *did* say that he was using Maddison's knowledge of Joshua's affair to blackmail him. He contacted Joshua to ask for the fifteen grand to pay off Freddie Sutherland, and made it very clear that he didn't expect to pay a single penny back, otherwise he was going to tell Rosanna.'

'So,' Lauren said, leaning forward, 'Maddison and Niall both had Joshua over a barrel. What if Joshua decided to come clean? Confess to Rosanna, burn the whole thing down. That'd make their whole blackmail scheme useless.'

Tom nodded. 'That's one of the working theories. Joshua's threat to confess could've triggered panic. Maddison and Niall might've decided to silence him before he exposed everything. That way, Tristan doesn't find out about the affair, and Niall doesn't have to pay a whole heap of money back.'

'And where does Evie fit in all of this?' Lauren asked. 'Is she just collateral damage?'

'Niall swears he didn't touch her. Says he was shocked when he heard she was dead. Reckons the last time he saw her was at the charity do.'

'So both he and Maddison want us to believe they were up to their necks in secrets and lies – but when it came to murder, they suddenly drew the line?'

Deborah gave a tired shrug. 'Apparently.'

They lapsed into silence, the sounds of cutlery scraping on paper plates and half-hearted Christmas music from someone's tinny phone speaker filling the void.

After a moment, Lauren took up the thread. 'The only reason I can see why they would've killed Joshua was if he threatened to go rogue. Maybe he already had, and told Tristan. Tristan confronted Maddison—'

'Which,' Tom said, 'might explain why Maddison was so terrified of seeing him alive again.'

'Right. So Tristan confronts her, maybe confronts them both. It gets out of hand.'

'And they attack him,' Deborah said.

Lauren frowned. 'But if they were capable of murder, why leave Tristan alive, knowing we might get to him at some point? Why not just finish the job?'

'Maybe they thought he *was* dead,' Tom suggested. 'His foot was the first gift. Maybe he was the first victim, and they've learned from their mistakes for the next two.'

'Too messy?' an eavesdropping DC said. 'Too scared?'

'Or maybe one of them got cold feet,' Deborah offered, then momentarily shuddered at the turn of phrase. 'Or didn't realise how far the other would go.'

'Maybe he escaped.'

'With a foot missing?' Tom shook his head. 'Unlikely. I know they found him in a barn in the middle of nowhere, so maybe they left him there to die, knowing there was little chance of him making it back to civilisation. And he had insulin in his pocket, enough to keep himself alive. That part makes no sense. If they wanted him dead, why leave him insulin?'

They fell quiet, thoughts spinning.

'Then what about the gifts?' Deborah asked, dragging her chair forward. 'They're still the strangest part of this.'

She motioned to the board.

Tristan's foot, addressed to Maddison.

Joshua's hand, addressed to Niall.

Evie's head, addressed to Rosanna.

'Could it be symbolic,' Deborah murmured. 'Punishment, maybe. One for each of them.'

'But who sent them?' Lauren asked.

Tom shook his head. 'If Maddison and Niall are the killers, why send parts of the victims to themselves?'

'To throw us off the scent?'

'Maybe, but it feels like too much of a swing and a miss.'

Deborah's eyes narrowed. 'If it's not them, it has to be Rosanna.'

Lauren turned to her. 'Go on.'

'Well, maybe she found out about Joshua and Evie's affair, and did something about it. She did tell us she suspected him of playing away. Maybe she snaps. Kills Evie in the heat of the moment. Then Joshua to cover her tracks. Then, she paints herself as the victim, vanishes to her parents' house and keeps well out of our way.'

Tom frowned. 'She's played the perfect grieving wife.'

'Maybe too perfect,' Deborah said. 'No press statements. No breakdowns. No demands for updates.'

'She's kept herself out of the spotlight,' Lauren agreed. 'If she *is* involved, she's played it smart.'

Tom stood. 'Tristan won't be ready for interview for a few more hours. One of the DCs called the hospital; they said he's awake but groggy, and under supervision. So if we're going to speak to Rosanna again, now's the time.'

Deborah stayed seated. 'I'll stay here, go back over the original witness statements. See if there's anything we missed the first time around.'

Tom nodded. 'If Rosanna *is* involved, this might be our last chance to catch her off-guard.'

'Let's do it,' Lauren said, reaching for her coat.

46

IF ROSANNA'S HOUSE WAS nice, her parents' house was out of this world – like something a celebrity would show off in *Hello!* magazine. Travelling up the private, cobbled drive, a Georgian masterpiece slowly revealed itself to Tom and Lauren. The façade gleamed in the winter sunlight, ivy snaking up the pale stone. The steps leading up to the grand black front door were swept clean of snow, flanked by stone lions and potted plants wrapped in twinkling fairy lights. Plus, the most enormous Christmas tree Tom had ever laid eyes on.

'Wow,' Lauren cooed, as she got out of the car.

Tom ascended the steps and rapped on the door. A moment later, it opened halfway, a woman with shoulder-length blonde hair wedged in the opening, her lips already pursed in disapproval.

'Can I help you?' she asked.

'I'm DI Tom Stonem, and this is my partner DS Rea. We'd like to speak to Rosanna.'

The woman's brow furrowed, offended rather than concerned. 'Really? Can't this wait? It's Christmas Day, for goodness' sake!'

'We wish it could, madam, but it really can't.'

'Is she in some kind of trouble?'

'We just need to speak to her.'

Before the woman could argue further, Rosanna appeared behind her, barefoot on the marble tiles. She wore a novelty

Christmas jumper with a grinning reindeer, a pair of tartan pyjama bottoms, her hair piled in a loose bun.

'Detectives?' she said.

'Hi, Rosanna. Sorry to bother you on Christmas Day, but we need to have a quick chat. Would you prefer to come down to the station, or…'

Tom let the sentence hang. On the car journey over, he and Lauren had discussed inviting themselves into Rosanna's parent's home. Psychologically, it wasn't as intense as an interview in a police station. It was more likely that, due to the interviewee feeling more comfortable in their own home, they would let something slip.

Rosanna glanced between them, her face unreadable. 'No, it's okay. You can come in. Just take your shoes off, if you don't mind.'

Tom and Lauren stepped across the threshold and started to unlace their shoes. Rosanna's mother released a sharp sigh, but said nothing more as they padded down a wide hallway under a crystal chandelier. Family portraits lined the walls – horseback rides, skiing holidays, black-tie dinners.

They entered a living room the size of Tom's Durham flat. It was awash with opulence: deep green walls, a roaring fire, velvet sofas arranged around a gleaming mahogany coffee table. The tree in the corner looked professionally decorated – white and gold ornaments, ribbons cascading like waterfalls, a star twinkling on top.

'Rosanna,' Tom said, once they were all sitting. 'I'm not sure if you've caught the news at all today.'

'I haven't,' she replied, curling her legs under her. 'We've been doing family stuff all day. No time for TV. Why?'

Tom couldn't be sure, but there was something in her delivery that made it sound like a lie: the slight tremor in her voice, the guarded look. He decided to press on, rather than tip her off to the fact they were here to potentially arrest her: that was a sure-fire way to get her to clam up and stop talking.

'Tristan has been found.'

'Tristan?' she repeated, an incredulous look on her face. 'Isn't he dead?'

Again, bad delivery. Tom was sure she knew more than she was letting on. Still, he decided to play along.

'That's what everyone thought, including us,' Tom said. 'But he was found in a barn with his foot chopped off. In a bad way, yes, but very much alive and breathing. He alleges that Maddison and Niall were behind it, but we're starting to think he might have got it wrong.'

Rosanna's eyes brimmed. For a moment she looked down at her lap, lips trembling. Then the dam broke.

'He's playing everyone,' she whispered.

'What do you mean?' Lauren asked, softly.

'Tristan killed Joshua and Evie.'

Tom felt his thigh muscles clench. *Could it be?*

Reality doused him as he remembered the state of Tristan in the barn.

'And what?' he said. 'Cut off his own leg? Come on.'

'He did! He—' She froze for a moment, before finishing the sentence. 'He made me help.'

Her voice cracked and she covered her mouth with both hands, shaking. Her shoulders began to tremble with sobs.

So Rosanna helped Tristan amputate his *own foot*…

Tom sat, stunned, unable to get beyond the thought: What the fuck had they just uncovered?

'Take your time,' Lauren said gently.

'I didn't want to! I swear to God. But he said if I didn't, he'd kill me, too. He said it was the only way I could make it up to him, the bastard,' she spat, her teeth bared. 'He did the amputation, but he made me suture and stitch it.'

Tom and Lauren exchanged a glance, letting the silence stretch.

271

'Tell us what you know,' Lauren said, finally. 'And start at the beginning.'

Rosanna wiped her face with the sleeve of her jumper, her breaths coming in erratic bursts.

'It started when Tristan found out about Maddison and Niall – about them sleeping together at that charity event. He blamed me. Said I'd orchestrated it. That I'd humiliated him.'

'Did you?'

'No!' she snapped. 'I swore blind that I had nothing to do with it, but he didn't believe me. He said he would have his revenge, and that I would have to make it up to him. I didn't know what he meant.'

She paused, pressing her fingers to her temple as if trying to erase the memory.

'And then what?'

'A few days went by, and then I got a message from him, asking to meet. I thought he meant for a coffee, that maybe he had seen sense and was going to apologise. But he sent me an address, which turned out to be a disused warehouse on an abandoned industrial estate. When I went in, Joshua and Evie were there – already dead on the ground, and he was cutting off Joshua's hand. *My* Joshua.'

She choked on the words, eyes wide, staring through the room as if seeing it again.

'I threw up, and then I screamed at him to stop, but he just kept going. Calm as anything. He told me he'd killed them to hurt Maddison and Niall – and me. He wanted to frame them for it. He said if I didn't help, he'd kill me, too. Said he'd already thought it all through. He was convinced that Maddison had postponed their Christmas wedding because of Niall, as she did it shortly after the charity ball. He thought Maddison and Niall were planning a life together behind his back! It was ridiculous, but he was paranoid. His ego bruised by her change of plans. So he wanted to punish them both – rather than getting married by Christmas, Maddison would be behind bars by then. Niall and Tristan always had a twisted rivalry, ever since school. My job was to help move the bodies, and deliver the … the gifts. I told him I wouldn't do it, that I wouldn't help him. That I'd go to the police. But he said he would kill me there and then if I didn't help. I was scared … I…'

'So if you did those things for him, he'd leave you be?'

She swallowed hard, clearly struggling with what came next.

'Not quite. There was one more thing. He wanted to fake his own death. He was going to cut his foot off, and send it as a present to divert attention away from himself. I told him he was crazy, but he thought that, since I am a surgeon, it was something I could do.'

'Why didn't he just disappear? Why go to the trouble of cutting off his own foot?'

'He had neuropathy. His foot had been giving him grief for years. I suppose he thought it would bring him some relief, and make his plan more real.'

Tom shook his head slowly. 'Jesus.'

'So, you hid the bodies, you stitched his amputation up and you delivered the gifts. What else?'

'I drove him to the barn where he wanted to lie low, and that was my last part in it. I told him I'd more than played my part, and he agreed. He told me that if he was caught, he'd play the victim and keep my name out of it.' She let out a shaky breath. 'Is he at the hospital?'

'Yes.'

'Right.' Her shoulders sagged. 'Then they'll find out, soon enough.'

'Find out what?' Lauren asked.

Rosanna looked up, a wild intensity to her gaze now. 'That I poisoned him. I spiked his insulin with calcium chloride. It acts slowly, but the accumulation over several days will guarantee death. It wasn't hard to swipe a batch from Joshua's company, Silver Skies.'

So *that* was why Duncan noted an order had gone missing.

'After I administered morphine for the amputation recovery, Tristan was out for a long time. I tampered with his insulin supply. I'm a doctor, it wasn't hard. I knew the poison would kill him by Christmas Day. I'd told him how to clean his wound, but I also suspected that as he grew weaker, as the delirium and vomiting took over, he'd forget. And that nasty wound of his would become infected, too.' Her hands balled into fists. 'He thought he could kill Joshua, just like that? I know my husband slept with Evie. But he *loved* me. We loved each other, more than anything. Tristan was scum for thinking he could do such a thing and get away with it.' She leaned forward. 'Speaking of, why do you think he addressed Evie's head to me? Because if Plan A: frame Maddison and Niall didn't work, he was going to opt for Plan B. Framing me. And all of us – everyone who went to school with him – knew how twisted he was. Do you really think he would have stopped with Joshua and Evie? That he wouldn't have pulled something like this again? The bastard deserved to rot. It's just a shame they found him before he truly did.'

Tom sat stunned at the spew of vitriol, and the admission that she had tried to exact her own revenge. Sure, Tristan's crimes were appalling, but hers was still devious and premeditated, and Rosanna would have further questions to answer very soon. While he tried to gather his thoughts, Lauren pressed on with taking Rosanna's story.

'Did you put your husband's finger in Maddison's flat?'

She sobbed harder now, nodding. 'It was part of the plan. He said it would clinch it.'

'And what was his grand plan when Maddison and Niall were arrested? Miraculously appear again and live a normal life?'

'No,' Rosanna said. 'He told me that he'd taken money from Joshua and planned to pay some loan shark to sort him a fake passport. A new identity. Obviously, I wasn't going to let that happen.'

He was a cunning fucker.

'So, what now?'

'Well, Rosanna, we appreciate your honesty. You'll have to come to the station for further questioning, and show us where you stowed the bodies, so the families can have a proper burial for their loved ones.'

Lauren stood, read Rosanna her rights and cuffed her. Then, she called for a team to come and collect Rosanna so she could show them where the bodies were hidden, to verify her story.

'Why tell us all this?' Tom asked, while they waited. 'Most people answer no comment.'

Rosanna gave a bitter laugh. 'Because I saw that he'd been found on the news this morning. I thought if he was backed into a corner and started to talk, he might use my name as some sort of leverage. I thought he might throw me under the bus, when the only reason I did his bidding was so he wouldn't kill me. I'd rather go to prison for my part in it, than see him get away with everything. You don't understand what I've been through. The nightmares. I'm exhausted. The guilt is like nothing I've ever felt.'

Just then, the sitting room door opened.

Her mother entered, holding a tray of tea and mince pies, a polite smile on her face. It dropped instantly when she saw the cuffs and her daughter's mascara-streaked cheeks.

'Rosanna?' she gasped.

Time froze.

Then the tray clattered to the floor. A fine china teapot shattered like a gunshot. Hot tea splashed across the cream carpet and up the lime walls.

Rosanna's mother uttered a strangled wail and crumpled to the floor.

47

An hour later, Tom and Lauren pulled into the car park of Carlisle hospital, the low winter sun bleeding gold across the tarmac, casting long, spindly shadows. They'd discussed the drama of Rosanna's mother's collapse, the officers carting Rosanna off in tears, and, hanging over it all, the damning implications of what she'd said. If she was telling the truth, then Tristan wasn't just alive – he was dangerous, and he was cornered.

As they got out of the car and started walking towards the hospital's entrance, Tom felt a sense of finality. The case, at long last, was coming to a close. Loose ends stitching together. Answers falling into place. Surely a bed-bound 'victim' couldn't put up too much of a fight – no matter how manipulative he'd proven himself to be.

Before they reached the door, Tom's phone buzzed in his coat pocket. He paused, shielding the screen from the sun's glare.

A message.

No words – just three images.

He swiped through them slowly.

The first: a grainy photo of a disused warehouse, most of its windows broken or missing entirely, graffiti scrawled across the brickwork. In the foreground was a burnt-out van, one Tom thought might belong with NW Technologies.

The second: two dead bodies, dumped unceremoniously on concrete, one missing its head.

276

The third: A close up of Joshua's arm, severed at the wrist.

He handed the phone to Lauren. She took one look at the photos, mouth tightening.

'Shit,' she muttered. 'Looks like Rosanna was telling the truth. How fucking grim is that?'

'It's her word against Tristan's for now,' Tom said. 'Let's hope forensics can match anything to either of them. Then, it's game over.'

'Let's just hope he's too weak to try anything stupid.'

They'd phoned on the way over and received confirmation that a high concentration of Calcium Chloride was found in Tristan's system and that the doctors were doing all they could to flush it out.

Inside the hospital, the bright lighting and the antiseptic tang of disinfectant did nothing to ease the tension threading through Tom's chest. They approached the reception desk, where a woman was typing furiously.

'We're looking for a patient – Tristan Watt?' Lauren asked.

The woman sighed, pushed her glasses up her nose, and clicked through a few screens. 'Watt, Watt...' She squinted, tongue poking out slightly. Then tilted her chin up. 'Yeah. Bed seven. High-dependency unit.'

Tom nodded his thanks. The directions she rattled off were vague enough to be useless, so he pulled out his phone and opened a map of the hospital. Even with it, they took a wrong turn down a sterile corridor that led only to a row of vending machines. The silence of the place unnerved him – it was too quiet for such a big building.

Lauren caught his sleeve when he veered off again. 'Not that way. You're heading back to reception.'

Eventually, they found the high-dependency ward, with a nurse's station just ahead.

'Is Tristan Watt in here?' Lauren asked the sole nurse behind the desk.

'There's just been a shift change,' she said, as she consulted a computer screen. After a minute, she said, 'Yes, bed seven. Can I ask why you need to see him?'

'We're police. We need to question him as a matter of urgency.' Tom reached for his badge.

'Okay, but I can't let you stay long,' the nurse said. 'He's in a bit of a state, and is due another check-up in about ten minutes—'

Tom was already moving.

The ward was dimmer than expected, its lighting subdued. Eight beds in total, four a side. One elderly man snored softly through an oxygen mask. Another patient at the far end was sitting up, reaching for grapes that were on a nearby table. The air was heavy with bleach and something underneath it – sickly-sweet, metallic.

They moved to bed seven. The curtain around it was pulled tight, the fabric rustling slightly thanks to the open window.

'Tristan?' he called out.

No response.

'Tristan?' he tried again, louder.

Again, there was no reply.

'Maybe he's asleep?' Lauren ventured, but her tone was uncertain.

The silence felt wrong.

Off.

Tom drew a breath, grabbed a fold of curtain, and peeled it back.

The bed was empty.

'What the fuck?' Tom noted the rumpled sheets, the pillow with the head-sized hollow in it, the two IV lines hanging uselessly on their holders, one swaying slightly as if recently disturbed.

He turned on his heel and stormed toward the nurse's station. 'Where the hell is Tristan Watt?'

'Bed seven,' the nurse said, after staring at him blankly for a second. 'You just asked me that.'

'Yeah, well, bed seven's fucking empty. Are you sure that's where he's meant to be?'

'Empty?' she repeated, looking rattled. 'He was there at the end of the last round – what do you mean? He's gone?'

'I mean he's not there. There's no one in the bed.'

She shot to her feet, scrambling around the desk, and followed them back into the ward. At the sight of the empty bed, she stopped dead, staring at it like it was a Tracey Emin.

'Give me a minute,' she muttered.

She moved briskly, checking the other beds, just in case someone had shifted him, but everyone else was where they were supposed to be. Then, she opened the door to the en-suite bathroom, but it was empty.

Finally, she turned to them, pale now.

'He's gone.'

'No shit, Sherlock,' Tom said, agitated. 'Where has he gone?'

Tom didn't wait for the nurse to answer his question, or finish sputtering excuses. Instead, he ran from the ward into the corridor.

'Lock the place down,' Tom barked at the nurse behind the station, while looking around.

'He can't have got far,' Lauren said. 'He wouldn't have made it out through the main entrance – not in that state.'

'No, someone would've recognised him, or at least, recognised the state he was in and stopped him.'

To the left of the station, there was a fire-escape door, the green light above it glowing and otherworldly.

That had to be where he had gone.

Tom ran to it and yanked the door open. A flight of concrete stairs spiralled both up and down, emergency lighting flickering along the walls.

'Up or down?' he asked Lauren.

'Up,' she said. 'Less people.'

They took the steps two at a time. Tom's heart thudded – not just from exertion, but from the sickening realisation of what Tristan might be trying to do. If he guessed that Rosanna had exposed him – if he knew the game was up – he wouldn't run.

He'd end it, like his plan had been all along.

There, on the stairs, spots clouded his vision.

His chest clamped tight. His throat constricted.

No, please no. Not now.

He knew what Dr Dougan would say – how he'd scold him for pushing himself too hard. Of *course*, this was the critical juncture when his body would fail him. Typical.

Just as he'd failed everyone last year with The Christmas List Killer.

Just as Archie Walker said, his failure in print for all the world to see.

His breaths were short and shallow gasps now.

It was his worst panic attack yet.

Then – he felt a hand on his shoulder.

Lauren had come back down the stairs. She knelt beside him, her eyes brimming with tender concern. 'It's okay, Tom,' she said, though her voice seemed to drift from the end of a tunnel. 'I'm right here. I'm with you.'

Somehow, in her words, in the touch of her hand, in the warmth of her gaze, he found the strength he needed for his panic to dissipate.

He breathed in a deep lungful. His head was clear.

In that moment, he knew what he would say to her, once this was all over.

But first: they had a killer to catch.

He stood up and they snapped back into action, covering the remaining stairs.

They reached the top of the stairwell, coming to another fire door. Tom slammed his shoulder into it, and it burst open with a metallic groan onto a flat rooftop.

The biting cold air hit them like a punch. The rooftop was flat and wide, littered with humming generators, vents, and rusted air-conditioning units. The city stretched out beneath a perimeter of steel railings: grey rooftops, cranes, spires, the river glinting coldly in the distance.

And on the far edge – beyond the railing, silhouetted by the darkening sky – stood Tristan Watt.

His hospital gown whipped around him. His one bare foot stood inches from a sheer drop, the stump bandaged but weeping. One hand clutched the railing.

'Tristan!' Lauren called out. 'Step away from the edge.'

He didn't turn.

'I'm not going to prison,' Tristan said quietly.

'Let's just talk this through,' Tom said, his voice as soft as he could make it.

'I have nothing to say to you.'

'We can get you help,' Lauren insisted.

'I *don't want* help!' Tristan roared. 'I want *out*! I want to stop running! You think I don't know? You think I don't realise it's all over? I bet by now you've spoken to Rosanna. I bet the moment she saw me on TV, that stupid bitch came running to you.'

'It's not like that—'

'Spare me. I know what she's like. By now, you'll know about the warehouse. You'll have found the bodies. You'll be working on pinning this on me.' He inched forward. 'But I'm not going to prison.'

He stood on the precipice, the toes of his remaining foot curled over the edge of the concrete.

Tom bolted forward.

'Tristan, no!'

He lunged, grabbing the back of Tristan's gown with one hand and looping the other around his chest, dragging him back from the edge. Tristan screamed, thrashed, his foot slipping off the concrete lip. For a heart-stopping second, his body teetered – then Tom hauled him backwards over the railing, crashing onto the roof.

Tristan kicked out instinctively.

'Let me go!' he groaned. 'Just let me go!'

But he had no strength left. His body began trembling violently. His breathing became shallow, his skin clammy.

'Lauren, get someone to help,' Tom called. 'Now!'

'It's too late for help, you know?' Tristan murmured, as Lauren crashed back through the fire escape. 'That bitch poisoned me. I heard the doctors say they didn't fancy my chances.'

'So, if you're going to die, tell me something: why did you kill Evie?'

'She was never part of the plan. She saw me. She came out of the bathroom after I … after I stabbed Joshua. She wouldn't stop screaming. I panicked. I had to… I couldn't let her go. She would have fucked it all up.'

Tristan groaned. Then, he started convulsing, his eyes rolling in his head.

Helpless, Tom shifted him into the recovery position and screamed as loud as he could for help.

48

Boxing Day

TOM AND LAUREN SAT alone in the office, trying to make sense of their days.

A couple of minutes after Tom had placed Tristan into the recovery position, Lauren had reappeared, with two paramedics in tow, their kit bags open and ready. They'd set about stabilising him, and his body had soon responded. When they were happy that he was out of the woods, they'd stretchered him off the roof. This time, when he was returned to the ward, he wasn't going anywhere. His wrists were cuffed to the bed rail, and Tom had arranged for a uniform to sit outside his door until further notice.

Before they'd left, Tom had apologised to the nurse for all the swearing he'd directed at her. She'd had the good grace to look a little sheepish.

In the car, on the way back, he'd received a call from his mum with good news: his dad's test results had finally arrived, and they were negative. Hearing it made him feel as euphoric as hiking the Pennines, all those days ago. He wiped away a tear as he told them he loved them, and would see them soon.

There was more good news to follow. Back at the station, Tom had rung the CPS, briefed them on the new evidence, and formally secured a charge of murder.

Now, with the fluorescent lights humming overhead and the station silent, Tom sat by the window. The sun had long gone, leaving darkness behind. Across the road, one of the terraced houses glowed with weak, flickering fairy lights. A tinsel-clad Christmas tree stood in the window – leaning slightly, like it was too tired to stand upright after a long month of celebration.

Tom barely saw it. Instead, he was ruminating on leaving Haltwhistle. Despite the grim circumstances that had brought him here, there was something grounding about the place – the red-brick charm of the high street, the green hills and twisting paths just beyond, the familiarity of the pubs. Even the local teenagers had given him the occasional respectful nod, which, in his book, bordered on affection.

Behind him, Lauren released a long breath and shut the folder in front of her with a satisfying thump.

'Do you think we can leave the rest of the paperwork until tomorrow?' she asked.

Tom turned. 'It's Boxing Day. Of course we can. There's no other sucker here, is there?'

She gave a dry laugh. 'I can certainly think of more festive ways to spend an evening.'

He walked across the room and leaned beside her on the desk, folding his arms.

'Thank you. For … helping me on the stairs. I don't know what would have happened if you hadn't been there. Maybe…' It was best not to dwell. 'It meant a lot.'

She smiled, tucked her hair behind her ear in an uncharacteristically coy gesture. 'Don't mention it.'

'Do you think you'll make it back in time to see Sophie before bedtime?'

'Maybe,' she said, checking her watch. 'I reckon she's had so much sugar today, it'll be a miracle if she goes to sleep at all.'

'If you can't munch a full selection box and a Terry's Chocolate Orange on Boxing Day while watching *The Polar Express*, when can you?'

'Well, there's that,' she admitted. 'Fuck, I'd love a Terry's Chocolate Orange right about now.'

'I can't help you there,' Tom said. 'But there's a couple of Mars Bars left in the vending machine. I could wrap one in paper towels and slap a Post-it note on it. I could even try to draw a little bow?'

'I appreciate the sentiment.'

They sat in silence for a beat longer. Then Lauren spoke, quietly.

'You know … I was going to tell you about the engagement. When it first happened.'

Tom glanced at her, unsure of where this was headed. 'Yeah?'

She nodded, eyes on her hands. 'But it didn't feel real. Not really. And somehow … telling you would've made it feel more real than telling anyone else.'

'Because of work?'

'No,' she said quietly, lifting her eyes to meet his. 'Because I care what you think. And I was scared you'd look at me differently.'

The air between them seemed to shift.

Tom glanced up.

'Have you noticed that before?' he said.

He gestured to a sorry-looking sprig of mistletoe, the cheap plastic kind that someone had Blu-tacked to one of the ceiling fans as a joke. It drooped pitifully overhead.

Lauren followed his gaze, then gave a soft laugh.

'God, it looks like it's about to die.'

'Maybe we can find its killer,' Tom said. And then: 'Is it bad luck to ignore mistletoe, like not saluting a magpie?'

Lauren didn't reply.

Her gaze returned to his. Her lips parted ever so slightly.

Tom leaned in, just enough to close the distance if she wanted him to.

The moment held. Balanced on a knife-edge.

Then—

The door banged open.

'Jesus Christ, are you two still here?' Deborah's voice cut through the air like a siren. She clutched her handbag and car keys like she was about to throw them at someone. 'I'm locking up. Some of us have families to get back to.'

Tom straightened instantly, stepping away. Lauren swivelled quickly in her chair, flustered.

'Right. Of course,' he said. 'Sorry. 'We were just finishing up.'

Deborah narrowed her eyes. 'You city lot have no off switch, do you? Go home. Eat something that didn't come from a vending machine. Be merry.'

She was gone a second later, muttering about unpaid overtime and the bright lights of Durham.

Lauren turned to Tom, a sheepish smile on her lips. 'I should go. Sophie will be waiting.'

Tom nodded, heart still thumping. 'You okay to drive?'

'Yeah, fine. Shall we meet back here on the twenty-eighth and really nail down all the evidence for the CPS.'

'Sounds like a plan.'

Lauren moved toward the door, then paused, glancing up at the mistletoe again.

'Let's hope no one tidies this place before we're back,' she said, and then, with a wide smile, she disappeared into the corridor.

Tom waited a few minutes to give her a head start. When he stepped outside, her car was already gone. Deborah was locking the doors behind him, shooing him off the steps like a mother hen who'd had enough of everyone.

The snow had started again – soft flakes falling in silence.

He hoped it wouldn't settle.

He had to get back to Manchester.

To Mum, Dad, Danny. His other life.

There was a game of football he needed to play.

Acknowledgements

The book is dedicated to the NHS, and I thought I'd explain why.

In January 2024, I was diagnosed with Type 1 Diabetes. I spent five days in hospital and was cared for brilliantly during a particularly hectic week by an incredible team of nurses, doctors, dietitians and diabetic specialists. By day two, I'd been fitted with a blood sugar sensor and was checked on constantly. The fact that I walked out with all the equipment that would keep me alive, and without a huge medical bill, still amazes me. It made me realise how much we take for granted. The diabetes storyline in this book grew out of that experience – though thankfully, no one has yet tried to poison me!

My diagnosis meant I had to postpone the sequel to *The Killer's Christmas List* by a year. Which brings me to the wonderful team at HarperNorth. I left a gap in their publishing schedule, but they were nothing but supportive and understanding, which made a tough time infinitely easier. Gen, Alice, Megan, Taslima and Jess – you'll never know how much your patience and encouragement meant. Huge thanks, too, to the editorial team whose ideas and suggestions elevated the book into what it is today, so thanks to Morgan Dun-Campbell and Emily Thomas.

A special thank you to Daisy Watt, my editor, whose sharp eye and guidance made this book so much stronger. Your insight and enthusiasm kept me on track when I needed it most, and I'm hugely grateful for the care you put into every page.

To David Headley – agent extraordinaire, wise counsel, all-round good guy and someone I'm very lucky to call a friend. Thank you for always being a phone call away, for your ideas, and for believing in me. Thanks, too, to the team at DHH for their support, the invites to the coolest parties (I got to meet Johnson from *Peep Show*! – a long-held dream), and for making me feel part of the team.

Steven Kedie and Jonathan Whitelaw. I think it's now contractual that I have to mention you two, but the truth is I'd do it anyway. Thank you for the music chat, the banter, and the encouragement. To the birthday cake of faithfulness – our WhatsApp group is more than a writing chat – it's a little family – and it's always a joy when we manage to meet in person.

To Chris, Kelly and all at Serenity Booksellers. What started with me shuffling into your shop and nervously asking if they'd like to do a launch event for *The Killer's Christmas List* has spawned an incredible friendship, and a festival in Stockport Noir. You guys are the best, and deserve every success your growing empire gets. I wouldn't be where I am without you!

To my new bandmates in WARPED – Fred, Fester and Thom. I love that there are three other guys embracing the midlife crisis with me, and am blown away by what we've done so far. Thank you for your support, enthusiasm and encouragement (and for lending your names to my next book!). Here's to many more years of making glorious noise together.

A heartfelt thank you to all the authors who so generously read the book and shared kind words about the first in the series, and to the readers who bought it in droves. Knowing that so many of you have taken Tom Stonem to heart means the world. I hope you've enjoyed his second outing – and I can only apologise for leaving you with a bit of a cliffhanger…

Finally, to my beautiful family. Sarah, Emma and Sophie – you are everything, and I couldn't do any of this without your love and encouragement.

Book Credits

Fionnuala Barrett

Peter Borcsok

Sarah Burke

Alan Cracknell

Jonathan de Peyer

Anna Derkacz

Morgan Dun-Campbell

Tom Dunstan

Kate Elton

Sarah Emsley

Andrew Furlow

Simon Gerratt

Imogen Gordon Clark

Lydia Grainge

Monica Green

Natassa Hadjinicolaou

Emma Hatlen

Jess Haycox

Megan Jones

Jean-Marie Kelly

Taslima Khatun

Holly Kyte

Rachel McCarron

Millie Morton

Alice Murphy-Pyle

Adam Murray

Genevieve Pegg

Amanda Percival

Dean Russell

Florence Shepherd

Colleen Simpson

Eleanor Slater

Hilary Stein

Emma Sullivan

Emily Thomas

Katrina Troy

Claire Ward

Ben Wright

For more unmissable reads,
sign up to the HarperNorth newsletter at
www.harpernorth.co.uk

or find us on socials at
@HarperNorthUK

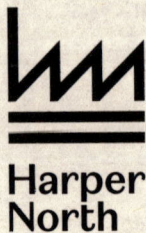

**Harper
North**